YESTERDAY'S NEWS

Margaret Allan

Severn House Large Print
London & New York

This first large print edition published in Great Britain 2003 by
SEVERN HOUSE LARGE PRINT BOOKS LTD of
9-15, High Street, Sutton, Surrey, SM1 1DF.
First world regular print edition published 2002 by
Severn House Publishers, London and New York.
This first large print edition published in the USA 2003 by
SEVERN HOUSE PUBLISHERS INC., of
595 Madison Avenue, New York, NY 10022

British Library Cataloguing in Publication Data

Allan, Margaret, 1922-
    Yesterday's news. - Large print ed.
    1. Country life - Scotland - Fiction
    2. Large type books
    I. Title
    823.9'14 [F]

    ISBN 0-7278-7201-X

Except where actual historical events and characters are being
described for the storyline of this novel, all situations in this
publication are fictitious and any resemblance to living persons
is purely coincidental.

Printed and bound in Great Britain by
MPG Books Ltd, Bodmin, Cornwall.

Author's Note

The first cases of foot and mouth disease in England were recorded in February 2001. By mid-summer, in spite of the stringent regulations then in force, the outbreak had spread to many areas of England, Wales and southern Scotland with devastating effects on the farming, tourist and other allied industries. When by December 2001 no new cases had occurred for three months it was hoped that the outbreak was over.

This book was written during that period of time. It is dedicated to all those people in the rural communities who suffered such terrible disruption in their private and business lives. My hope is that they will soon know better times.

One

Grace was smiling as she turned the Volvo smoothly out of the lane and into the wide curve of the drive that led to her home. Soon the leaden sky from which a steady downpour was descending would be left behind and they would be enjoying long lazy sun-filled days in Italy. Looking forward to that was what had kept her going through the days of worry before the operation and the long weeks of slow recovery which had followed.

'We'll go to Italy when it's all over, my darling, and put these awful months behind us,' Paul had promised in the days when her strength and her courage had been at low ebb.

Now her courage was no longer at low ebb. She had come through all the stages of fear, despair and hope supported by Paul's love and the faith inherited from her childhood spent in a Scottish manse. Inside the beautiful Cotswold stone house which she had shared with Paul for the last ten years her luggage was waiting to be collected. She had only to attend to a few last minute things, to leave a key with their neighbour and check that all the windows and doors were secured and the alarm systems working. Then she would have time for a quick coffee and a sandwich before the taxi came to take her to the airport. Paul would meet her there on his way back from the conference he'd been attending that weekend.

For a moment, after she had parked the car in the double garage and locked the door, she glanced around her at the garden which encircled the house, seeing the bright yellow splash of colour made by the daffodils which crowded together beneath the rowan tree and the strong green spikes of tulips which would be in bloom when she and Paul came home from Italy in April. As always she would be so glad to be home again then, and ready to go back to full time work in her floristry business. With that thought in her mind she moved quickly up the few stone steps which led to the carved oak front door and let herself into the hall.

Her matching pale grey suitcase and flight bag were waiting there. Paul had taken his luggage with him when he went to Bournemouth for the conference which would end this morning. Doing that would save time today, he had decided. While she had been having a last-minute hairdo he would have been on his way to the airport. A glance at her watch showed her she would need to drink her coffee on the hoof, and dispense with the sandwich. She wasn't very hungry anyway.

It was after she had checked everything and was reaching for the key she was to leave next door that she saw the envelope with a single name, her own name, scrawled across it in the large flowing script that belonged to her husband. She stared down at it, frowning. Where had it come from? Certainly not through the post. Neither had it been lying there on the hall table since Paul had left for his conference on Friday morning because one of the things she had done on Saturday evening was to go through all the accumulated, mostly unwanted, papers which had been piling up there for a couple of weeks and consign them to the waste bin.

Paul must have come home while she was out having her hair done, but why? If he had come home why was he not here now? Why hadn't he phoned her to let her know of his change of plan? Uneasiness stirred inside Grace as she picked up the thick white envelope, weighing it in her hand while the questions about it churned about in her mind. Her fingers were trembling when she at last slit open the envelope. They began to shake visibly as she read the words her husband had written.

Darling Grace, I came home so that I could talk to you before you left for the airport but when I found you were not here I lost my courage and simply could not stay to face you with the truth. You don't deserve what I have to say to you, and you are going to hate me for it. I hate myself for what I'm about to do but I have to do it while there is still time for me to start again. I just can't think of any other way to do things.

What did Paul mean? What was he talking about? Grace shook her head in bewilderment as she read on.

We always said it didn't matter that we had no children as yet, because we had each other and our careers. Perhaps we both hoped that one day if we didn't worry too much about it a child would come along. Certainly I did, even if I didn't say so. Your operation finally cancelled out that hope, and until you recovered that was all that mattered to me. Now, though, the whole scene has changed for me because of what happened while you were in hospital.

Sickness began to rise inside Grace as she turned the sheet of notepaper over.

Because I was so worried about you I couldn't sleep. So I spent most of the night hours thinking about our future. At first my mind was full of relief that your operation was over and you were going to recover completely. Then I found myself full of anger because there was now no hope of us ever having children. I couldn't stop myself from envying my brother, and my sister, for the kids they have. I knew then that it was what I've always wanted too, to have children and a family way of life. Even though I tried to push such thoughts out of my mind I became obsessed with them. Now they have taken over most of my waking thoughts and I feel cheated because a family life isn't going to happen for us. So I am asking you to give me some time and space to find out whether I can go on with our life together now that I know there'll only ever be the two of us. What I need is for you to agree to a trial separation. Please agree, and please forgive me. Please believe that I still love you.

Grace was unable to read the final words

11

clearly because of the moisture that was invading her eyes. Paul's signature wavered. The first tear slid down her cheek and made a blotch on the bold lettering. She dropped on to the bottom step of the elegant staircase and covered her face with her hands as shock engulfed her. Her fight to regain her health and strength, and to remain cheerful for Paul's sake, had all been for nothing. Paul was asking her to let him go, to end their marriage because there was no chance of her being able to give him a child.

She was still weeping when the telephone began to ring a few minutes later. Her first thought was to let it go on ringing. Then the hope leapt into her mind that it could be Paul, ringing to tell her he was sorry about the note he had written and that he didn't mean what he had said. Hope surged strongly enough within her to bring her to her feet. It had to be Paul ringing her. It must be him.

'Hello, Paul!' she gasped.

'Did you get my letter?' His voice was sharp, almost curt.

'Yes.' She waited for him to speak again; waited for him to say he did not mean what he had written.

'I can't begin to tell you just how sorry I am, Grace,' he began.

A great wave of relief washed over her.

'I guessed that was why you were phoning,

darling.' The words raced out of her throat so fast that she was unable to stop them. She was aware of a ringing in her ears as she waited again for what he would say next. A glance at her watch showed she would still be able to get to the airport in plenty of time for their flight.

'I should have told you in the letter that I had cancelled the flight, and the holiday. I didn't think you would want to go there on your own.'

A long moment of silence followed while Grace tried to take in what her husband had just said. Then she found her voice again. 'I don't understand what you're saying, Paul. I thought you were ringing to tell me that you didn't mean what you said in the letter.'

'I'm sorry, terribly sorry, but I do mean what I said. I've thought a lot about it and I feel I must sort things out in my mind before we are able to start living together properly again. If we ever start living to-gether properly again, I mean.'

Pain scourged her as the realisation finally hit her that without a child she was not enough for Paul now. Perhaps she never had been enough for him?

'If that's how you feel, of course we must separate.' The effort of saying that so calmly was almost more than she could bear.

'I'll get in touch with you, once I've got myself—' he started to say, but she was

13

beyond being able to go on listening, and she replaced the instrument before he could utter any more hurtful words.

'It's for you, Laurel. Hurry up!'

There was no need for her mother to urge her to hurry because Laurel was already geared up to dash downstairs as soon as she heard the phone start to ring. Perhaps this time it would be Daniel. The thought, the hope, gave wings to her bare feet as she sped down the wide staircase that led into the hall and almost grabbed the phone in her haste to speak.

'Hi!' She could feel her heart thudding as she waited, feeling almost sick with anxiety.

'It's Calum speaking, Laurel. I wonder if you could do me a favour and come in tonight to do the meal for the Rotary Club? That's if you've nothing planned, of course.'

Disappointment hit her like a blow so that she was unable to answer at first. It was only when Calum McLeod spoke again that she managed to pull herself together.

'I'm sorry to have to ask you again so soon, Laurel. I know you stepped in last time James went sick, but I'm running out of time now. If you can't help I'll have to try the agency.'

'There won't be any need for that. I'll come in, Calum. I'll be in by six, as usual,' she managed to answer cheerfully, because

14

it wasn't Calum's fault that James was so often unwell, and it wasn't Calum's fault that Daniel was taking so long to get in touch with her.

'Thanks, Laurel. Thanks a lot!' her boss replied. 'I don't know what I'll do without you when you go to join Daniel.'

'I expect you'll manage.' She even forced a short laugh as she said that.

'I'm not so sure about that. You're a bit special—' He broke off, sounding embarrassed, as though he felt he had said too much. It wasn't like him to do that. Then she heard the click that signalled the end of the conversation.

It was time then to tell her mother of the change in plans. 'I have to go in to work tonight because James has gone sick again and there's the Rotary Club coming for a meal.'

'Calum will miss you when you go to Daniel, won't he?'

Laurel was aware of her mother's perceptive eyes watching her face as she spoke. They were full of an expression she had seen in them too often recently. Was it sympathy? Did her mother know how anxious she was becoming about Daniel's failure to call her?

'It seems quite a while since you heard from him. Or is it my imagination?'

'I can't remember exactly when it was.

15

He's not someone who enjoys letter writing,' Laurel hedged as she stared down at the three small emeralds set in a narrow band of gold that Daniel had given her when they became engaged.

'There is the phone,' her mother pointed out.

'I'd better get ready and go right away. I don't know how much James managed to do before he was taken ill.'

As she finished speaking Laurel was on her way back up the stairs to her room, glad to get away from her mother's questions. Of course it was quite a while since she had heard from Daniel. Far too long for her to be easy in her mind. He had rung her a couple of times during his first week in the new job, just to let her know he loved her, he had said. Since then there had been nothing, no phone call, no letter, not even a postcard. Surely by now Daniel should have been able to find a flat they could share within travelling distance of the new job? That was what they had planned before he left Yorkshire. So why wasn't it happening?

Next week she would be on holiday, and all her hopes had been pinned on Daniel having found a flat for them by then so that she could go down and start getting it ready for them to move in. Now, since there had been no word from him, she was uncertain of what to do. She wondered yet again

16

whether perhaps the job he had been so enthusiastic about in the first few weeks after he left the Skellkirk Abbey Hotel had not come up to expectations, but surely if that were the case he would have told her by now? Why didn't he let her know what was happening?

Calum McLeod, changing into an immaculate dark lounge suit with a pale lilac shirt and darker purple patterned tie in the bedroom of his suite in the annexe of the Skellkirk Abbey Hotel, was still thinking about Laurel Appleby. His thoughts were causing him some concern. He was not looking forward to her departure from his hotel because she was a gifted and imaginative chef who had brought added prestige to the business in the time she had worked there. On a more personal level she had brought feelings to life inside him which he had never expected to experience again. Since Laurel had eyes for no one but Daniel Dailey he had kept those feelings under strict control.

What was Daniel Dailey playing at? He ought to know that sooner or later the gossip about him would filter back to Laurel, especially since the two hotels belonged to the same group and there was from time to time an exchange of staff. Laurel would be deeply upset if she became aware that Daniel had become involved with Sian, the glamorous Welsh head reception clerk. Rumour had it that he had moved into Sian's flat within a month of his departure from the Skellkirk Abbey Hotel. There was trouble brewing, and Calum did not want to have to stand by and see Laurel get hurt.

There was Laurel now, parking her small car in the staff car park beneath his window and sliding gracefully out of the driving seat. His eyes rested on her small, slim figure clad in pale blue cotton pants and a blue and white checked tailored shirt. Her mass of silky golden brown hair was secured in a top-knot by a dark blue velvet band. As always, the sight of her sent his emotions into overdrive. Then he told himself not to be a fool. Laurel was not for him, and the sooner he came to terms with that the better. There was work waiting for him in the hotel, and work was the main thing he had to live for nowadays.

'You've done a good job, Laurel,' he told her later as he came over to where she was dropping a tea bag into a mug and pouring boiling water over it. 'The Rotarians' President asked me to say how much they had enjoyed their meal.'

Laurel allowed her tired shoulders to relax while the tea brewed. 'I suppose you can't go wrong with the traditional roast beef and

Yorkshire pud,' she replied with a smile.

'You certainly can't the way you cook it. The sherry trifle came in for high praise too.'

Laurel laughed. 'You can't really go wrong with that either, not when it's made to my mum's recipe. I was making that when I was still at junior school, and having a crafty sip of the sherry at the same time.'

'So your mother taught you, before you went to college?' He knew so little about Laurel Appleby, other than that she was a gifted chef and a conscientious employee who never let him down in emergencies like they had been faced with tonight when James, the head chef, had been hit by a severe asthma attack. The attacks were coming more frequently these days. It was worrying Calum now he knew Laurel would be leaving once Daniel found a flat for them to share in London.

'Mum taught me a lot about traditional cooking because she was a food technology teacher before she married Dad and became a farmer's wife,' she explained.

'Your mother isn't looking for a job by any chance, is she?'

Laurel laughed. 'Why? Are you thinking of sacking me and taking her on?'

His grey eyes lit with humour and his long, lean face relaxed as he pushed aside the worry about James' health and Laurel's imminent departure.

'No, far from it! I was just wondering how I'd cope without you, when you leave here.'

'You've no need to worry yet, Calum. There doesn't seem to be any sign of Daniel managing to get a flat for us as yet.'

'You must be disappointed?'

She shrugged her slender shoulders but did not reply. Instead she took a long drink from the mug of tea.

Watching her, Calum felt a wave of anger scorch him. Daniel Dailey was a bloody fool to risk losing Laurel. He'd made sure he got her, cutting out everyone else from the time he set eyes on her the first day he came to work at the hotel. Calum had fancied her himself, but he was of a much more cautious nature and was afraid of making another mistake.

'You'll have plenty of time to find a replacement for me, Calum,' she said quietly. 'Apart from the time specified in my contract, I mean. Because there'll be the wedding to arrange as well.'

'You're planning to marry as soon as that?' He was amazed that she was prepared to marry so quickly a man she had known for so short a time.

'Yes. I must seem a bit behind the times to you, but I come from that sort of family. My parents set great store by traditional things and I suppose, since we are such a close family, that I take after them.'

'Do they like Daniel?' He had to ask that, with all the doubt about Daniel Dailey that was in his own mind.

Laurel frowned. 'I expect so. I hope so. They haven't seen such a lot of him with him going off to the new job so soon after we got engaged.'

'Will we be doing your reception here?'

Her reply was drowned by an outburst of laughter that exploded in the room next door, the private dining room where the local Rotary Club held regular meetings. Calum was proud of that fact, since they were known always to choose the best hotel in the locality.

'You'll be wanting to get home. You must be very tired after doing the extra shift. Thanks again, Laurel, I really do appreciate it.'

Laurel took off her whites and thrust them into the laundry basket after the manager had gone. Calum was a nice man, but a very private one. It was not often that he lingered to talk to her when the work was done. As she walked slowly out of the staff entrance, heading for where her car was parked, cigar smoke came drifting out from the open windows of the dining room. It hung about her as she bent to retrieve her shoulder bag, which had slipped down from her arm and landed on the gravelled surface of the car park.

What she overheard as she bent to pick up the bag caused the breath to catch in her throat. The voice that spoke so clearly was that of the local businessman who was sitting closest to the open window. He was well-spoken, so she had no difficulty in catching every word. Even so, she could hardly believe what she was hearing.

'Yes, I agree. The girl is a superb cook. Calum says he'll be sorry to lose her when she goes to join her boyfriend in London. Though she might not be going now, because it looks as if the boyfriend has something going with the receptionist where he's working now. He works at the place where I stay when we have London meetings, and that receptionist really is something!'

Laurel straightened up slowly, having gathered together a collection of small objects which had fallen out of her bag and were scattered about her feet. Was that why Daniel had not written to her after the first couple of weeks he had been working at the London hotel: because he had something going with a head receptionist who was 'really something'? Was that why Daniel had not even telephoned her during the last three weeks? Was that why he had not yet found a flat for them to move into? Maybe he wasn't even trying, if what she had just heard was true?

These questions, and a dozen others, milled around in Laurel's mind as she made her way to her car. On any other night she would have been eager to switch on the engine and drive the three miles to her home in the hope that when he finished his duties Daniel would phone her, but not tonight. Tonight she took her time, finding it difficult to concentrate on her driving while she was still trying to cope with the shock that the words she had heard Alistair Whitby say had given her. Soon she decided she had better pull off the road and get control of herself before she arrived home and had to face her parents.

When she switched off the engine in a parking area close to the river Skell and allowed her hands to rest on the steering wheel she became aware that they were trembling slightly, and that her heart was racing. Was what she had overheard out there in the car park true? Or was it just idle gossip? She had to know, because how could she go on defending Daniel's failure to contact her to either of her parents until she knew the truth?

How could she discover the truth though? Her first instinct was to drive straight down to the London hotel right now and confront Daniel with what she had heard, but that would mean making explanations to Mum and Dad, and to Calum, about why she was not available to go to work tomorrow. She could try ringing Daniel at the hotel, and hope that he would be there to answer her, but if there was nothing in the gossip she had heard he would be angry and upset at her lack of trust in him.

There was only one other option open to her, but she was reluctant to use that as it would mean admitting to Mr Whitby that she had been eavesdropping on his conversation tonight. For a long, long moment she argued with herself about the wisdom of taking such action. Then, even though she guessed she would probably regret it later, she used her mobile phone to call Skellkirk Abbey Hotel and asked if she could speak to Mr Whitby.

It seemed an age to her before his voice came to her. His surprise when she identified herself to him was evident.

'I hope you don't mind me calling you, Mr Whitby,' she began with a rush.

'No, my dear, of course not. It gives me the opportunity to tell you how much I enjoyed the dinner you cooked for us tonight.'

'Thank you, I'm glad you enjoyed it. I couldn't help overhearing something you were saying as I left by the back door of the hotel to go to my car.' She stopped, wondering how to go on. In the silence she heard his exclamation of dismay.

'I dropped my bag, you see, and while I was gathering up the things that fell out of it I heard ... I heard what you said about Daniel.'

'Oh dear! I'm terribly sorry about that. I don't quite know what to say to you now.'

'Just tell me if what you said is true.'

He hesitated, because he was a kind man, and a family man who knew her father. George Appleby would want to kick the backside of Daniel Dailey if he guessed at what was happening down there in the London hotel.

'I think you should ask Daniel about that, my dear.'

'How can I when he never seems to be available when I telephone him, and when he never seems to have time to ring me?'

She did not wait for him to answer. Instead she started the car engine and set off to drive the remaining mile or so to her farmhouse home. Fern, the working collie, came to give her a boisterous welcome as she made her way wearily across the cobbled yard to the back door which led into the farm kitchen.

'You look tired out, love,' her dad said. 'Come and sit down.'

Her mum poured a cup of tea for her before speaking. 'There was a call for you from Daniel while you were out.'

'Is he going to ring me back?' she wanted to know.

'No. He said would you ring him on this number.' Her mother handed her a scrap of paper with a telephone number scribbled on it.

It was not the familiar hotel number which she had used before, so perhaps Daniel had managed to get a flat at last. Hope surged into her heart and pushed away all her doubts. 'I'll go and call him now,' she said, already on her way into the hall to do just that.

The buzz sounding on the other end of the line seemed to go on for a long time before she heard a voice answering. It was a woman's voice, and it sounded sleepy.

'I'd like to speak to Daniel Dailey, please.' Laurel was aware of her own rapid heart-beats as she waited.

'Dan! Dan! Here's the call you're expecting.' The voice held the musical lilt of Wales.

Then there was Daniel's voice, clipped and impatient. 'How are you, Laurel?'

'Fine, thanks. I've been very worried about you, with not hearing from you for so long.'

'It isn't that long. I've been very busy since I came down here,' he said defensively.

'Have you got a flat now? Is that where you were ringing from?'

'Sort of. I'm sharing a flat with someone.

We work together, and since I met her everything has changed.'

It was true then, what she had overheard earlier that evening.

'What are you trying to tell me, Daniel?' she broke in.

'There's someone else. I've moved in with her.'

Fury took possession of Laurel as she listened. 'So it's true, what I heard at the hotel tonight?'

'I don't know what you heard, but as I said, I've met someone else so—'

'So you won't be marrying me?' Laurel spoke quietly even though she was hardly able to control her anger.

'I don't know what to say—'

'Then don't say anything or you'll only make it worse. I'll send your ring back—'

'There's no need. I'd like you to keep it.'

'What makes you think I'd want to keep anything that reminds me of you, when you couldn't even stay faithful to me for a few months?'

Laurel slammed down the phone, then took a deep breath before going back into the kitchen to tell her parents that her engagement was off.

Grace stretched her cramped legs and dragged herself to her feet. It was quite dark now, and it was time she decided what to do. She was empty of tears, for the time being, so she must pull herself together and try to get on with her life, a life without Paul. First there were those three weeks of holiday to be got through.

As that thought hit her, she knew she must get out of this house which held so many memories of her life with Paul. Not just out of the house, right away from this small beautiful Cotswold town where she and Paul were both so well known that gossip would soon begin to circulate about their separation. People would begin to feel sorry for her, a barren woman who could not manage to hang on to her husband. If she stayed she would have to keep meeting those people once she was back in her florist shop.

A new thought crept up on her then to bring more dismay. How would her parents cope with the news that her marriage was in ruins? It was bound to upset them, especially her father. He had married her to Paul in the little church at Rowankirk where he had spent so many years as a minister. At least they would not need to be told the news yet since they would be in New Zealand with her sisters and their families for several months They had only just gone out there, having waited for her to recover from her operation.

The relief brought on by this thought was

followed swiftly by a longing to be in the place where she had spent so many happy years as a child and a young girl. Rowanmore Manse, the grey house set close to the larger of the two churches where her father had been minister. A new minister would be living there now but her parents had bought a cottage for their retirement, and they had left a key with her. She would take refuge in the cottage while she got over the events of this day and worked out what to do with the rest of her life.

Minutes after making the decision, Grace was emptying her suitcase of clothes meant for Italy and refilling it with garments more suitable for Scotland. Within an hour she was driving away from the pretty Cotswold town and heading for Rowanmore.

As the hours passed slowly after her parents had gone to bed, Laurel stayed on in the big chair that was set close to the Aga with Fern draped across her feet. The anger had all been used up now and only the heartache remained. Her parents had been sparing with words, though Laurel was aware of her father's disgust with Daniel.

'It's probably all for the best,' was all her mum had said, almost as though she had been expecting it to happen. 'At least you didn't give up your good job at the hotel for him.'

What would it be like at the hotel though when everyone heard that her engagement to Daniel was off? When she had to explain to Calum that there would be no wedding breakfast held there after her marriage to Daniel. Though maybe it would not be so surprising to some of her friends there, or to Calum, if they had also heard the rumours about Daniel and the receptionist moving in together.

It was then, as her mind was still on the Skellkirk Abbey Hotel, that Laurel knew it was time to move on. Time to leave behind the place where she had met Daniel, and lost him. With a good reference from Calum she could apply for a chef's job at another hotel, a hotel somewhere far away from Skellkirk.

She reached out for her father's *Yorkshire Post*. It was yesterday's news now, but all that interested her were the pages that listed career opportunities.

Two

Victor was instantly awake as the sound of an explosion penetrated his consciousness. God, where was he? What was happening? He was aware then of the film of cold sweat which lay on his forehead. It began to trickle down into his eyes, so that he was forced to rub it away with his knuckles. A moment later he was out of bed and staring into the blackness of the night. The blackness exploded suddenly into a fountain of coloured lights shooting up into the sky above the village. Fireworks! Thank God it was only fireworks and not what he had at first imagined. His shaking hands began to steady as he gripped the window-sill, trying all the time to shut out the sound of Shona's voice, so loud in the momentary silence after the bomb blast.

'Take care of Robbie for me, please! Stay with him, Vic, stay with him!'

As always, her final words became lost in the remembered noise of sirens from the ambulances and police and fire rescue vehicles which had come racing to the

31

scene. Tears mingled with the sweat that ran down Victor's cheeks as he tried to push away the memory of that friendly little town where death had come so suddenly in the middle of a bright autumn morning.

When the tears had been dried and the sweat banished Victor reached into his travel bag for the bottle of Highland malt which went everywhere with him, his consolation in a world that no longer held any joy for him. His fingers were unscrewing the cork when the sound of a child's voice drifted up to him through the open window. It was a boy's voice. A voice that held the same hint of Scottish accent which he had so loved in Shona's voice. Victor slowly replaced the top of the whisky bottle and switched on the tea-maker the hotel had provided.

The drinking would have to stop if he was to look after Robbie, and he was determined to do that. It was not going to be easy though because Isla and Ruth were set on keeping Robbie with them in Rowankirk. They were convinced that Victor would not be able to care for the boy properly while he was serving with the army. What they didn't know yet was that his army days were over. His injuries had left him unfit for further service with his regiment. That was what he had come here to tell them, and it was not going to be easy.

While the tea was brewing, Victor, calmer

now that the fireworks were over and the Highland village had settled down for the night, began to look ahead to the difficulties that faced him. He had no job, no home, and no wife. Nor was he fully recovered yet from the injuries he had sustained in the explosion which had killed Shona. There was a chance he would never fully recover. What he did have was an eighteen-month-old son, a lump sum as recompense for his fifteen years in the service, and a pension to help him live out the rest of his life now that he was no longer one hundred per cent fit.

By the time he had drunk the strong sweet tea, he had reluctantly accepted that he would not be able to take proper care of Robbie without some help, and that the most likely people to be able to provide that help were the two women who had been looking after his baby son during the time he had been a patient in two different hospitals. So he would have to sell the house close to where he had been stationed with his regiment, and where he had lived so happily with Shona and Robbie, and find a place to live here in Rowanmore or in Rowankirk. Then he must find some work to do. The skills he had acquired during his service years would surely help him there.

Things would work out for him and Robbie. He would make sure that they did. Victor wanted his boy to know the same

happy childhood that he himself remembered. His own father had been based in Edin-
burgh and they had shared many holidays
here in the Scottish Highlands, walking,
climbing, fishing and golfing. He had met
Shona on one of those holidays.

Shona should have been with him now as
he planned this new civilian life for himself
and their son. Instead, her ashes were
scattered in the place she had loved, the glen
of sorrows where the Highland Clearances
of long ago had banished earlier generations
of her family from their homes and their
livings as crofters. Shona, Shona, his heart
wept, how can I go on living without you?

Laurel Appleby stopped to consult her map
when she came to a parking bay close to the
edge of the loch. She must be nearly there
now because the road that led to the hotel
turned off to the left in between the villages
of Rowankirk and Rowanmore, and she had
already come through Rowankirk. The
journey from Yorkshire had been a long one
and she was very tired now. There was a
strong temptation inside her to put her head
back on the rest and close her eyes for a few
minutes, but if she did that and overslept
she could find herself lost in the mist that
was descending from the mountains. So she
started the car again and began to move
slowly on until she could just catch a

34

glimpse through the swirling mist of a building ahead of her.

When she drew closer to this, Laurel was dismayed to find not a huddle of farm dwellings set at the foot of the towering hills but only the remains of what must at one time have been homes for people or animals. There was a small notice set close to these. She was forced to stop the car again in order to discover whether she was on the right route for the Glen View Hotel.

It was not until she was out of her vehicle and staring up at the notice board that she discovered that this was a site of historic interest, one of the places in the Scottish Highlands where the crofters had been driven from their homes by absentee landlords who had claimed the land for the raising of huge flocks of sheep. A few sheep grazed there now among the ruins. There was a man there too, a shepherd perhaps? Laurel began to walk towards him, her feet making no sound on the damp grass. Then she spoke to him.

'Could you tell me how to get to the Glen View Hotel, please?'

The man spun round, startled because he had been unaware of her presence, unaware of everything except what he had come here to do. The flowers he had brought were still in his hands, white roses and white heather in a small heart-shaped arrangement.

'Next left and up the hill,' he replied curtly before turning his back on her.

Laurel saw the flowers a moment after she had glimpsed the desolation in his eyes. She bit her lips as she struggled to find words of apology for intruding.

'I'm sorry,' she muttered at last. 'I didn't realise...'

As she walked the short distance back to her car she saw, on the bend of the road, the notice board advertising the Glen View Hotel and just past it a signpost indicating the road to Rowan Glen. This proved to be a narrower road turning off to the left and winding uphill to where the hotel was shrouded in thick mist. It was a road to be treated with care, a road which wound ever upwards, a road where sheep wandered freely on unfenced moorland. The sheep had a way of wandering from one side of the road to the other, which would have been alarming for her if she had not been accustomed to the unfenced moorland roads in North Yorkshire.

When she reached the hotel Laurel found the car park held a motley collection of vans and lorries belonging to the army of workmen who had spent the last few months renovating the place, ready for reopening shortly. The manager, who had interviewed her in York when she applied for the position of head chef, had mentioned that a fire had almost gutted the building a couple of years earlier. There was little evidence of that to be seen as Laurel entered by the front door and walked across a carpet of dust sheets to where the reception desk was being put into place.

'Miss Appleby?'

'Yes.' Laurel recognised the copper-coloured hair of the man who had interviewed her in York six weeks ago. He had been wearing a dark lounge suit then, now he was clad in casual gear.

'Did you have a good journey?' he asked. 'I was afraid you might have got lost in the fog.'

'I thought I had, so I stopped to ask someone the way.' Laurel found herself able to recall vividly the strong face and the desolate expression in the eyes of the man she had spoken to down there in the ruins of the old Highland village.

'I'm not going to keep you talking because I'm sure you'll be tired and ready for some tea. I'll show you the kitchen, then I'll take you to the cottage where you'll be staying. We can discuss everything else tomorrow morning.' Fergus McLeod told her.

Laurel was relieved to hear that. She was desperate for a cup of tea and her shoulders were aching after the long drive. When she followed him into the spacious kitchen she discovered that it appeared to be almost

37

ready for action, with the gleam of brand-new polished steel appliances and worktops everywhere. Very different in fact from the kitchens of the Skellkirk Abbey Hotel, where although everything was maintained to a very high standard of cleanliness some of the equipment was in need of replacement. Her spirits began to lift as she gazed around her. She was going to enjoy working in this superb kitchen.

'Will it do for you? Can you work here?' Fergus asked with a grin as he saw her expression brighten.

'Oh, yes! I can't wait to get started.'

'Not tonight though. Our housekeeper, Mrs Reid, has a meal prepared for those of us who are already here. So if you come across to eat at about seven you'll meet the others then. Now I'll take you to your cottage.'

He led the way to a door opening out into a wide corridor where he walked alongside Laurel until they came to a glass-covered porch where an elderly labrador lay sound asleep in a basket and where a collection of walking boots, shooting sticks and golf clubs cluttered up one corner beneath a coat rack that was draped with Barbours, fleeces and dog leads. The dog lifted his head and stretched before coming to greet his master.

'Lie down, Mull,' Fergus ordered quietly.

After going stiffly to welcome Laurel, who

stroked his smooth head, the dog obeyed.

'He's nice,' Laurel said.

'You like dogs?'

'Yes. I'm used to them. My father's a farmer in the Yorkshire Dales. He trains collies for the sheepdog trials,' she told him.

'Mull is a gun dog, a good one, but he's getting on a bit now.' They were out in the mist again as Fergus told her that, walking across a paved square to where three single-storey cottages could be seen.

'This is yours, Laurel. It's the smallest of the three but I thought you wouldn't mind that as you are on your own.'

There was a small carriage lamp casting a glow of light over the blue-painted front door, on each side of which was a square many-paned window. Fergus opened the door and switched on a light before stepping aside to allow Laurel to enter the middle cottage of the three.

'This is Kingfisher Cottage,' he told her. 'The others are Heron Cottage and Wagtail Cottage. They were converted from the old stable block, and fortunately were too far away from the main house to suffer any damage in the fire we had. We're planning to let the other two for self-catering holidays. I'll be living in the Coach House, which is closer to the main gate, when all the work is finished and my cousin arrives.'

The doors that opened off the tiny hall

revealed a cosy living room to one side and a plainly furnished bedroom on the other. At the rear of the cottage was a shower room and a small kitchen.

'I'm afraid it's not very large but I hope it will be adequate for your needs,' Fergus was saying as Laurel looked about her.

'I don't suppose I'll spend a lot of time in here, with working most evenings. I'll hope to be out in the fresh air when I'm not on duty in the daytime. I like walking,' she told him.

'You should enjoy living here then because there are some wonderful scenic walks you can do without needing to use your car. There's room to park your car near the cottage so you can get your luggage out. I hope you'll be happy here,' he added as he made for the front door again. 'I'll see you later for supper, about seven.'

When he had gone, Laurel moved her car closer to Kingfisher Cottage and brought her bags into the house before filling the electric kettle and setting it to boil. She was too tired to unpack but she would probably feel better after having a hot drink. Someone had been thoughtful enough to put a carton of milk, coffee, tea, sugar and short-bread biscuits ready for her on a tray. Soon she was in the living room sipping gratefully from a mug of steaming tea and munching a piece of the delicious buttery shortbread while the warmth from an electric fire helped her to relax.

This was not where she had expected to be in early March 2001, taking possession of a home for one in the Highlands of Scotland. Where she had hoped to be by now was in a London flat for two, sharing with Daniel and looking for a job somewhere near to him. It was best to put thoughts like that right to the back of her mind though, because they were still able to bring an ache to her heart. In the days immediately after she had found out about Daniel she had twice overheard him described as a two-timing rat by members of staff at the Skellkirk Abbey Hotel. Everyone, especially her parents and Calum, had been very kind to her, but their sympathy had been hard to cope with so she had tried to close her mind to it. The fact that they all pitied her so much was the main reason why she had jumped at the chance to move so far away from Yorkshire when she had been offered the job here after Fergus McLeod had seen the excellent reference provided for her by Calum.

'I'm sure you'll love Scotland, Laurel, and the change of scene just now will be good for you,' Calum had said. She knew then that the news of her break with Daniel had got back to him.

Laurel was not sure that she would love

Scotland. Already she was feeling homesick for the farmhouse she had gone home to every evening when her stint of duty at the hotel was over, and for her mum and dad. There was a huge lump in her throat and a tear trickling slowly down her cheek when exhaustion took possession of her and she fell asleep.

Because of the extreme tiredness Grace began to experience after a couple of hours of motorway driving she booked a room for the night in a motel, thankful to be away from the intermittent fog which had plagued her for the last hundred miles. Her head was throbbing and her eyes ached still from the long session of weeping which had preceded her departure. All she longed for now was sleep.

Yet in spite of her weariness sleep refused to come to her. Instead, she found herself going over and over what Paul had said to her during his phone call, and what he had written in the letter that she had brought with her. She simply could not believe that they had lived together for so long without her ever guessing just how important it was to him that they should have children. They had discussed having children before they married, but since they were living at that time in a small flat above the florist shop where Grace was working while Paul was studying for his final examinations, the decision about just when they would start a family was not high on their list of priorities. They wanted to be well established first in their respective careers and living in a house which would provide plenty of space for children and pets.

Their move to the Cotswold town where Paul became a partner in one business while she established her own small shop had brought them both busy years when the question of children was something to be left to the future. Until a routine health test brought the possibility that she might need an operation which would put an end to any hope of pregnancy. It was then that Grace began to wish they had not waited so long to become parents. She voiced her regret to Paul when the operation became a certainty. Paul told her that all he wanted was for her to get the operation over with and be well again.

He hadn't meant that though, had he? At least not for long. All the time she had been recuperating it must have been on his mind that he would never be able to have children of his own. Why had he not told her? Why not suggest they adopt a child?

She would never know. All she did know was that she must give Paul his freedom, because to hang on to a marriage where she was unable to give him what he wanted so badly was something her pride would not allow her to contemplate. Even if Paul changed his mind it would not work out, because she would always wonder if she was really enough for him. How was she going to go on living without Paul?

There was water in a glass on the bedside table, and a packet of aspirin she had bought to cure the headache that was still thudding away at her temples. The two tablets she had taken before coming to bed had not worked. If she took more aspirin, a lot more, it would put an end to her pain for good. It would also set Paul free to find a new partner who could give him children.

Once that thought had entered Grace's mind it would not be banished. Did she possess the courage to reach out for the tablets and swallow them all? Or was she too much of a coward to do that? It would be easier if she released all the tablets in the pack from their foil containers and put them in a pile ready to be swallowed quickly. Then she would wash them down with a long drink of water. She got out of bed and took the half-empty glass into the en-suite bathroom so she could fill it right to the top.

The glass was so full when she reached the bed again that some of the water splashed over on to her bare feet. There were the tablets, waiting for her to pick them up. Her hands were shaking so much that she was unable to hold the glass steady. She reached out to pick up the first aspirins, and a stream of water cascaded on to the surface of the bedside table and began to run from there to the floor. Grace stumbled back to the bathroom to find a towel to mop it up.

As she started dabbing with the towel, she saw something she had not noticed earlier: a small copy of the New Testament placed in hotel bedrooms by the Gideons. It was very wet. When she lifted the book a swift stab of guilt came to her, along with a memory of her father wearing his preaching robe and reading from the huge bible in the tiny church at Rowankirk. If she were to open the pages and start to read she might find comfort there, and so change her mind about swallowing the tablets. She did not want to change her mind, so she dried the dark leather cover and replaced the little volume where she had found it. Then she went back to refill the glass.

She felt quite calm as she slipped beneath the duvet again, calm and determined to take every one of the tablets. Sitting up with a couple of pillows behind her, she put out the hand that wore the wedding and engagement rings placed there by Paul and reached out for the pile of tablets. Only there were no tablets. All that was left on the bedside cabinet was a pool of cloudy water which spread beneath her fingers and began to slide downwards towards the wet patch on the carpet. The aspirins, all of them, had dissolved in the water she had spilled.

A tearing rage took possession of her then because fate had cheated her. She beat her knuckles together to stop herself from screaming out her fury. She did not want to go on living without Paul. There would be no point to her life without him. Yet she knew when she looked again at the pool of water, where a few specks of white powder were all that remained of the aspirin, that she would indeed have to go on without Paul.

Outside the motel a new day was dawning. Rose-tinted light began to colour the sky and a blackbird started to sing. Grace heard the birdsong, and it calmed her. She drew back the curtains from the window so she could watch the light strengthen. Within minutes she was dressed. An hour later she was on the motorway again and heading for the country of her birth.

Victor showered and dressed carefully before going down to tackle the hearty breakfast he had ordered for eight thirty. He had a lot to get through during the day: first the meeting with his son, his mother-in-law and Shona's sister, Isla; then would come the search for work and for somewhere to live. He had little heart for any of it, except for the reunion with Robbie, but he had lost too much time already with spending so many months in hospital. It was time he got on with his life in civvy street, for Robbie's sake. When he had laid his small posy of white roses and heather in the place where Shona's ashes had been scattered he had made a silent vow that he would give Shona's son a good life, a happy life. It was time to begin that life today.

He began to wonder whether the boy would remember him. It was months since they had met, months during which Robbie had begun to walk and to talk. Victor found himself feeling quite nervous as he approached the large stone house where his in-laws lived. With so much of his life having been spent as an army officer, he had never got to know Shona's family very well.

'Hello, Victor! It's good to see you. Are you feeling better now?' Shona's mother greeted him. He was saddened to notice how much the tragic loss of her daughter had affected her. The black curly hair was streaked with white now, the face was thinner, the eyes lack-lustre.

'I'm much better, thanks.' Victor kissed her cheek as the door behind her opened to reveal Isla.

Pain struck Victor when he was close enough to get a good look at his sister-in-law. Isla had lost weight since he had last seen her. This slimmer, quieter twin sister of his beloved Shona was so much like her that he could hardly believe what he was seeing. The twin daughters of Ruth and Alexander Summers had never before appeared to him to be identical, but now the likeness was undeniable.

'How are you, Isla?' he asked when his heartbeats had steadied enough.

'The way we all are, just getting by one day at a time.' Isla managed a smile that did not quite reach her eyes.

'How's Fergus? Have you got the wedding sorted yet?'

The long, silky black hair, so like Shona's hair, moved about her too slender shoulders as she shook her head. 'Not yet. There's no hurry.'

Victor frowned. That wasn't what they had said when they got engaged a month or so before the bomb blast had shattered all their plans for the future.

'I hope looking after Robbie hasn't delayed your wedding. I wouldn't want that to happen,' he told her.

'No, it wasn't just that. The work that had to be done up at Glen View took much longer than we expected,' she answered. 'We thought it best to wait until that was finished to move into the Coach House, and leave the wedding till after that.'

Victor was perplexed. Surely Isla and

Fergus had gone to live together in the converted coach house behind the hotel when they became engaged? They had been childhood friends at the village school and neither had ever wanted anyone else. Probably if it had not been for the fire which had devastated the Glen View Hotel they would have been married much earlier.

'How long will it be now before everything is finished?' he wanted to know.

'The reopening is scheduled for next month. Fergus has been interviewing staff and the first of them, the key people, are already here.'

Victor remembered then the girl who had asked him the way to the hotel, the exhausted-looking girl who had been so distressed when she became aware that he was taking flowers to place on the ruins of the old kirk for Shona.

'I'll be looking for work myself, and for somewhere to live,' he said.

'Are you fit enough to work? You don't look—'

'I'll be better working. I've had too much time on my hands,' he broke in.

'What will you do? I mean, after so many years in the army.'

'I'll find something. I've got skills I can use even if I'm not as fit as I used to be.'

There was a silence then while each of them waited for the subject of Robbie to be voiced.

'What about the boy?' That was Shona's mother, moving closer to him. 'You'll not be taking him away from us, will you, Victor? Not now!'

There was all the pent-up anxiety in her voice that he had been expecting. The fear that after losing her daughter, Victor would take Robbie, the wee boy who had become such a comfort to her, far away to some place where they would not often see him. Victor recognised it and knew he must reassure her without delay.

He put an arm about her shoulders. 'No, Ruth, I'll not be taking Robbie right away from you. In fact I'll still need your help with him, if you are prepared to have him for some of the time while I'm at work. When I get a job that is, and somewhere to live.'

'You could stay here,' Shona's mother suggested.

'Thanks, Ruth, but I really need to get a place of my own where I can bring all my things when the house over there is sold.'

'What will you do? For work I mean?'

'Something out of doors. That's what I need. I don't want to be shut in.' The daylight nightmares came back at times when Victor found himself alone in a small room.

'They need someone for the gardens up at the Glen View,' Isla broke in eagerly. 'The man who was given the job has changed his mind about moving so far north. It could be right for you, Vic. Shona was so proud of the lovely garden you made for her over there.'

Yes, Shona had loved the huge garden which surrounded the bungalow. The place where he had planted a bed of flowering shrubs and a rockery. Also made a water feature and a large patio with a pagoda-shaped summer-house. There was a swing, and a sandpit too. With such a garden the place would sell easily and for a good price, the estate agent had promised.

'Shall I talk to Fergus about it before he asks anyone else?' Isla's voice broke into his wandering thoughts.

'Yes, it might be a good idea. I've been hanging about for too long already since the army got rid of me. As soon as I've fixed up some work I can find somewhere to live. In the meantime, where's Robbie?'

'He'll be back any minute,' Ruth told him. 'He's gone for a wee walk to the paper shop with his grandpa.'

After spending a couple of hours with his son, who did not at first remember who he was, but later did not want to be parted from him, Victor drove up into the hills that stood guard all around Rowanmore. When he came to the big parking area close to the gates of the Glen View Hotel he brought the car to a halt and got out to spend a few minutes admiring the view which had given a name to the McLeods' hotel. He was early for his appointment with Fergus so had a few minutes to spare. There was snow on the distant mountains beneath the deep blue sky. How Shona had loved this place! Even though she had enjoyed some of the places they had gone to during his service career, whenever they had leave she would want to come back here.

The sound of a dog barking somewhere close at hand startled Victor. A moment later the dog was there at his feet, dropping a hefty stick into a slight hollow where primroses grew thickly.

'Mull! Come here, Mull!'

The labrador glanced to where the voice came from, but stayed where he was. His amiable amber eyes challenged Victor to pick up the stick and throw it for him. Victor could not resist doing that. It was a long time since he had done such a thing. It was yet another of those ordinary, everyday things which were no longer part of his life. One of those things which had ended that day when he had been shopping with Shona.

'You're a bad boy, Mull! Come here at once.'

This time Mull obeyed, bounding over the springy brown heather towards the girl who was standing close to the gates of the hotel.

A small girl, perhaps in her early twenties, whose golden brown hair was caught up on top of her head with a bright blue scarf which matched her eyes.

'I'm sorry,' she said breathlessly. 'About him bothering you, I mean.'

There was something vaguely familiar about the girl; something he remembered about her voice.

It was like watching the past replay itself, except that the big brown dog had been a young black dog then, and the girl with him had not been small and brown haired but tall, beautiful, and black haired. This was where he had met Shona all those years ago when she had been walking one of the McLeod dogs. They had looked at each other for a long time and the attraction had been instant.

Dear God, was there to be no end to the agony of remembering? The familiar shaking began deep inside him. He turned his back on the girl and the dog and the view and went back to his car.

Three

Grace had travelled to the Highlands many times before, but never in the state of mind that she was experiencing now, when only one part of her gave the concentration she needed for motorway driving. The other part where all the hurt was, along with the anger at failing in her effort to evade a future without Paul, waited to envelop her every time she paused in her journey to fill up with petrol, visit a toilet or drink scalding coffee. Low cloud was covering the mountain tops by the time she reached the familiar landmarks and knew that her long drive was almost over.

There was the loch, gleaming dully through the swirls of mist. There were the ruins of the old village which were all that remained after the Highland Clearances of long ago. There was the bell tower of the little church at Rowankirk where she had married Paul. She felt tears gush into her eyes as she tried to push remembrance of that day out of her mind and look out instead for the cottage her parents had bought for their retirement. The cottage she had not yet seen. It was on the far side of the village, her father had said, just off the Rowanmore Road. It was whitewashed, as so many cottages and farmhouses were in this part of Scotland, and had a large garden. They had named it Faith's Cottage.

She got her first glimpse of Faith's Cottage just when she was beginning to think she had missed it. Seconds later she was pulling her car off the road and into a parking space beside the house. It was quite large, though not as large as Rowanmore Manse, where her parents had lived for so many years. Grace had to push open the sturdy wooden double gates so that she could take her car on to the drive that led to one side of the property. A couple of minutes later she was inside the stone porch unlocking the front door and letting herself into the cottage.

How strange it felt to be arriving at her parents' home without them being there to greet her. It was so silent, so empty. Everything was abnormally tidy, quite unlike the usual clutter of books, newspapers, discarded letters and leaflets, gloves and scarves that spoke of the lifestyle of two busy people. There were no flowers, no plants, no cats or dogs. Grace shivered, and wished she had not come to Rowankirk.

It was too late now though to have second thoughts because she could not face any more hours of driving. She was exhausted.

All she wanted was to crash out and drift into a world where nothing mattered except the oblivion of sleep. So she brought in her suitcase and carried it up the stairs to what was obviously a guest bedroom. The bed was not made up but there was a duvet and pillows in place for her to use as she slumped down and let utter weariness take over.

Sunlight woke her many hours later, along with the sound of a dog barking. She yawned and stretched, aware at once of how dry her mouth was after so many hours without anything to drink. Stumbling down the unfamiliar stairs with her head still full of sleep, she went in search of the kitchen, hoping to find some long-life milk to go with the tea she knew would be in one of the cupboards. She was sipping the tea in the big living room at the front of the cottage when the telephone rang.

Her first thought was not to answer it. Then a spurt of hope sent her hurtling out into the hall in case it was Paul, who had guessed at where she might have gone. When she heard a woman's voice her hopes collapsed as swiftly as they had risen.

'Is that you, Mrs Hastie? We didn't realise you were back already until we saw your car this morning. We thought you'd gone away for a few months. Is everything all right with you?'

Grace took a deep breath. Why hadn't she

56

realised that in a village as small as Rowan-kirk the locals would be quick to notice her unexpected arrival? Now there would be questions to answer, and she was not ready for them yet.

'Who's speaking?' she hedged. 'My mother isn't here.'

'Isla Summers,' came the answer. Then: 'Is everything all right, Grace? You've been ill, haven't you? An operation, your mother said.'

'Yes, I did have an operation at the end of last year but I'm fine again now, thanks.'

'We were concerned when we noticed the car, because Mrs Hastie hadn't said anything to Mum about you coming up. I thought she said you were going abroad somewhere for a holiday.'

'Yes, we were, only Paul had some urgent work to do and couldn't manage to get away just now so I decided to come up on my own. He'll be joining me later,' she added. How easy it was to lie, once you got started, Grace thought as she listened to Isla's words of sympathy. It was easier than telling the truth though, because the truth would arouse even more sympathy and she knew she could not cope with that. How stupid she had been to come here of all places without Paul. She would have to move on fairly soon, before the truth leaked out.

'If you are on your own I expect you can

do with a bit of company until Paul arrives. Why don't you come up to the ceilidh we're having at Glen View tomorrow night to celebrate the reopening of the hotel?'

'Oh, I don't think...' Grace sought around wildly in her mind for an excuse not to go. If she said she was not feeling well enough yet for anything like that, either Isla or her mother would want to come along and look after her, and really they had enough problems to deal with after the death of Isla's twin sister a few months earlier in a terrorist attack.

'It'll be good for you to meet up with everyone again, and you won't need to bother with cooking your own supper either because Calum has brought a super young chef up from the hotel where he was working in Yorkshire, and she's doing a buffet supper,' Isla added.

'How is Calum?' Grace wanted to know.

'I don't know. He's not here yet. He's coming up tomorrow in time for the ceilidh and the hotel will open the day after.'

'I haven't seen him since the night of the fire.'

'He hasn't been here. Or hardly ever. Fergus has been supervising all the renovation.'

'How is Fergus?'

'Busy. Always busy,' Isla answered shortly.

'What about the wedding? Have you got it

all planned again yet?' It was much safer to talk about Isla and Fergus, Grace thought, than to have Isla ask any more questions about Paul.

'No. We had started to think about it, until what happened to Shona brought it all to a standstill again.'

'I'm so sorry, Isla. It was such a dreadful thing to happen. So awful for all of you.'

'Yes, it has been hard to cope with, especially for Victor and wee Robbie. You might see Vic around. He's looking for somewhere to live around here so that Mum can still help by looking after Robbie while he's at work.'

'I thought Victor was still in the army?'

'Not now. His injuries have left him unfit for army service. I expect he'll be at the ceilidh tomorrow night. At least I hope he will. Do come too, Grace. If your parents had been at home they would have been with us. It's going to be a good night. We'll be celebrating a new start for some of us, and putting the past behind us. We all need to do that, I guess. Any time after eight. I'll see you then!'

Before Grace could say that she did not think so, Isla had rung off.

Laurel's first couple of weeks at the Glen View Hotel were so full of new people, new places, and new ideas that during the daylight hours she was able to push the thought of Daniel and the collapse of her plans for a future spent with him to the back of her mind. It was very different at night. Then all the heartache and disappointment still haunted her, making her restless and unable to sleep a whole night through. Sometimes she blamed herself for what had happened, telling herself that if she had taken a chance on getting the sort of job she wanted down in London Daniel would never have become involved with the glamorous Sian.

Yet it had not only been that she was unwilling to take a chance when Daniel had urged her to go with him. There had been the fact that James, the head chef at the Skellkirk Abbey Hotel, was on his winter holiday break for two weeks with his family in Orlando. Daniel had argued that someone else would fill in for her if she went with him to London but Laurel knew that Calum was relying on her to be there when some of the big seasonal functions were taking place. She felt a debt of loyalty to Calum for taking a chance on her capabilities when she was only in her first year out of catering college.

The experience she would gain here in this very different hotel, where most of the guests would be residents rather than local people eating out, would stand her in good stead even if she did not want to stay on when the season here was over. They would be very busy at Easter, Fergus had told her, then quiet for a month or so except for some short Bargain Break bookings which he hoped would come as a result of the advertising they were putting into a couple of Scottish newspapers. After that people would come for the golf, the fishing, the mountain walking and to see the rhododendrons, which were so spectacular in June. Then there would be the Highland Games and the open gardens at the nearby castles to draw them into the district during late summer and autumn.

Already Laurel was planning menus in consultation with Fergus, ordering supplies of food for the store cupboards and freezers, and visiting local firms who were eager to supply the hotel regularly with fish, game, pâté or haggis, cheeses and lamb or beef. Yes, the days had been busy and quite enjoyable even though the nights had been wearisome. There had been little opportunity for her to explore the two nearby villages: Rowanmore, where she had found some good local shops, or the smaller village of Rowankirk. Both villages were situated far below the hotel so that on clear days she could look down on them from the hotel garden or when she was walking Mull for Fergus, who was working the clock round now that the opening of the hotel was so close.

There was to be a ceilidh on the evening before the opening. All the people who had been involved in restoring the hotel and the gardens to their former glory had been invited, along with the staff members such as herself, Mrs Reid, and others who came daily to work at the Glen View, plus some local people.

'Some of them used to work here before the fire,' Mrs Reid told Laurel when they were putting the finishing touches to the buffet table just before the start of the ceilidh. 'Some of the older ones worked here earlier than that when this place was still just a family home for the McLeods.'

'How long ago was that?' Laurel wondered.

'Twelve years or so. Most of the family were still here then, though they were not here for long once they were finished with university. All over the world they went then, Australia, New Zealand, Africa, the USA. Only Calum stayed to take over the place and try to make it pay its way when the older McLeods needed to go into the nursing home.'

'Calum? Don't you mean Fergus, Mrs Reid?'

'No, I don't mean Fergus. I mean Calum! He met this girl, while he was at the university, and they set about putting Glen View House to rights so they could turn it into a country house hotel. There was plenty needing doing, I can tell you. A new roof, new windows, some new floors and the whole place modernised and redecorated from top to bottom. All that money spent, and then ten years later it was nearly all destroyed in the fire. Och! What a tragedy!' Mrs Reid shook her head. 'I was working here then, and my Wally too, and we could hardly believe what had happened to the place when we saw it the next day. We'd had such a grand time up here for Hogmanay. The place was full of visitors that night, and then some friends too, staying over from Christmas. Fergus was here, and Isla, celebrating their engagement at the same time.'

Mrs Reid's reflections were interrupted by Fergus, come to tell them that his cousin had just arrived.

'Och! It'll be grand to see Calum again. It's been a long time since he was here.' Already she was bustling out of the dining room and into the hall.

Fergus grinned. 'We go back a long way with Mrs Reid, Calum and me. She was here when we were both children. I spent all my school holidays at Glen View House when I was at boarding school while my parents were working abroad,' he told Laurel.

'No wonder she's excited—' Laurel's words came to a halt and her eyes widened with surprise when she recognised the man who was hugging the elderly housekeeper. 'It's Calum McLeod,' she whispered. 'What's he doing here, Fergus? He can't be—'

Fergus laughed at her astonishment. 'He certainly can! Calum is my cousin. I've just been overseeing the renovating for him until he was ready to...' He hesitated, then went on. 'Until he was ready to come back here again.'

Laurel frowned. 'I don't understand...' she began. Mrs Reid had spoken about the hotel being owned by Fergus's cousin, Calum, but she had never indicated at any time that Calum had been working as manager of a hotel in Yorkshire. All she had said was that Calum was 'away from here just now' as if his absence had been only a short one. It was puzzling.

'You will understand, in time,' Fergus told her. 'Now come and say hello to him.'

Already Calum was walking towards them, his tall slim figure moving gracefully. His light grey eyes, meeting her own bewildered blue glance, held an expression she was unable to fathom. Was it that same warm compassion that she had recognised on that day a few weeks ago when she had asked him if he would supply her with a reference for the position she now held here in his hotel? Calum had not seemed to be at all surprised when, after asking her if she was going to join Daniel in London, he heard that she was going instead in the opposite direction, up to the Scottish Highlands. She had assumed that he had heard the gossip about Daniel. He had asked no questions after that, not even seeming interested in where she was going. In fact she remembered feeling just a little hurt about that.

'Of course I'll be delighted to give you a reference, Laurel,' he had told her quite cheerfully. 'I can hardly do otherwise after the way you've worked here at this hotel.'

Again, she had been disappointed that he hadn't said he would be sorry to lose her. Of course, he would have known at that stage that he was not losing her at all! Why had Calum been acting as manager of the Skellkirk Abbey Hotel all the time she had worked there when he was the owner of the Glen View Hotel? Her mind was teeming with questions, but they were not about to be answered because Calum was holding out his right hand to take her own fingers in a firm grasp as he smiled down at her.

'How are you, Laurel?' he asked quietly. 'Are you beginning to enjoy life up here?'

'Yes, I am,' she heard herself reply before he released her hand. All at once she knew it was true, that she was starting to enjoy her life here with so much beauty around her and the challenge of her work to give her plenty to think about.

'I'll be seeing you later,' Calum told her. 'After I've unpacked and had a shower. Don't wait for me to start the ceilidh, Fergus, now that most people are here.'

He was walking away from her then, his stride purposeful, his travel bag slung over his shoulder as he made his way swiftly up the beautifully restored staircase to the tower flat on the top floor of the building. A lift had been installed, but Calum ignored it because he needed to stretch his legs after the long drive up from North Yorkshire.

'Och! It's good to see him looking so much better!' Mrs Reid beamed as she made this observation to Fergus and Laurel. 'I was aye feared for him, at one time—'

'It's over now, Maggie. You've no need to worry about him any more. At least, no more than you do about all of us McLeods.' As he spoke, Fergus put an affectionate arm about Maggie Reid's plump shoulders and gave her a hug. 'What would we do without you, Maggie?'

'Away with ye! There's nothing I do that some other body couldna' do just as weel.' With that, Maggie Reid slipped away from them to go and greet some new arrivals from Rowankirk.

'I think you embarrassed her,' Laurel murmured with a smile. 'She's quite reserved,

66

isn't she?'

'She's also quite special to us,' Fergus replied. 'Incredibly loyal to us.' He left her then to join Isla Summers who had just arrived at the hotel with the man Laurel had seen working in the hotel garden, the man she had first seen down at the site of the Highland Clearances when she was at the end of her long journey north. The man whose face had shown such deep desolation when he turned to answer her, holding his posy of white flowers. When Laurel had met him again while she was walking Mull for Fergus he had not appeared to remember her. She watched him exchange a few words with Fergus then stroll away from the engaged couple towards the main reception room. He had quite a pronounced limp, she noticed then, yet his bearing was upright and his shoulders were held very straight.

The ceilidh turned out to be a night to remember, a night when Laurel knew she had made the right decision in taking the job at this hotel. There was no one here in this remote spot who knew that the man she loved had so quickly found another love. No one except Calum McLeod, she corrected her thoughts ruefully. Yet she felt certain that Calum would not gossip about her past, because all the time she had worked for him she had been aware that he was a very reserved man, a man who would respect her privacy as he would expect her to respect his own.

Yes, she had done the right thing to leave Skellkirk and all her memories of Daniel behind. Here she was making a new start and beginning to make new friends. Already some of the staff who lived locally had asked her up to take part in some of the dances, which were set to the music of fiddle and accordians played by a quartet of men attired in tartan kilts and frilled shirts. This was a form of dance she had never attempted before but the rhythm was irresistible and she found herself adapting to the movements surprisingly quickly.

She was recovering from her third such dance with three different partners and enjoying a long, ice-cold lemon and lime drink when the tempo of the music changed from the lively reels and became slower. It was then that Calum appeared before her to invite her to partner him. He had changed from the casual gear which she had seen him wearing when he first arrived at the Glen View and looked splendid now in a kilt of his clan tartan and a dark-coloured velvet jacket. On his feet were knee-length socks and black pumps. Her eyes must have shown her surprise because he laughed as he took her hand and drew her to her feet.

'I'll apologise in advance for the times I'm probably going to tread on your toes,

Laurel,' he said. 'It's so long since I took to the floor that I'll be way out of practice.'

'You'll be better at it than me, because I've never even tried this sort of dancing before,' she assured him. 'There was no opportunity down in Skellkirk.'

'Then we'll muddle through together,' Calum murmured as he led her to the edge of the floor and put his arm about her.

The dancing was taking place on the polished parquet flooring of the reception hall, with the ceilidh band playing above them on the first-floor balcony. A dozen or so couples were circling to the lilting music of the waltz. Any more would have been too many. Laurel felt her spirits lifting. It was so long since she had done anything like this, and Calum was a graceful mover and light on his feet.

'You're not really out of practice, are you?' she teased him as he spun her round at the end of an old-time waltz.

'It's years since I did anything like this,' he answered.

'I've never done it before, but I'm enjoying it. It's great!'

'You'll have plenty of opportunities to do it again, once we start our regular ceilidh nights. Now I'll get you another drink before Fergus and Isla take the floor.'

When Calum returned from the lounge bar with two glasses and a bottle of wine on

69

a tray, Laurel was in for another surprise as Fergus, also in Highland dress but with a cascade of lace falling from the neck of his shirt, led his fiancée into the centre of the room. Isla wore her long black hair loose about the shoulders of her long white brocade gown. A dark green and scarlet silk sash covered one shoulder and draped to one side of her waist where it was held by a heavy silver brooch.

'Oh, doesn't she look lovely!' Laurel exclaimed.

'Yes, it's like old times again having the place full of family and friends. Like it used to be before the fire, before everything started to go wrong.' Calum's expression changed as he spoke. He looked quite stern now and was certainly not the same man who had appeared so pleased to be her partner in the dancing, Laurel thought. She cast about in her mind for something to say. Then the aloof expression cleared from his face as suddenly as it had arrived.

'It's time to put the past behind us now, Laurel, and think about making a new start, don't you think?' he said with a smile.

Laurel could not speak for the lump in her throat. Even though she had made a new start in her working life here in Calum's hotel, there would never be anyone who could bring back the joy and hope for the future she had once shared with Daniel.

70

Four

As Calum moved to the centre of the floor to announce that Fergus and Isla, as requested, would delight their friends with a couple of favourite Scottish ballads, Victor hovered in the entrance gathering up courage to listen to them. He should not have allowed himself to be persuaded to come here tonight. His first instinct, to make the excuse that there was no one to sit with Robbie, had been the right one. Only he had been overruled by his in-laws, Ruth and Alexander, who had said it was time he had a night out and that they were happy not to go to the ceilidh..

Now, as he stared at Isla, Victor felt pain tearing at his guts. It was the same relentless pain, the same immense sense of loss, which had never left him since the day of the terrorist attack which had cost him his lovely Shona. The likeness to Shona that Isla bore now was quite startling, and hard for him to take. A year or so ago Isla had been the more lively twin whose bubbling sense of humour was never far away, in contrast to

71

Shona's quieter, more thoughtful nature. A year ago Isla had possessed generous curves about her hips and shoulders, and had worn her hair in a short and curly style that was very different from Shona's long silky black tresses.

Now Isla was almost too slender. Her face showed high cheekbones from which the flesh had dropped sharply, and her hair was dressed in an exact copy of Shona's style. Even her long white dress revived memories of the one Shona had worn when they were married in the little church at Rowankirk. There was no way he could stay and watch, or even listen, as Shona's sister sang one of the songs that the sisters had so often sung together. He had to get out of here before he broke down and spoiled the evening for all those who had come to enjoy themselves after the long winter of hard work renovating Glen View.

Spurred on by the tears that burned behind his eyes and threatened to overflow, Victor turned so abruptly to make his way through the half dozen people who were gathered close to the main entrance that his shoulder caught in the folds of the dark blue wool cape that Grace had slipped over her long blue skirt and matching blue-patterned silk shirt. The cape slid smoothly over the thin silk and fell in a heap at Victor's feet. As he bent to retrieve it, Grace also reached down to pick it up. Their hands brushed momentarily, and Grace felt the tear he had not been able to stop splash down on to her hand. Startled, she looked up into his face and was appalled by what she saw there.

Victor knew he could not escape into the hotel garden until he had apologised for his clumsiness. For a long moment he stood facing her, attempting to utter the few words that his inherent good manners demanded. Only the words were trapped by the swelling inside his throat. There was no way he could force them out. All he could do was stand there while another couple of tears slid very slowly down either side of his tightly closed mouth.

Grace looked away from his anguish and down at the fine woollen cape which showed a smudge of dust where one of his shoes had caught it. She noticed that Victor's hands were grasping the garment so tightly that his knuckles showed white. Another wave of pity for him washed over her.

'It doesn't matter,' she whispered. 'Please don't be upset. The dust will brush off.'

He found his voice then, though it came out rough and husky. 'I'm very sorry. It was clumsy of me. I wasn't looking where I was going.'

'It really doesn't matter,' she insisted. 'I'll take it into the cloakroom and it'll be as good as new in a few minutes.'

She managed to force a smile as she held out her hand to take the cape from him. He recognised her then, as he rubbed the moisture from his cheeks with the back of his hand.

'It's Grace, isn't it? Mr Hastie's daughter.'

'Yes, I'm surprised that you remember me though; we can't have met very often.' Grace hesitated before going on. 'How are you Victor? Are you still in the army?'

'Not any more. I'm not fit enough,' he replied so brusquely that Grace was left in no doubt that having to leave the army life he had loved was yet another blow Victor had been forced to endure since she had last seen him.

'I'm sorry to hear that. Sorry about everything that's happened to you.'

He shrugged the powerful shoulders that were clad in a dark green suede jacket. 'At least I'll be better able to look after my son now I've left the service.'

'I suppose that will be your priority now. Is he with his grandparents tonight?' She asked the question because she was anxious to move away from the difficult subject of his bereavement.

'Yes. I didn't want to come tonight but Ruth and Alexander more or less insisted on it,' he found himself confessing.

Grace smiled. 'I wasn't too keen myself,

but I was afraid that if I used the excuse that I wasn't feeling up to it Isla or Ruth would have come dashing along to the cottage to find out if I needed looking after.'

He frowned. 'Why should they do that? Aren't you staying with your parents?'

'No. They're in New Zealand for a few months visiting my sisters. They've been wanting to go out there for ages but it wasn't possible until Dad retired from his ministry at the end of last year. Then there was the move from the manse to Faith's Cottage.' After that there had been her own illness and operation to delay her parents' departure but she was not going to mention that.

'You'll just be up here for a short visit then. Is your husband with you?' Grace knew Victor was only being polite, pretending an interest in her that was not really there.

'No. He couldn't manage it.' Oh, how it hurt to say that! How much more it hurt to remember that Paul could no longer manage to go on living with her.

'Well, I won't keep you from the entertainment, now that you are here.' He was about to move on, out of hearing of the hauntingly beautiful Scottish ballad being sung by Isla, when he turned back to speak again to Grace.

'Why didn't you want to come to the

ceilidh, Grace?'

Grace swallowed. How could she answer that one? She was not going to tell Victor that her main reason for not wanting to be here, where there were so many people she had known for much of her life, was that some of those old friends would ask the sort of questions about Paul that she would find it impossible to answer. It would be time enough for the news of their separation to get round when her parents were back.

It must be so much worse for Victor, having to face all these people who would not know what to say to him. Vividly into her mind came remembrance of the headline from the local newspaper which her parents had sent to her just after the tragedy. 'Local Ceilidh Singer Dies In Bomb Blast.' No wonder Victor's emotions had become too much for him when he heard Isla singing. It made her own situation seem just a little less hopeless. At least Paul was still alive; still able to make a decision about whether or not he cared enough for her to accept the fact that she could not give him children.

Victor was still waiting for her to explain her own reluctance to put in an appearance at the ceilidh. It had better be something near to the truth, she decided. 'I've been ill recently and I soon get tired. So I'm not all that keen on going out in the evening.'

76

'And I'm keeping you standing here when you ought to be sitting down. I'm so sorry, Grace!' he broke in. His dark grey eyes were full of compassion for her. 'I hope you'll soon be quite well again.'

With that he strode away, down the steps and into the garden, moving quickly as though he could not get away from the sound of the music soon enough. Grace noticed that he had a pronounced limp. What would he do with the rest of his life now that he was not fit enough for the army? Her last sight of him hurrying away from the party atmosphere to the solitude of the hotel grounds stayed in her mind as she took a seat on the edge of the dance floor.

Soon there were people coming to greet her, and inevitably to ask about her husband. By the time she had answered several of these well-meaning enquiries Grace found it slightly easier to make it appear that the only reason Paul was not at her side was because his business was so successful that he could not spare the time to get away just now. Her own presence alone here in her parents' cottage was, she explained to several different people, because if she had stayed at home she would have been tempted to go back to work too soon. It was a relief when the supper interval arrived and an old friend of her father's came to escort her to the buffet table. He asked no awkward questions, for which Grace was more than thankful.

Victor Thorpe did not come back into the hotel until after Isla and Fergus had sung their second set of songs. As she watched them singing together Grace was able to guess at his anguish: since she had last stayed in the area Isla had taken on a startling likeness to Shona. Her loss of weight had something to do with this, but so had the hair style too. Could it be that Isla was finding comfort in deliberately highlighting her likeness to her twin? There was no disguising the similarity in the sisters' voices. No wonder Victor had been forced to escape into the garden.

'It's like going back in time a couple of years, isn't it?' Calum McLeod said quietly as he came to stand close to Grace.

Grace shivered in spite of the warmth of the room. 'Yes,' she whispered. 'Like that last ceilidh, the night before the fire. So many things have happened since then. The terrible things that happened to Shona and Victor, and you being injured that night. How are you now?'

'I'm fine. Completely recovered.'

'I'm glad to hear that.

'The time I've spent working down in Yorkshire has helped me a lot.'

'Why did you decide to do that?'

Calum took his time answering. 'I just

78

couldn't face seeing this place in ruins after all the time and effort, and money, I'd put into it. At first I didn't intend to bother restoring it, since Katharine had taken a job over in the States and told me she had no intention of coming back here either to work or to marry me.'

'I was sorry when I heard your engagement was off, after all you'd been through,' Grace said into the silence that had grown between them.

'It was for the best. All in the past now; yesterday's news.' He said that as though he meant it, which surprised Grace, even though she had never really liked Katharine.

'So you went to manage someone else's hotel?'

'Yes. It took so long to sort out the insurance claim that when I was fit to work I thought I'd widen my experience by taking the job in the Yorkshire Dales.'

Grace frowned. 'That can't have been easy to do, after being your own boss for so long.'

'I needed the money, as well as to get away from here.'

'Why did you wait for so long to come back?' Grace wanted to know.

The stern lines of Calum's face softened. 'Because of something that happened to me down in Yorkshire. Something that has helped me to come to terms with what happened here.'

'Are you going to manage Glen View? Or will it be Fergus who does that?'

'I'll be owner-manager and Fergus will be my deputy. He may become my partner, if he stays on here. I suppose that will partly depend on what Isla wants to do.'

'Maybe they'll get married now Victor has come here to look after his son?'

Calum frowned. 'Maybe. I thought they would have been married long before now. Isla seems to have changed quite a lot since Shona died. I noticed that when I came up for a short visit a few weeks ago.'

'I don't suppose Isla could face having the wedding without her twin sister as her bridesmaid. They were always so close, weren't they?'

'Yes. I know Isla missed Shona tremendously when she first married Victor and went with him to Ireland. They had the wedding already planned when Shona was killed, but poor Ruth was so ill with the shock that Isla was needed to help look after wee Robbie. So they decided to put the wedding on hold for the time being.'

'I had a word with Victor, just after I arrived tonight. He's devastated, isn't he? Do you think he'll be able to cope with looking after the little boy and finding work here?'

'He's already found work, here at Glen View. Didn't he tell you?'

'No, we didn't talk for long. He was finding it hard to listen to Isla singing.'

'Yes, he would. Life would probably have been easier for him now if he had been able to stay in the army, but he's not fit enough.'

'What will he do here?'

'Look after the gardens. Fergus and Isla were so impressed with the garden he created at the house he bought in Ireland that Fergus offered him the job here. I just hope it works out for him,' Calum ended.

'I hope things work out for you, too, Calum,' Grace said then. 'It'll be a new start for you, won't it, from tomorrow when your first guests arrive?'

'Yes, I think so.' His eyes scanned the room as he spoke. Who was he looking for? Grace had a feeling it was the girl he had been dancing with earlier in the evening. The small, brown-haired girl who was so unlike the woman who had been Calum's partner for so long.

'We've spoken about everyone except you, Grace,' Calum said then. 'Is your life going so well that you can't wait to get back to your lovely home and your flower shop, and to Paul?'

Grace waited too long to answer him. She was finding it almost impossible to tell a lie to Calum, who had been her friend since her childhood. 'I've been ill, so I needed a break from my home and my shop,' she

81

began hesitantly.

Calum frowned. 'I didn't know that. I've got a bit behind with the news while I've been living down in Yorkshire. How are you now?'

She tried to force a smile, but didn't quite make it. Nor could she come up with the right sort of words. All at once she felt desperately tired and tearful. All she wanted was to be away from Glen View and back in Faith's Cottage where Calum could not ask the question which was certain to come next.

Calum took a step closer to her, his eyes full of his concern. 'What is it, Grace? Are you feeling unwell right now?'

It was much easier to nod her head, to take that way out before words and tears came together and spoiled Calum's evening.

'Let me take you home. Or you can stay the night here if you'd rather.'

'I'd rather go home,' she managed at last. 'I'll be fine once I've had some sleep.'

'I'm not easy in my mind about you, Grace. Why don't you leave your car here and let me drive you home, then you can collect it tomorrow when you're feeling better. What do you say?'

Suddenly it seemed easier to give in and nod her head. 'Thanks, Calum.'

He spoke little and drove carefully on the short journey down to the village. At the bottom of the hill he stopped the car and turned to her 'I'm not sure which way to go. I know your parents bought a cottage in Rowankirk but I can't remember which one it was.'

'Faith's Cottage,' she murmured. 'It's on the Rowanmore Road.'

When they reached the cottage he got out of the car and went to open the door and help her out. 'I'll see you to the door,' he said firmly when she would have protested.

She was standing in the porch, with her key in the lock, and was about to thank him and say goodnight, when the question came that she had been dreading. It was asked quietly.

'Why isn't Paul here with you?'

'He's very busy just now.'

'Surely if you've been ill—'

'Things are always hectic in his business at this time of the year, and I'm over the worst now,' she added hurriedly. 'Thanks, Calum! Goodnight!'

She was inside the cottage and closing the door even as he said, 'Goodnight, Grace.'

He walked slowly down the drive but did not get into his car until he had seen lights come on in the windows. Uneasiness went with him as he made his way back to Glen View. There was something worrying him about Grace. Something he could not dismiss from his mind long after the last guests had departed and the hotel was quiet. Grace had looked not just ill but almost in a state of shock. In all the years he had known her there had been about her not just the beauty and vitality of a healthy young woman but something more than that, a sort of inner radiance. At one time he had been strongly attracted to her and they had started going out together, then she had met Paul and gone overboard for him. She had been stunningly lovely then in her joy, and the happiness appeared to have lasted when they had met on her visits to her parents. Where had it gone now? Why had she never once mentioned Paul during their conversation? Dawn was bringing a rosy tint to the sky above Glen View before Calum was able to banish his uneasiness about Grace and drift into sleep.

For Grace there had been a night of weeping, on and off, with intervals when she had got out of bed to make tea and drag her thoughts away from Paul and towards a future that he was no part of. A future where she must make a fresh start somewhere far away from their Cotswold home. The few hours spent in this cottage, bought at the end of her father's long service to the church, had brought vividly into her mind what her Dad would have said if he had guessed that she had even contemplated taking that aspirin overdose.

'That's not the way, my wee girl. You know well what the way is.'

So many times she had heard him say that, in the minor and major crises which had beset her in childhood and early adulthood. If she had succeeded in her bid to end her life in the motel room, what would it have done to her parents? Grace shuddered as she recalled piling up the aspirin tablets and filling the glass with water. If she hadn't spilled the water, hadn't waited to dry off that small New Testament while the tablets were dissolving, the police would have been contacting Paul now. Already Paul would be feeling the burden of her death on his conscience.

It had not happened though. Something, some strange set of circumstances, had saved her. Her father would say she had been saved for a reason. As yet she did not want to know what that reason was. All she wanted to know was what she was going to do next. What was to be the first step in making a new life for herself?

Five

Victor was working in the vast rear garden of the hotel, sorting out the raspberry canes which were furthest away from the building and which seemed to be recovering now from being trampled underfoot first by firemen then by workmen. The April sun was warm on his back and somewhere close at hand a blackbird was singing his sweet springtime song. Later, once the guests began to arrive, there would be the sound of motor engines to disturb the peace, but for now Victor was grateful for the quiet and the solitude to be found in his new job.

Shona would have smiled at the way he was going about his task of untangling dead wood and allowing the new green shoots more light and air. They had grown raspberries in their garden in Ireland, because wee Robbie loved them. So did Shona. This gentle reminder of her did not hurt as much as some. Until, from one of the open upstairs windows at the rear of Glen View, he heard the sound of her voice. Only it couldn't be Shona's voice, could it?

'We've been over it all before, Fergus! I told you, I'm not ready yet. We'll wait till this place is properly back in business, and till Vic finds a home for himself and Robbie. Maybe at the end of the season, late October or November...'

The voice belonged to Isla, of course. An Isla who was impatient, upset, almost on the verge of tears by the sound of it. Victor felt guilty for listening but could not help himself since the sounds were reaching him so clearly through the still air.

Now the voice was Fergus's, angry enough to send every word striking a blow at Victor's heart. His hands, strong and supple, gripped the cane he was holding so tightly that a spurt of blood from one of the thorns ran down his thumb.

'You're using Shona's death as an excuse, Isla, so don't try to deny it!'

'I'm not! I'm not, Fergus. It's just that—'

'It's just that you've changed your mind about wedding me, now that he's back.'

'No! No! You're wrong! It's wee Robbie I'm thinking about.' Isla was crying now. 'You know it is.'

'I know nothing of the sort, and I'm fed up with waiting for you.'

'You haven't been waiting for me, have you?' The words came in a burst of anger from Isla.

Victor bit hard on his lips. Dear God, what

87

had he done, what problems had he caused by coming back to Rowankirk when he ought to have stayed in Ireland and found someone there to look after Robbie?

'I'm talking about waiting to marry you, and to have a family of our own.' Fergus shouted.

'There's plenty of time for that. When this place is properly back in business. Be reasonable, Fergus. Things'll be easier for us then.'

'They won't. You'll be finding another excuse then for putting it off. I want the wedding arranged for early June. Or not at all.'

Victor did not know what came next. Pushing his way through the jungle of overgrown plants that separated the vegetable garden from the rising ground of the mountain, he stumbled away, wanting only to leave the discord which had arisen so unexpectedly between these two people who had been so staunch in their support of him. The ground was rough now, with tree roots and outcrops of stone waiting to trip him if he moved carelessly. He was heedless of that hazard in his desire to get himself speedily out of range of those furious voices and the quarrel he knew he was responsible for.

On and on he strode, crushing the springy tufts of heather beneath his boots while a pulse beat fiercely inside his temples. In the end it was an unbearable surge of pain burning into his damaged ankle that brought him to an abrupt halt, forcing him to sink to his knees while he beat at the nearest outcrop of rose-coloured rock with his fists and, unaware, gave voice to a string of curses.

'Bloody hell! Bloody sodding hell! Why didn't I die instead of Shona? Why was I left alive to cause trouble? Why? Why?'

From somewhere fairly close, as though responding to his words, came the sound of a large dog barking. The sound brought Victor to his feet, bent on escape, but not quickly enough to prevent the dog from bounding towards him. It was Fergus's labrador which often came to keep him company while he was working. Certain of a welcome, the animal came to thrust a cool nose into his hand. Victor instinctively reached out to stroke the silky head.

'Did you hurt yourself?' Laurel asked as she reached him. 'You had me worried when I heard you shouting.' She was frowning, and out of breath too, as she stared at him.

Victor was not pleased to see her. 'No,' he replied sharply, 'I'm all right.' At least he would be when she called the dog to her side and left him alone.

'I thought ... I wanted to make sure...'

'If you mean you heard me cursing, I apologise for that.' What else had she heard him say in his torment? He didn't even want to think about that.

'There's no need to. You thought you were alone. I'll be on my way, now I know you're not injured.' She stopped, then rushed on, 'I mean, not in need of any help to get back to the hotel.'

It was the girl Calum had brought up here from the hotel in Yorkshire, the young woman chef. Plainly, she was afraid she had said the wrong thing.

'It was good of you to come and find out. Thanks,' Victor said as she called the dog and began to walk on.

She turned back then and smiled at him. 'Enjoy your walk.'

He sighed. 'I'm not supposed to be walking, I'm supposed to be working. I *was* working, on the raspberry canes in the back garden, until I overheard something I didn't want to hear. So I made my escape up here.'

Laurel took a step back towards him, speaking her thoughts without being aware of it. 'How strange! That's why I came up here to work, because of something I overheard when I was working in a hotel in Yorkshire. I didn't want to hear it either, because it made me face up to the truth about someone.'

'Maybe what I overheard will help me to face up to the truth that I made a mistake in coming here to live.' Victor's voice was sombre.

'But you've got family here, haven't you? People who can help you to look after your little boy. So it can't really be a mistake, can it?' Mrs Reid had told Laurel why Victor was working as a gardener at the hotel.

Laurel's words made him aware that she knew who he was, and why he had come to live in Rowankirk. Perhaps even why he was so full of anger. Somehow that helped him to relax enough to say, 'Time will tell, for both of us, I expect.' He smiled at her, and she suddenly noticed how handsome he was. 'I'd better get back to work. I'll be seeing you around.'

He watched her walk away, a small dainty girl who held her head high and moved gracefully. He wondered briefly what she had overheard down there in Yorkshire that had brought her so far away from her home to work, and what sort of truth she had been forced to face up to. Then he left the thought behind and began to walk back to the hotel garden, moving carefully this time. Back by the raspberries, he took up the knife he had dropped and listened for a moment before starting to use it. The upstairs window on the first floor was still wide open but there were no voices to be heard from there now.

Grace knew she would have to walk up to

the Glen View Hotel that morning to get her car back, but she was not looking forward to the possibility that on her way she would meet more people she knew. People who would ask first how, she was, then go on to ask about her husband. Should she leave the car where it was in the hotel car park and go for it later when she felt better able to deal with these well-meant questions? The temptation was so strong she almost gave way to it, until she realised that if she did not collect her car Calum might think she was not feeling well enough to walk up for it.

Before she could lose her courage, she slipped a warm fleece jacket over her sweater and slacks, put on a pair of sturdy walking shoes and left Faith's Cottage to start on the mile long uphill walk from the village to the hotel. The first part of the walk took her very close to the little granite church where she had married Paul. Her first sight of the plain, sturdy-looking building brought a physical pain so severe that she almost turned back and made for the safety of the cottage again.

She was totally unprepared for the surge of longing that hit her when a vivid memory of Paul, there, holding her close, took possession of her. They had arrived too early for the rehearsal on the night before their wedding, found the church locked, her father delayed at a meeting. So they had waited in the porch, lost to everything in the world except one another.

'When we leave here tomorrow you'll really belong to me, Grace. I just can't wait for that,' Paul had whispered.

They had shared a tumult of passionate feeling for each other in those few precious moments before her father arrived. That passionate feeling for each other had still been an essential part of their marriage ten years later. Their working lives had been shared with other people, as had some of their leisure time, but their nights in their home had belonged only to themselves and their love for each other. Until her illness had started a year or so ago.

Grace had hated the difference her illness brought to their marriage. Yet Paul had told her it did not matter, that one day it would be a thing of the past and the passion, as well as the tenderness of their love, would be shared again. The sharing was to have begun on their holiday in Italy. Only instead there had been his letter and his phone call confirming that there would be no shared holiday, and no shared love, now that she was unable to have children.

For a few seconds despair enveloped her and she saw the little granite building through a mist of tears. Then, as she was about to move on, she saw Ruth Summers walking towards her with a small boy holding her hand. Grace knew she would have to meet Ruth sooner or later while she was here in Rowankirk, but she could not face meeting her right now when she was fighting to hold tears at bay. There was only one place she could go to avoid a meeting, so she pushed open the lych gate and hurried down the path and into the church.

Once inside the building she let her breath go on a long sigh. She was safe here. As she dropped into one of the worn wooden pews at the back of the church she found herself trembling with relief at her escape. It was a cold little building, with that indefinable scent of dust, wax polish and old flower arrangements that seemed to belong to empty churches.

So many times she had been in this particular church over the years her father had been a minister; as a child trying not to giggle at the sight of Mrs Mactavish's weird Sunday hat; as a young girl gazing with calf-love at Calum McLeod, handsome in his tartan kilt and best jacket; at her own wedding aching with love for Paul. It had been a mistake to escape to this particular place. There were just too many hurtful memories here. Almost choked by the size of the lump in her throat she rose from the seat and made her way back to the porch. So eager was she to get out that as she pulled the heavy door inwards the man who

was already holding the handle on the outside was taken by surprise.

'Sorry!' he said. 'I didn't realise there was
someone inside. In fact the door is usually
locked at this time, I don't know why it isn't
now.'

Grace swallowed. 'I wasn't expecting anyone to be here either at this time. There
never used to be anyone around this early.'

'So you're not a stranger here? Not a
visitor, I mean?' the man said, still holding
the door open for her to leave.

'No. I used to live here. My father was the
minister at this church and the one in
Rowanmore until he retired last year.'

'So you're Gordon's daughter? The one
who lives in the Cotswolds?'

'Yes. You sound as if you know my dad.'

'I do. I'm Donald Muir, the new man.'

He held out a hand to her and she found
her fingers held firmly in his. She hoped he
would not be noticing the evidence of her
recent tears.

'Grace Hardy,' she introduced herself.
'I'm just here for a few days' stay in my
parents' cottage.'

'I hope we'll meet again then. You'll know
the times of the services as well as I do. I
haven't got round to changing them yet.' He
smiled as he told her that, and the smile
banished from his face the lines of weariness.

Grace found herself smiling back. 'This isn't a place that accepts change without a fight,' she remarked. 'Though you'll have discovered that for yourself by now.'

His smile deepened. 'I'm not afraid to fight for what I believe in. I had plenty of experience of that in my last parish.'

'Where was that?' politeness made her ask.

'Manchester. Inner city. For five years.'

'Did you win your fight there?'

'I was winning until...' He stopped, then went on, 'I mustn't keep you, Mrs Hardy, but I'm glad to have met you. You know where I am, if you should need any help while you're here.'

What made him think she might need his help, Grace wondered as she walked through the neat churchyard to the gate. Surely the news of her and Paul had not already got around? Then the thought came to console her that her father might have mentioned her illness and operation. So Donald was only doing his job in the conventional way by telling her that he was there to help if she needed him.

Not that she would be asking him for help, she told herself as she followed a bridle path that would lead eventually to the Glen View Hotel. Her help now must come from within herself. She was a mature woman of thirty-five, well-educated and with the skill in her hands and the ideas in her brain to

have built up a small but successful business. The crying and feeling sorry for herself
had to stop now. She must direct all her
thoughts towards the future, a future far
away from the place where her life had gone
wrong.

The first step would be to phone Alison,
the friend who had taken over the managing
of her little shop when she first became ill.
They had met at the county flower club,
where Grace had been so impressed with
Alison's talent for creating unusual arrangements that she had offered her part-time
work soon afterwards. Alison, a divorced
mother of two school-age children, had
been delighted, and they had worked well
together in building up a name for their
complete wedding service.

Making that first decision, to sell her shop,
gave new impetus to Grace's feet and helped her to enjoy the bracing mountain air.
Soon she was walking through the hotel
gates and looking round for her car. She
recalled then that on the previous evening
all the parking spaces in front of the hotel
had been occupied so she had been forced
to drive round to the rear car park. As she
turned the corner she could see her car, the
silver Volvo that had been Paul's gift on their
tenth wedding anniversary last year. It
would probably have to be sold when she
was a single woman again, needing to buy a

home as well as a business.

'How are you feeling today, Grace?' Calum asked, coming out of the back porch while she was searching her bag for her keys.

'I'm fine.' She gave him such a brilliant smile as she said the words that he began to wonder whether the uneasiness he had felt about her last night had all been in his imagination. 'All I needed to put me right was a good sleep.'

'You certainly look more like yourself. I was worried about you last night.'

'Thanks a lot for taking me home. Did you enjoy the rest of the ceilidh?'

He laughed. 'I certainly did. There wasn't much of the night left when I finally got to bed. Now there's plenty of work ahead of me. We've a full house here from today until after Easter, but we haven't quite got a full staff – the girl who was going to share reception duty with Isla hasn't arrived yet. Her car has broken down.'

'Is there anything I can do to help?' Grace found herself asking.

Calum surveyed her thoughtfully before answering. 'There might be. Why don't you go in and have a word with Isla? The last time I saw her she was beginning to lose her cool a bit, so she may be glad of a helping hand from someone she knows.'

'I'll do that right now. Have you any idea where I'll find her?'

'She ought to be in the staff-room taking a coffee break but she's probably on the go somewhere now she knows the other girl won't be here today. I'd better warn you that she's on a short fuse just now.'

'I expect you all are at this stage. I mean after all the trauma of the building work.'

'I've missed out on most of that, with working down in Yorkshire. It's Fergus and Isla who've had all the problems to cope with.' Calum was frowning as he said that, then added, 'I think perhaps I ought to have come back sooner.'

'Have they set the wedding date, now that Victor's out of hospital?' Grace wanted to know.

Calum shook his head. 'No, I mentioned before, it's on hold, and it might be better if you don't mention it when you talk to Isla. As I said, she seems to be really stressed out just now.'

'Thanks for the warning. I'll go and see if I can find her.'

'I'm looking for Victor. He was out here earlier this morning but he seems to have vanished.'

Plainly, Calum had come back to the hotel which had once been his family home to any number of problems. Grace found herself wondering again why he had not come back to Glen View much earlier. Dropping her car keys back into her bag, she went into the

99

building by the back entrance.

Everywhere she looked there was new paint, new wood, new floor coverings, new furniture and soft furnishings. It was all so very different from the way Glen View had looked in the days when Calum had converted it. The country house look had still been retained in the earlier hotel, while more en-suite bathrooms had been added and the kitchen extended by taking in the former dairies and pantries. Now, while the exterior looked very much as Grace remembered, inside it had become a modern hotel with the spacious front hall made larger by the incorporation of the old breakfast room on one side and the library on the other.

There was no sign of Isla in any of the rooms which opened directly off the reception hall, so Grace made her way into the kitchen. The dainty young chef Calum had brought up from Yorkshire was concocting a luscious looking cold pudding at one of the stainless steel worktops while a young lad whose face reminded Grace of someone was stirring something in a pan on one of the immense cookers. He did not look round as Grace spoke.

'Could you tell me where I'll find Isla, please?'

The girl looked up and smiled at her. 'She could be anywhere, the way things are this morning. I suppose you'll have already looked everywhere on the ground floor?'

'Yes.'

'Do you know what she looks like?'

'Yes. I used to live here, a long time ago.'

'You could try the bedrooms then. Isla might have gone to make sure all the tea-makers are fully stocked, even though Mrs Reid said they were. I think panic was beginning to set in,' Laurel said with a grin.

'Thanks, I'll take a look.'

'Do you know the way?'

Grace laughed. 'I could find my way upstairs in this place blindfolded. You see I used to come up here to play when it was Calum's family home.'

'You'll be a family friend then?'

'Yes.'

'I should be offering you a coffee...'

Grace shook her head. 'No, thanks all the same. I need to find Isla first to see if she needs any help from me.'

'I'm sure she does. Everything seems to be going wrong this morning. Maybe we were all up a bit too late last night at the ceilidh. Though we all had a great time,' she added.

'Yes.' Everyone except her, and Victor Thorpe. Grace pushed the thought away and went in search of Isla.

It was very quiet up on the first floor, with all the bedroom doors closed so that it was not possible to tell which room Isla was in. Grace hesitated before a low table on which there was a tall lamp and a bowl of flowers. The flowers had been too hastily arranged. She could not resist putting them to rights before moving further along the corridor. At the far end of that wing, after she had passed many closed doors, she stopped again. This time she called Isla's name. There was no response. Then the sound of glass or china breaking above her head sent her up the second flight of stairs at speed.

'Are you there, Isla? It's Grace,' she called when she reached the topmost step.

What she heard then sent her hurrying along another wide corridor to the area where the old nursery suite was situated. Her feet made no noise on the thickly carpeted floor as she drew nearer to where she could hear faint sounds that she found disturbing. Someone was crying. Not the sort of unrestrained weeping that would cause instant alarm, but more like barely stifled sobs which someone was unable to control. Grace held her breath as she drew nearer to the old nursery where she, Isla and Shona had played so often with the McLeod children. Yes, the sobs were on the other side of that door. What should she do, ignore it and go downstairs again? How could she do that when she suspected that the unhappy person was Isla?

'Oh, Isla, whatever's wrong?' A few steps into the spacious room brought her to where the younger girl was slumped on the dressing stool with her head on her arms amid a litter of broken glass from the crystal candlestick she had knocked over.

'Everything. Absolutely everything, and I can't do anything about it,' Isla muttered.

'I might be able to help—' Grace began.

'No one can! So you might as well leave me alone,' Isla went on, in between her stifled sobs.

Grace ignored her and began to carefully gather up the pieces of broken glass and drop them into the waste paper bin.

Six

Why don't you go away and leave me alone? I told you there's nothing you can do.'

The words were less certain now. Isla was scrubbing her eyes, still bending over so that Grace was unable to see her face. What she could see was the trickle of blood which was running slowly down from Isla's knuckles to drip on to her skirt.

'I'll leave you when I've found something to stop you from bleeding all over your clothes, and the new carpet,' Grace told her. 'It wouldn't have mattered when it was the carpet that used to be in here, but it won't do this new pale green one any good, will it?'

Isla replied only with a sniff and a gulp while Grace fished around in her shoulder bag for a tissue and a plaster. She handed them to the distraught girl, then went back to gathering up shards of broken glass, this time from the carpet around Isla's feet.

'I'll go if you want me to, as soon as I've finished doing this,' she said. 'I only came to look for you because Calum said you might be glad of some help.'

Alarm flared in Isla's face as she looked down at Grace. 'What made him say that?'

'He mentioned that the girl who was supposed to arrive today to help with reception wasn't coming because her car had broken down. So I asked him if there was anything I could do.' Grace got to her feet, ready to leave if that was what Isla wanted.

Isla sighed. 'Oh Grace, I'm sorry I was so rude. It was just that my smashing the candlestick was the last straw. The final thing to go wrong for me.'

'It's not the end of the world though, is it? Unless the candlestick was something priceless which can't be replaced?'

'No, it wasn't really the candlestick. It was everything else. All the things I can't put right ever again.'

'It can't really be as bad as that, can it? I expect you're tired out after all the work you've done, and the late night last night.'

Isla sighed again. 'I wish it were only that, but it isn't.'

'What then? Or would you rather not talk about it?'

Isla got to her feet, still scrubbing at her eyes. 'You might not understand.'

'You could try me. After all, we are old friends.'

'I'll think about it, but for now I've wasted enough time and I'll never have everything finished before the guests start arriving this afternoon. The new girl was going to do the flowers and the menus. I've made a start on the flowers, but I'll never have the dinner menus done in time.'

Already she was on her way to the door, a tall graceful girl with a curtain of silky black hair falling to her shoulders. She looked so like Shona, Grace thought. Was it that she hadn't yet started to come to terms with Shona's death?

'Would you like me to finish doing the flowers?' she offered.

'Oh, would you? Please! I'm hopeless at arranging them. I was going to enrol for some classes, but when wee Robbie came to live with us I didn't have enough time.'

'Are there any more flowers to do up here?'

'You could tidy up the ones I've already done. They'll need it,' Isla told her with a rueful smile. 'The rest of the arrangements are for the downstairs rooms. You'll find the boxes and containers in the small conservatory. If you'll do that I can get on to the computer and start the menus. I'll see you later, for lunch at half twelve.'

Isla had pulled herself together remarkably quickly, Grace thought as she watched her go out of the room carrying the bin with the broken glass. So what was it all about, that terrible weeping and her mood of utter

106

despair? Had there been a row with Fergus? Was the tension between them becoming unbearable now that they were working together all the time?

Before the fire Isla had worked as head receptionist at a large Glasgow hotel and Katharine had been behind the desk here at Glen View. When the engagement had been announced on the night of the fire, Isla and Fergus were already preparing the Coach House and planning their wedding for the following summer, until Shona's sudden violent death had thrown their plans into chaos. Was that what was at the heart of Isla's despair? Did she feel unable to go ahead with her wedding without her twin sister there to take part? If Isla chose to confide in her she would listen, but would talking about her problems be enough to banish the haunted look from Isla's lovely eyes? She would have to wait and see.

There was little time, once Grace had put to rights the bowls of spring flowers which stood on the window-ledges and old oak chests in the corridors and landings of the first and second floors before moving to the ground floor where the local women who had been recruited by Mrs Reid had now finished vacuuming, dusting and polishing. Here again there were large arrangements of daffodils, narcissi and forsythia to be placed on the reception desk, in the windows and on small tables in the lounges. For the dining tables dainty vases of spray carnations were required.

Grace was in her element, giving all her attention to this work at which she was so highly skilled. Then it was noon and the time had flown without her being aware of it. Fergus found her placing the final bowl of mixed flowers in the entrance, standing back from it to make sure the balance was right.

'You've made a wonderful job of those, Grace,' he said warmly. 'I'm glad you were here to come to the rescue.'

Grace smiled back at him. 'I expect someone else would have come to help out if I hadn't been here. Someone from one of the local shops or nurseries, I mean.'

'There isn't anywhere that local now,' he told her. 'We have to go as far as Fort William to find a decent florist, and I don't think they'd have been prepared to send anyone as far as this at short notice. We order the flowers by phone to be sent from there. These were delivered early this morning, but Isla didn't have time to do them.'

'What happened to the flower shop in Rowanmore? The florist there was quite good.'

'She certainly was, and she was prepared to come out here after the shop closed if we had a wedding or party booked,' Fergus agreed. 'Until her husband was transferred to London and she had to move with him.'

'Didn't anyone else take over the business?'

Fergus shook his head. 'No. The name stayed the same but it was turned into a gift and card shop, then rented by someone selling their own beauty products, but neither lasted long and the place is empty again now. We could really do with someone like you setting up shop here, but that's not going to happen, is it?'

Grace remained silent, robbed of the power of speech for a few moments by what Fergus had just said. Ideas were chasing one another so madly round and round in her head that she was unable to cope with them at first. The ideas were rubbish, of course, because from what she could recall of the florist shop in Rowanmore it had been very small and a bit run-down, despite the proprietor's talent. She had probably only been renting the place, Grace surmised.

'Are you all right, Grace?' Fergus asked with some concern. 'You haven't been too well, have you? It's probably time you had a rest and something to eat. There'll be soup and cheese ready about now in the staffroom, so come along and take a break.' He put his arm about her shoulders and led her through the foyer to the room at the back of the building where the staff took their meal breaks.

Grace was still preoccupied as she took her seat on one side of the big square pine table from where she was able to get a good view of the huge back garden of the hotel. Victor Thorpe was at work there, planting out something in neat rows. She wondered if he would come in for his lunch or if he would have brought a packed lunch to eat on the bench which backed on to the brick potting shed. He might feel embarrassed if he came indoors and found her sitting here, after the mishap he had had with her cape last night.

Her thoughts returned to that small empty shop in Rowanmore, and whether there was any living accommodation behind or above it. Certainly there would not be the profit to be made up here in this thinly populated Highland region that she was used to making in the prosperous and busy Cotswolds. Probably the rent of the shop in Rowanmore would not be so high though, and there would not be the wages of Alison and the young girl trainee to pay. It just might be worth taking a look.

'Hello, Grace. Did you manage to get those big footmarks of mine off your cape?' Victor asked quietly as he slid into the chair next to hers.

Grace turned her head to smile into his dark, serious eyes. 'There was no damage

110

done,' she assured him truthfully. 'I told you the dust would brush off, and it did.'

'I didn't see you later, so you must have left early?'

'Yes. I'd had a long journey the day before, followed by a sleepless night. Tiredness just caught up on me so Calum drove me home.'

'I didn't realise you worked here,' he began.

Grace laughed softly. 'Neither did I, until I came up to collect my car this morning and Calum told me that the assistant receptionist was delayed. So I offered to help out by doing the flowers.'

'That was good of you, when you're on holiday.'

She laughed again. 'It isn't hard work for me. I'm used to working at it all day, in my own business, and sometimes into the evenings too at busy times.'

'Is someone else looking after your business for you while you're away?'

'Yes, my friend Alison. She's been marvellous at coping with it all while I've been ill.'

Fergus had brought a covered dish of soup to the table on which a basket of warm bread rolls, a dish of butter and a platter of cheeses were already set out. He was frowning so heavily that his rusty eyebrows almost met. Behind him was Isla, whose lovely eyes were still red-rimmed. When he took his

111

place at the table on the other side of Grace, Isla did not go to occupy the chair next to him but instead went to sit beside Victor and open up a lively conversation with him. Plainly, Fergus was not pleased at this. Grace began to feel uncomfortable.

'Why didn't you bring wee Robbie up here with you this morning, Vic?' Isla wanted to know.

'I thought he might be in the way when everyone had so much to do.'

'He'd have been fine with me, and Mum could have caught up on her work while he was here.'

'You were complaining a couple of hours ago that you would never manage to get everything ready before the first guests arrived,' Fergus broke in. 'That's why Grace offered to help, isn't it?'

Isla did not answer the challenge in his stare. Grace began to feel even more aware of the tense atmosphere that was building up around the table. It was only the arrival of Calum and the dainty little chef, who were sharing a joke, that helped to lighten the atmosphere. Calum seemed to be in very good spirits. The day the Glen View Hotel reopened for business was a day he must have looked forward to all the time he was working in Yorkshire.

'Have you two met, Grace?' he asked. 'This is Laurel Appleby from the Skellkirk

Abbey Hotel in Yorkshire. She's a superb cook. Laurel, this is Grace Hardy, an old family friend who lives in the Cotswolds with a husband whose business is so successful that he can't get away just now. Her parents are away too, visiting her sisters in New Zealand, so we must make sure Grace is not lonely while she's here.'

'We've already met, Calum, when I was looking for Isla. Haven't we, Laurel?'

The two girls exchanged smiles across the table. Grace guessed that Laurel was too shy to be able to easily make conversation with a stranger. She also guessed that Calum was in love with the girl, since he seemed unable to tear his glance away from her. Laurel was very pretty, with her long golden hair tied up in a knot of blue velvet on the crown of her head. Her eyes were the vivid blue of the bluebells that would soon take the place of the wild daffodils on the wooded lower slopes of the hills. If her guess was right and Calum was in love with Laurel Appleby, was Laurel also in love with him?

Soon, as the talk turned to the events which had been arranged at the hotel for the start of what they all hoped would be a successful season, the hint of discord which had been hanging about the room faded, and Grace began to wonder whether she had just imagined that Fergus was intensely jealous of Victor Thorpe.

By mid-afternoon the visitors were beginning to arrive and Grace was driving back down the narrow winding road that led to Rowankirk. She did not stop at Faith's Cottage but drove on, taking the wider road that led to Rowanmore, the larger of the two villages. When she left the Glen View she had not intended to do this, but curiosity about that small empty shop would not be banished from her mind. Looking at the place did not commit her to deciding that she would return to live in the place where she had spent so many happy years, she told herself. Though she would certainly have to find somewhere to live.

The long main street of Rowanmore looked unchanged from when she last visited it a year ago. Many of the tiny single-storey cottages opened directly on to the High Street, which widened out midway down into a square, where rowan trees were beginning to show their spring foliage and rustic benches invited passers-by to linger and enjoy the first warm days of the year. The sun brought a glint of silver to the stonework of the village school and the larger dwellings which were set back from the square. Grace parked her car in one of the bays placed handily for the shops and got out to explore the place on foot.

Shops, cafés and substantial houses whose front gardens were colourful with spring flowers all looked the same as they had done ever since she had been a pupil at the village infant school. Rowanmore did not seem to hanker for change and modernisation. Tourists came to wander through the peaceful thoroughfares because they liked the slower pace of life to be found here, so why change it?

There had been a few changes though, Grace discovered as she walked slowly down the length of the High Street until she reached the granite church and the manse where her parents had lived. Scaffolding spoiled the appearance of the church. Next door to it the manse wore an air of neglect that Grace knew would have upset her mother. She walked on until she came to the hotels and guest houses which lined the route to the larger resorts, where skiing was possible for most of the winter and dry slopes were on offer all year. She turned back then, not wishing to progress as far as the main road where traffic would be heavy on this fine day.

The empty shop she had come to look at was on the other side of the road, one of six low-roofed buildings which were attractive to the tourists because of their look of belonging to years long gone. There was a newsagent, a wine shop, a greengrocer, a bookshop, an art shop – and there was the empty shop. It was a tiny place with one main window and a glass door. Also a pitched slate roof where a dormer window could just be glimpsed poking through the lichen. It was the end property of the terraced row, and there was a poster in the main window which looked as if it had been there for rather too long.

Grace moved nearer to the window and began to peer at the interior of the shop. From here it didn't look too bad. There was a counter across the far corner and shelves built into the alcoves. To her surprise, the floor area was larger than she remembered, so perhaps the place had been extended. She might as well take a look at the back of the premises to see if this was so.

There were side windows let in at both the ground-floor and upper levels. Through the ground-floor one she could see that her guess had been correct. An arch led from the original shop through to another room of roughly the same size. Her inspection of the back showed that another room had also been added at first-floor level. Behind the extension was a long, narrow back garden with a greenhouse and a shed. For a long time Grace stood in the back garden staring at the building and wondering whether to take the next step and contact the agent with a view to looking at the inside of The Flower Basket, High Street, Rowanmore.

If she took the drastic step of selling her

Cotswold business and moving up here she would be acknowledging to herself that she had given up any hope of Paul having second thoughts and coming back to her. It would also be sending out the same signal to Paul. Did she really want that?

No! No! What she wanted was for Paul to get in touch with her and tell her he couldn't live without her because he loved her too much. Would that ever happen though? Paul was not a man who acted hastily; he was a man who made decisions only after long and careful thought. While she had been in hospital he had had plenty of time to consider, long and hard, how much it mattered to him that never, while he was married to her, would he become the father of a family. Paul would not have found it easy to come to that decision, Grace knew. So if she really loved him and wanted him to be happy she would have to let him go.

Slowly, with footsteps that dragged, she made her way back to the front of The Flower Basket and stared again through the window. That was when she saw something she had missed earlier, a single flower container which had somehow been forgotten when the stock had all been cleared from the shop. It stood forlornly at the far end of one of the shelves, a pale blue crib, faded to almost white by the sun, the sort of thing proud fathers or grandparents sent to a new mother. Grace had filled many such containers with spray carnations, freesias, lily of the valley or rosebuds and delivered them to homes and hospitals without having to endure the reaction that came over her now as her eyes remained glued to that forlorn-looking crib.

There was a huge lump growing ever larger in her throat and threatening to choke her; there was a fierce burning behind her eyes that she knew was about to explode into a storm of tears. Yet she was unable to move on, away from where people were passing and repassing her on their way to the other shops in the parade. She'd be fine in a minute, she told herself. The shaking would stop and she'd blink away the tears and get a hold on herself. All she had to do was turn round and make her way back to the rear of the building. Only it was already too late because the tears were gushing out so fast they were blinding her.

'Hello! It's Miss Hastie, isn't it?'

The voice was vaguely familiar to her but Grace couldn't quite place it. Or even wanted to place it. All she wanted was for the voice, and the man, to walk on and allow her to regain control of herself before anyone she knew came along the busy main street. So she hastily opened her shoulder bag and began to search inside it, hiding her face as the tears still ran unchecked down her cheeks.

'Of course, you're not Miss Hastie at all. I do know that, but I'm afraid I can't remember your married name.'

Grace choked back a sob and had to take a deep breath before she could manage to answer, her face still almost hidden in her bag.

'It's Grace. Grace Hardy.'

'You seem to be...' the man paused, then went on, '...having some difficulty. Have you lost something, Grace?'

That was ironic, Grace thought. Yes, she had lost something. She had lost the most precious thing she had ever possessed. She had lost her husband.

'Have you lost something?' the man prompted when she did not reply.

Grace made an immense effort to come up with an answer. It was impossible. All she could do was to shake her head, and that did not seem to be enough to satisfy the man and send him on his way.

'There's something wrong, isn't there, Grace? Something very wrong,' he said quietly as he stared down at the tear which had flown on to his outstretched hand when Grace shook her head.

Then he placed his hand gently on her shoulder.

'Yes,' she admitted on a long sigh that

ended in a sob. 'There is something wrong, but there's nothing anyone can do about it.'

'Are you quite sure about that?' Donald Muir asked.

There was a long moment of silence while Grace thought about it. Suddenly the burden of it all, and of having to keep it to herself, became too much for her to contain. She wanted quite desperately to share it with someone. If her father had been here she would have shared it with him, and been helped by him. But he wasn't here, he was in New Zealand.

'I'm not sure about anything, now,' she muttered, not looking at him.

'Do you have any idea of why you are here, staring into an empty shop?' Donald asked.

She lifted her head then and turned on him the full gaze of her large silvery grey eyes. They were very beautiful eyes even when they were pink-rimmed, Donald Muir thought.

'I came to look at the shop,' she said, as though surprised by his question.

'And found it empty? Was that what upset you?'

'No. I knew it was empty. That's why I came.'

He shook his head. 'Now you've lost me, Grace.'

'I came to see if it was the right place for me.'

He frowned. 'The right place? But surely you have a successful business near your home?'

'It isn't my home any more. Not without...'

He waited for her to complete the sentence, feeling a great well of compassion for her growing inside him. He was able to guess at what would, almost certainly, come next because he had heard it so many times before, from so many different men and women in so many different places. It was always painful to hear, and this time for some reason it was even worse than usual. Perhaps his superiors had been right in saying he had been overstretched in Manchester and must wind down before he broke down.

'Not without...' he probed, determined not to put words into her mouth.

'Without Paul, my husband.'

It was said so calmly, so unemotionally, as though all at once the pain had been accepted and taken on board. Only the slight trembling of her lips betrayed her inner grief, and all the time there were people walking past them laughing and talking, discussing what to buy for their evening meal, what to watch on the television, while this woman was trying to decide how to go on living without the man she loved.

'Why won't Paul be there?' Donald asked

when he felt the time was right.

Grace pointed to the abandoned cradle in the window of the empty shop. 'Because, since my recent operation, there won't ever be any babies coming into our home,' she told him in a whisper. 'And Paul wants children.'

'Oh,' he sighed. 'Now I understand. But there's the possibility of adoption, you know.'

'Not for us. Paul won't even consider it. So he's asked me to agree to a separation while he decides whether he can settle for a marriage without children.'

Donald took out a handkerchief and wiped away two tears which remained on her cheek. 'So you are wondering whether it will help if you move up here to live and work?'

'Yes. I only heard about this shop today when I was helping at the Glen View. So I decided to come and take a look at it.'

'Don't do anything in a hurry, will you, Grace?'

'I have to give Paul his freedom, if that's what he wants.'

'It may not be what he wants when he's had time to realise what his life will be like without you. Take your time about making a decision as important as this. That's what your father would say to you if he were here, Grace.'

'Dad doesn't know yet. I don't want him to know. I don't want anyone to know that Paul's left me. I've told everyone here that he couldn't spare the time to come with me because of pressure of business. You do understand, don't you?'

For some time he did not answer. Then he put the handkerchief in his pocket and turned his head away from her to gaze instead beyond the grey granite tower of his church.

'Yes, I do understand, Grace. Only too well,' he said.

Seven

Grace turned her gaze to where Donald Muir's eyes were still resting on the mountain tops. She knew in that moment that her own cry of despair had awakened for him memories that he would perhaps rather not have had thrust back on him.

'I'm sorry, Donald,' she told him hurriedly. 'I shouldn't have burdened you with my problems, which you can't do anything about anyway. I feel ashamed I've embarrassed you like this, but when you showed such concern for me I suddenly felt I couldn't go on keeping all the hurt to myself any longer. Do forgive me, please?'

He turned his head and looked into her face again. She saw that the stern lines had softened and the firm mouth showed tenderness as he spoke.

'There's nothing to forgive, Grace. In fact I'm glad you shared your burden with me. That's what I'm here for.'

'All the same, you could be off duty today.' That seemed possible since he was not wearing a dark suit or his dog collar. 'Is it

124

your day off?' she asked.

He smiled, and she saw then that though she had taken him at first glance to be in late middle-age he was younger than that.

'It is. As a matter of fact, I came here to have a look round the bookshop and to buy some food at Mackenzie's and the Highland Oven. Then I was going to have a cup of tea in the Wee Scone tea-shop. Why don't we both go to the Wee Scone? I'm sure we'll feel better for a cuppa. What do you say?'

Grace hesitated. If she went with him she might open up and say more about how desperately unhappy she was. Yet if she did not accept his invitation it might look as if she was snubbing this new friend of her father's. So she made her mind up.

'Yes, Donald, I'd love a cup of tea. Though I can't remember where the Wee Scone is. Maybe it wasn't here on my last visit to Rowanmore.'

'When were you last here?' he asked as he led her away from the empty shop and back towards the top of the High Street.

'About a year ago. I came for Easter.'

'Before my time. I came here last autumn.'

'Just as my father retired.'

'Your father had been here for a long time, I believe?'

'Since I was a small child. I went to this little school,' she told him as they came to where the granite school building, the church and the manse occupied one side of the market square. When she saw the manse she wondered why he was taking her to tea at a café when his home was so close at hand.

As though he was able to guess at her thoughts, Donald supplied the answer to her question. 'I'm not really settled in at the manse yet. In fact I'm more or less living in one room, my study. So I eat out for much of the time.'

It was taking him a long time to get settled in, she thought. Was that because he had no wife to get things organised for him? There was a vaguely untidy look about his appearance that a wife might not have tolerated. His hair needed cutting, even though long-ish hair suited his long, lean face, and she noticed that his open-necked shirt was slightly frayed around the collar.

'Did you say you came here from an inner city parish?' Grace asked as they reached the tea-shop and Donald waited for her to precede him through the door.

'Yes. It was in the heart of Manchester.'

They were seated facing one another at a small table in a corner of the room before she voiced her next question. 'How long were you there?'

'For five years. The first five years of my ministry.'

'You must find it very different up here. I

mean the quietness, the slow pace of life.'

'That's why I came, because of the quietness.'

A waitress wearing a short tartan kilt and a white blouse came to take their order. Donald asked for a pot of tea and some home-made scones.

'Aren't you afraid it might be too quiet for you? That you'll get bored after all that must go on in a big city?'

Donald hesitated before replying thoughtfully, 'I need that sort of quietness just now. Because I have decisions to make that I couldn't make when the phone or the doorbell were always ringing, and when there were too many meetings and far too much pressure on my time.'

'You'd have very different problems to deal with in Manchester from the ones you get here. At times, when things were particularly quiet here, Dad used to hanker after a more challenging parish, but my mother began to suffer from a heart complaint when she was only in her forties so he was afraid that city life might not be good for her. That's why he stayed here for so long.'

'Your father has been a hard act to follow, Grace. Very hard. People here seem to think the world of him. They are always telling me about how he helped them when they were in trouble. It isn't easy to take over from someone so well-loved as him. Especially

127

when you're an outsider and at a crossroads yourself,' he added in a low voice.

The young waitress came back at that moment with a large pot of tea and a dish of fragrant hot scones with butter and strawberry jam. Grace thought Donald looked relieved that she had appeared just then.

'Will you pour, Grace?' he asked, then began to remark that the tea-shop would soon be much busier when the Easter visitors began to arrive. 'Some of the ladies from the church guild are quite keen to provide home-made teas for the tourists in the church hall when the scaffolding comes down from the building,' he told her. 'What do you think of that idea? Will it be likely to upset the people who are trying to make a living in the hotels and cafés, do you think? I don't want to cause any problems in Rowanmore and then have to go away and leave someone else to sort them out. That wouldn't be right.'

Grace found his last remark puzzling. Surely he was not already thinking of leaving Rowanmore when he had only been there for six months? Or was his just a temporary appointment until someone permanent was available?

'I don't see why it should cause any problems, having teas served in the church hall,' she told him thoughtfully. 'After all, at busy times of the year there are hardly enough places open to cope with all the visitors, and I'm sure the money raised will be useful.'

'Yes, there are going to be some big bills to pay. The storm damage from last autumn, just after I came here, will be covered by the insurance but there are other things needing to be done which will all have to be paid for. So I must give my approval with that in mind and hope that it doesn't cause friction at some time in the future. I wonder what your father would have done?' he ended with a wry smile.

Grace smiled back. 'Dad's a great believer in common sense decisions. Even if they're not popular.'

'Gordon could get away with that. I'm not sure that I can. Don't forget that I'm the new boy here and I've not been tested yet as your father has been over the years. He was the man they could lean on in their trials and tragedies, and they haven't forgotten him.'

Grace sighed. 'He was certainly that. Having to conduct the funeral of Shona Thorpe so soon after the baptism of wee Robbie certainly took its toll on him.'

'It's part of the job, but always so hard to do when the death was sudden and the person young. I believe Shona's husband has come back here.'

'Yes. He's working on the gardens at Glen

129

View, and looking for somewhere to live.'

'And are you thinking you might come back here to live and work, Grace? Is that why you were looking at the empty shop?'

'Yes. When I was helping Shona's sister Isla do the flowers at the hotel this morning Fergus was saying how inconvenient it sometimes was that they had to order flowers from a shop in Fort William. I asked about the flower shop here, and he said it was empty. So I came to take a look at it.'

Donald frowned when she said that. 'What if your husband changes his mind? Don't rush into anything in a hurry, Grace.'

Grace bit her lip and looked down at her hands which were moving restlessly from her knife to the teaspoon she did not need. 'I have a feeling he won't change his mind; that he'll suggest we have a divorce so he's free to find someone else,' she muttered.

'Does he know where you are, if he should want to get in touch with you?'

She looked up at him, startled by the urgency in his voice. 'No. We should have been in Italy now, together. Paul left me a note while I was out. Then he phoned to tell me he'd cancelled the holiday because he knew I wouldn't want to go to Italy on my own.'

'That must have been a shock to you, if you had no idea of his feelings?'

She nodded. 'It was. You see I thought

when my operation was over and I was feeling well again that we'd be as happy as we had been for ten years. Only it didn't happen like that.'

He looked at her sadly. 'It so often doesn't. That's something we have to come to terms with. I think you ought to let your husband know where you are though, and your parents too if they believe you are in Italy right now.'

Grace took her time about answering him. It was not something she wanted to agree to. 'I'll let Paul know where I am when I've come to a decision about the shop, but I don't want Mum and Dad to know what's happened until they are back in England,' she said at last.

'When will that be?'

'The end of August.'

'Nearly five months! That's a long time. Don't you think it would be better—' he began.

'I think they should have their holiday in New Zealand without having to worry about me,' she broke in. 'I'll be ringing them from time to time, but I don't want them to know about my marriage break-up,' she insisted. 'If they do get to know they'll probably come dashing back to look after me, and I really don't need that.'

He sighed. 'It's your decision, Grace, and I hope it's the right one. Now shall we taste these scones while they are still warm?'

For the rest of the time they were in the tea-shop they did not refer to her problems or to his work but talked instead about some of the beautiful places which brought people from all over the world to this part of Scotland. Grace began to relax and push thoughts of the shop to the back of her mind. She would go back to it later when she was alone and able to give all her concentration to it instead of wondering why this man who had come to serve this parish, and the smaller one of Rowankirk, gave her the impression that he was out of his depth here and as uncertain of his future as she was of hers.

When they parted company Donald reminded her that if she felt the need to talk to him again he would be there for her, and again advised her not to be too hasty. 'Things could all be very different for you by next week, Grace,' he said. 'Try to hang on to that thought, won't you?'

'Yes,' she promised, even though she knew that with every day that passed there was less chance of her damaged marriage being mended. Because it was not as though she and Paul had quarrelled and said cruel things to each other which would be cancelled out as soon as they were reconciled. It was so much more serious than that. Nothing could change the fact of her failure to become a mother, and nothing could lessen the pain for her as she forced a smile and thanked Donald Muir for his kindness.

'I expect I'll see you around before long,' he said before he walked swiftly away in the direction of his manse while she came to a sudden decision and made her way back to take a second look at The Flower Basket.

There would be no harm in having a look at the interior of the living accommodation. That would not commit her to anything. She had to do something; she could not just sit around feeling sorry for herself and waiting for a miracle which would not happen. So she noted the address and telephone number of the agent from the faded poster inside the shop window. His premises were in Fort William. That would give her something to do tomorrow. There were no tears on her face when she took her second look at this place which just might give her a start in making a new life for herself.

At the Glen View Hotel the car park was filling up by late afternoon. Orders for afternoon tea were keeping Laurel, Mrs Reid and young Ben busy in the kitchen. Isla was behind the reception desk presenting the hotel register for guests to sign and handing over keys while Calum and Fergus helped carry luggage to the lift. Calum felt confident and in control of the situation as he welcomed the guests but Fergus seemed to him to be in a strange mood, irritable and morose. Quite unlike his usual outgoing and optimistic self.

What was getting at Fergus, Calum wondered for the third time that afternoon. He appeared to be looking for things to find fault with, and especially things that had their origin in the reception area. Isla was coping well, even without help, yet Fergus was nit-picking at every opportunity. There was trouble brewing there and waiting to explode. Calum became more certain than ever of that when Victor Thorpe offered to abandon the garden and help indoors with duties the missing girl ought to have been carrying out.

'Victor said if we needed him he'd give a hand with the luggage or showing guests to their rooms till the girl from York arrives to take up her duties,' Isla said as she, Calum and Fergus took a hasty tea-break.

'We don't need him. Tell him to stick to what he knows,' Fergus replied tersely.

'Victor knows about much more than gardening. After all, when he was in the army he—' Isla began, but Fergus did not allow her to finish.

'He's not in the army now. He's here to work in the gardens. That's where he belongs.'

Calum listened to the two of them with

some concern. They were certainly well and truly at odds with one another. How long had they been like that? Since he had been working down in Yorkshire he had seen little of them together. His contact had been mainly with Fergus, who had been supervising the restoration of the burnt-out building. During his brief mid-week visits Calum had stayed in one of the holiday cottages so that he was able to catch up easily on the way the renovation was going. There had been no time for socialising. He had sometimes asked how Isla was and if the wedding plans were going smoothly. Fergus had said only that Isla was busy helping her mother care for her twin sister's little boy and that they had decided to postpone their marriage until the child's father was well enough to look after him. Perhaps that delay had put too great a strain on their relationship. Or maybe the partnership had been a mistake anyway. If so they were better to find out before it was too late. He knew what it was like to discover too late that you had made a mistake. Calum pushed the thought away from him as another car turned into the curving drive and pulled into a parking space.

Victor was surprised when Isla hurried out to speak to him as he was about to get into his car and drive back to the guest house in

Rowanmore, after spending a couple of hours with Robbie. That time with his little son had become so precious, so vital to him, that he did not mind having to wait until late evening before he had his meal. Robbie knew now when he would be arriving at his grandparents' home and was on the lookout for him, waiting to share a new game, a new skill, a new word he had learned to say since yesterday.

They could not go on like that for much longer though, Victor knew, because Shona's mother was looking tired and complaining sometimes of the pain in her back, even though every time Victor spoke of booking Robbie into a nursery school she begged him not to do that just yet.

'He's no trouble, Vic. No trouble at all,' she would hasten to assure him. 'He's a good wee boy, is our Robbie. Wait until he's a bit older.'

So Victor had pushed his uneasiness aside and decided to wait until he found a house to buy in Rowankirk before booking his son into a nursery school. As yet he had not even begun his search for a home because the hours of hard physical work every day at Glen View were leaving him so utterly weary that all he wanted to do after he reached the guest house was take a shower, have a late meal and then fall asleep. That was the plus side: instead of lying sleepless far into the night grieving for Shona, he was now always instantly asleep.

'Are you staying to have a meal with Mum and Dad tonight, Vic?' Isla wanted to know. 'If you are, I'll see you then. I'll be late though because of this girl not turning up.'

'I'll probably have gone by then,' Victor told her. 'I want to take a look in the property supplement from the local paper tonight. It's time I made a move from the guest house and found a home for Robbie.'

'You don't need to do that in a hurry, do you? I mean, we can go on helping out with Robbie, Mum and me.'

'No, you can't. Not now this place is open and you'll be working long hours during the season. Your mother looks very tired, and I know she's having trouble with her back. So I must get on with finding a house as soon as possible,' Victor insisted.

'You might be able to have the Coach House here,' Isla said thoughtfully. As she spoke she was staring into his face. He was struck again by how much she reminded him of Shona. There were the same dark violet eyes beneath the same gracefully arched eyebrows, and the same long, shining black hair. Even the slenderness of her tall body bore a striking resemblance to Shona's. Yet once Isla had been much more rounded and had worn her hair in a smooth, short style quite unlike that of her twin sister. She had appeared in those earlier years to have made a conscious effort to be very different from her twin. Now it seemed obvious to Victor that she was striving to be identical to Shona. Victor felt uneasy about why Isla was doing that.

'The Coach House!' His voice betrayed his astonishment at the idea. 'I can't see Fergus agreeing to me living there, Isla. Surely it's always been agreed that you and Fergus were to make your home there after you married.'

Isla brushed a lock of hair back from her forehead nervously. 'You may have been given that impression, Vic, but things have changed since the fire.'

'What do you mean? I don't understand what you are saying.'

'I'm saying that I'm not so certain now that I'll be marrying Fergus.' The words were said in a voice so low that Victor was not sure if he had heard aright.

'Do you mean that Fergus has changed his mind?' Victor did not believe that, after the conversation he had overheard earlier in the day.

'No. I mean that I'm not so certain any more that I want to marry Fergus.'

'Does Fergus know that?'

'Not yet.'

'How long have you had these doubts about him?' Victor frowned as he asked that.

'Oh, for ages now.'

'Why haven't you told Fergus how you feel?' Uneasiness was growing inside Victor.

'I wanted to wait till this place was open again and Calum was back here. I thought Fergus wouldn't be under quite so much pressure then.'

'But it's been you and Fergus ever since you were kids, at least that's what Shona always said.'

'We're not kids now, Vic. Things have changed. I don't want the same things now that I wanted when I got engaged to Fergus.'

'Do you mean that you don't want to stay here, where Fergus's work is?' Victor asked thoughtfully. 'Is that why you suggested I might have the Coach House?'

Her answer came quickly. Almost too quickly. 'No. I do want to stay here, but not to marry Fergus.'

Victor tried to make light of her doubts. 'It could be just last-minute nerves,' he suggested with a smile.

'It isn't. It's something quite different.'

A thought came to Victor then as he remembered what he had overheard. He tried to push it away but it refused to go. So he put the thought into words that were quietly spoken.

'Is it to do with my Robbie, Isla?'

For a moment Isla hesitated. He knew

then that it was as he had feared.

'It is in a way.'

'He'll be going to nursery school soon, and I'll be buying a house. So I won't be needing the Coach House,' he told her.

He saw then that her beautiful eyes were glistening with tears. 'Can't you guess what I'm trying to say, Vic? Don't you realise that it's because of you, not Robbie, that I can't marry Fergus?'

Victor was stunned. Amazement kept him silent for a long, long moment. Isla's next words were so unexpected that he could only clench his hands and close his eyes while dizziness threatened to bring him to his knees.

'I've been in love with you for years, Vic, but I wouldn't admit it to myself when you were married to Shona. Now I can't keep it to myself any longer.'

Victor took a deep breath and regained control of his emotions. 'You don't know what you are saying, Isla, so please don't go on. You'll only regret it later.'

'I won't. I can't marry Fergus when I love you and want to help you care for Robbie, can I?'

Victor was lost for words. Abruptly he turned his back and opened the door of his car. He hurled his body into the driving seat and switched on the engine. Without a backward glance he sped downhill to the village.

Eight

Isla watched Victor drive away through a mist of tears. He was very angry with her, and it was all her own fault. Of course she ought not to have let her feelings spill out as she had done. Now he would be trying to avoid her because she had embarrassed him. Maybe she had hurt him too by assuming that he would even think of becoming involved with anyone else after Shona's death. It was nine months now since that terrorist bomb had killed her. Perhaps nine months was too soon for him to have realised that he could not spend the rest of his life mourning Shona. After all, there were still moments when grief for her twin sister crept up on her and pierced her with swift stabs of pain.

Why hadn't she waited another few weeks before revealing her love for Victor? The answer to that was not far to seek. Fergus was putting so much pressure on her now to arrange an early date for their wedding that she seemed to be living in a permanent state of tension. Every time they were alone together he would return to the subject, so much so that she found herself trying to avoid being alone with him because he was permanently on a short fuse these days and ready to fly off the handle at any moment.

There had been such a scene this morning when he had accused her of making Victor and Robbie the priority in her life rather than him. Isla had been on the point of giving him back his ring then, but they had been interrupted by Calum. Then, during their lunch break, Fergus had refused Victor's offer to help. His attitude had made Isla wonder whether he was beginning to guess that she had fallen in love with Victor.

Soon she would have to tell Fergus that she had stopped loving him and could not marry him. She ought to have done that before now. Even though she knew she no longer loved Fergus in the way she had done before Shona's death she cared for him deeply enough not to want to hurt him. If she told him – when she told him – one of them would have to leave the Glen View. Probably it would be she herself who had to find a job elsewhere because Calum would not want to lose Fergus just as the tourist season was beginning. Finding another job would mean moving to somewhere away from Rowankirk, moving away from Victor. How could she bear to do that?

★ ★ ★

Victor did not stay to share a meal with his in-laws that evening as they invited him to do. He made the excuse that his leg was playing up and he needed to take pain-killers and go to bed early. It was not easy to lie to Shona's parents, who had been so good to him and Robbie, but he dare not risk still being in their house when Isla came home from Glen View. He certainly had no desire at all to come face to face with her again while her words were still so fresh in his mind. So he cut short his visit to Robbie and drove to the guest house in Rowan-more, stopping at a newsagent's shop in the High Street to buy a copy of the local paper. After his shower and the meal for which he had little appetite he retired to his bedroom. There he did not switch on the television and promptly fall asleep, as was his usual habit, but opened the paper and began his search for a house which he could make into a home for Robbie.

Soon he was going through the eight-page property supplement that offered every type of dwelling from cottages and small apartments to substantial residences which were way beyond either his means or his desires. They would not need a house as large as the one he had bought in Ireland, the home that was spacious enough for Shona, Robbie and himself plus the two other children they had hoped to add to their family. So cottages with only two or three bedrooms were the ones he ticked as being possibles. A vital requirement was a garden of a size to provide somewhere safe for Robbie to play. The other requirement was that the place he bought must not be in Rowankirk. That would be too close to Isla. Tomorrow, Saturday, he would not be working in the hotel gardens so he would go out and look at some properties, starting with the four that were available in Rowanmore.

Grace made an early start and was ready to enter the premises of the estate agent in Fort William soon after they opened for business. There she learned that though The Flower Basket was available for quite a reasonable rent the owner was now thinking of selling it. This news caused her to think again, but not for long.

'I'd like to look at the inside,' she told the negotiator.

'You'll find it in good order. It's only been empty for a few months,' he told her.

'When can I view it?'

'Later this morning.' He glanced in an appointment diary then smiled at her. 'I could take you there about ten thirty if that would suit you?'

'I won't need a lift because I'm staying in Rowankirk. So I'll meet you at The Flower

Basket at eleven o'clock,' she decided.

The inside of the property might be a disappointment, she argued with herself as she made her way back to Rowankirk, driving along the shore of the loch where sunshine sparkled on the still water and brought a touch of gold to the grey stone of the castle, which could just be glimpsed set among the spring foliage of the forest on the far side. When she reached the site where the ruins of the crofts were all that remained after the Highland Clearances she caught a glimpse of some white flowers placed among the stones. Her father had told her that Victor had asked him to scatter Shona's ashes there while he was still in hospital recovering from his injuries.

Poor Victor, what a terrible way for their happy marriage to come to an end. There was no hope left for him now, nothing to live for except his child. At least she had the hope, however slight, that one day Paul would get in touch with her and tell her that he still loved her. If she did decide to take the Rowanmore shop and make her home there she would need to let Paul know where she was. Maybe she should have done that already, but she had been unable to even consider doing so. The hurt had gone too deep for her to be able to think of Paul without becoming overwhelmed.

When she had inspected the interior of

The Flower Basket she knew that there was certainly a possibility that she would take it. Not only was the price right but the accommodation above and behind the shop was better than she had hoped for. At ground-floor level behind the extended shop premises a tiny kitchen had been added. Upstairs she found a spacious living room, a kitchen, bathroom and two bedrooms. The bedrooms were small, but since she would only now need a single bed that would not be a problem. The problem would be to get used to sleeping alone, and without love. An aching sense of loss swept over her as she contemplated a life without the tenderness and passion of Paul's love.

She swallowed the lump in her throat and blinked the burning moisture from her eyes, then followed the agent down the stairs to look again at the shop section of the building. At the end of the inspection she told him that she would come to a decision within a few days and get back to him. They had other properties she could look at, mostly in Fort William, he told her, but she showed no interest in these because there was something about the little shop in Rowanmore High Street that stirred a faint excitement in her and brought a glimmer of hope to her future.

When she was back at Faith's Cottage she took the step she knew to be inevitable and sat at her father's desk to compose a short letter to Paul. It was one of the most difficult things she had ever undertaken. How could you write off ten years of happy marriage to a man you loved with a few sentences stating your intention of letting him go so he could find what he needed while you set about making a new life for yourself? Words were written, and crossed out. Pages were screwed up and tossed in the waste bin. Ink was smudged as tears fell on the letter that Grace had never thought she would have to write.

Darling Paul, I am writing to let you know that you can contact me for the time being at Mum and Dad's new home. Faith's Cottage, Rowankirk, Inverness-shire, is all the address you need. I intend to agree to a divorce and will probably buy a home for myself up here when I have sold my business. Yours, Grace.

She would walk to the post box and send the letter on its way before she changed her mind and tore it up, she decided, even though the last collection of the day went at noon and it was now mid-afternoon. The fresh air would cool her burning eyes and might even lift her dark mood. A few minutes later she was walking briskly in the

147

direction of the post box which was set into the wall of the tiny village store and post office.

'Hello, Grace!'

The words penetrated the fog of depression that hung over Grace as she dropped the envelope into the mouth of the box which still bore the VR insignia of Queen Victoria. Grace swung round, not recognising the voice.

'Oh, it's you!' There was relief in Grace's voice because the speaker was not someone who had known her since her childhood; someone who would cause her pain by asking questions about why her husband was not with her.

'Sorry if I startled you,' Laurel was saying.

Grace managed a laugh. 'I was miles away, and I didn't hear you coming.'

'I've got a few hours off duty before I start cooking the dinners. So I thought I'd get away from the hotel for a while by walking down here to post this card to my parents.' Laurel dropped the card showing a view of the hotel and the loch far below it into the post box.

'It must have been quite traumatic for you, getting used to a strange place at one of the busiest times of the year. Especially when that girl didn't make it,' Grace added.

'It certainly was! Isla was really pleased that you were able to help yesterday, Grace.

148

Everyone has been admiring the flower arrangements you made up so quickly. I don't know how you manage to get them to stay in place – when I do them at home they always seem to fall apart.'

This time Grace found it easier to smile at the younger girl. 'It's everyone to her trade, isn't it? You see I'm a professional florist.'

Laurel sighed. 'I'd love to be able to make a better job of doing flowers, especially when I'm at home helping Mum with her farmhouse bed and breakfast. She grows most of the flowers but she isn't very good at arranging them properly. So she hasn't been able to teach me to do it.'

'She's obviously taught you to cook very well,' Grace pointed out, sensing that Laurel was a bit homesick. 'If the other receptionist doesn't turn up and I come to Glen View to help out you could maybe spare a few minutes to see how I do it.' Why on earth had she made that offer? It seemed to have come out without her thinking of what she was saying, Grace thought crossly.

'Oh, I'd love to do that. How long will you be staying here?'

Laurel was probably afraid she was only in Rowankirk for a short visit. 'I'm not really sure. It all depends...' It depended on Paul. Because without him Grace knew she would not go back to live in the Cotswold house.

'Perhaps I shouldn't have asked. I didn't

mean to be...' Laurel's lovely ivory skin flushed a warm and very becoming shade of pink as she made her apology.

The girl was shy, and perhaps feeling lonely so far away from her family and friends when she did not have her work to occupy her. It would be a kindness to try and make her feel at home here, as Grace knew her parents would have done. Their manse had always been open to the lonely, the sad or the needy.

'Have you time to come for a coffee, Laurel?' she found herself asking, and was unexpectedly pleased when the girl accepted.

'Oh, I'd love to! You see I don't know anyone here yet. Except Calum, of course,' she said.

'I'm staying in the cottage my parents bought for their retirement. It's only a short walk away, on the Rowanmore Road,' Grace told her.

As they walked to the cottage she encouraged Laurel to talk about her home and her parents. She learned then that there was a family farm in a village three miles away from the small cathedral city of Skellkirk and that Laurel's mother had been a home economics teacher who ran the farm guest house and a bunk-house for walkers to help keep the farm a viable prospect for Laurel's only brother, who was studying at agricultural college.

'I worry about Mum and Dad a lot of the time now that there's the foot and mouth outbreak in the country,' Laurel told her as they sat in the conservatory at the rear of the cottage drinking coffee and eating the shortbread biscuits Grace had bought in the village.

'Are there any cases close to the farm?'

'There are some less than thirty miles away, which means that Dad can't move his animals and that many of the public footpaths are closed so the walkers are not booking in like they usually do at this time of the year. That means their income will be reduced quite drastically. I feel quite guilty about coming so far away to work just now when I might have been there to support them, but I just had to get away. I couldn't stay on at the Skellkirk Abbey Hotel any longer after...'

Laurel's voice died away and she stared down into her coffee mug so that Grace might not see the distress in her eyes. She was too late though, because Grace had already seen her blink away the moisture and noticed the way her fingers were gripping the handle of her mug as she fought to keep her emotions under control. Grace searched her mind for something to say that would fill the silence, and remembered the way Calum had gazed at this girl on the night of the ceilidh.

'I should think Calum was delighted when you agreed to come up here to work for him at Glen View,' she said quietly.

Laurel managed a smile then. 'I didn't know, when I applied for this job, that the Glen View belonged to Calum. I was sitting beside the Aga in the middle of the night because I couldn't get to sleep when I saw Dad's *Yorkshire Post* lying there. It was yesterday's news by then, but that didn't matter because I knew there would be columns of jobs on offer in it. I wrote my application at once and was interviewed in York soon afterwards by Fergus, who had already seen the very good reference Calum had given me. I remember being surprised, and a little bit hurt, because Calum didn't try to persuade me to stay on at the Skellkirk Abbey. Though of course once I knew that he was the owner of the Glen View I understood.'

How much did Laurel really understand, Grace wondered. Had she any idea of how much her boss was attracted to her? Grace did not believe she had. Calum was a very reserved man, at least ten years older than the girl sitting opposite her. He had been badly hurt when Katharine had taken the job in America instead of staying to help him recover from the effects of the fire, Grace suspected. So maybe he would take his time about growing closer to Laurel.

'Do you think I did wrong to come here, Grace? Ought I to have stayed at home, once I knew that the foot and mouth disease was spreading?' Laurel asked, with a frown wrinkling her brow.

Grace took her time about answering. It was difficult to know what to say when she had no knowledge of why Laurel was so desperately anxious to leave a happy home and a job she enjoyed. During the pause in their conversation she was able to hear quite plainly the ever-present murmur of the countless sheep which grazed the lower slopes of the glen. That sound would inevitably be reminding the troubled young girl of her home so far away, and the threat that was hanging over it.

'I don't think anyone ever dreamed that the situation would become so serious so quickly,' she began, 'and if you were desperate to get away from your job down there I don't suppose you were able to focus on anything else. When things go badly wrong you tend to lose sight of everything except your own unhappiness. You just aren't able to think straight.' That was the state she had been in herself when she had decided to take an overdose. If the water had not spilled out of the glass and dissolved them she would not have been sitting here now trying to find the right words to bring comfort to this worried girl. A wave of thankfulness swept over her.

'That's exactly the state I was in when I agreed to take the job here,' Laurel confessed. 'All I wanted was to get away from the people who were feeling sorry for me and telling me what a rat Daniel was. I'd waited all those weeks for Daniel to ring and tell me he'd found a flat for us in London and I had all the arrangements made for us to get married quite quickly before I went to join him.' She stopped and bit her lip. 'Only what I didn't know, and I seem to have been the only one kept in the dark, was that Daniel had met someone else and moved into a flat with her.'

'Oh, Laurel, I'm so sorry! It must have been such a blow for you,' Grace murmured.

'Yes. I felt so humiliated. I'd been making excuses to Mum and Dad about why he hadn't rung me. I knew they were worried, but I trusted Daniel and felt sure there was a good reason why he hadn't rung or written to me. When I heard what people at the hotel were saying afterwards I knew how naive I'd been. I just couldn't get away from the place quickly enough then.'

'You probably did the right thing to get away, and I'm sure your parents understood why you had to do it.'

'I feel better for talking to you about it, Grace. Thanks a lot for listening to me. I must go now because I'm not quite sure how long it will take me to walk back to Glen View from here.' Laurel stood up as she spoke and picked up her bag. She looked brighter now, more confident, Grace was pleased to notice.

'I could drive you back,' she offered. 'I don't have anything else to do.'

Laurel shook her head. 'The walk will do me good, help to keep my weight down,' she laughed. 'I seem to have eaten more since I've been here than I was eating down in Yorkshire.'

'If the new girl doesn't turn up, ask Calum to give me a ring and I'll come and see to the flowers,' Grace said as she walked with Laurel to the gate of Faith's Cottage.

As she walked away Grace found herself wondering whether Laurel would find new happiness at Glen View with Calum, who was so plainly in love with her. Calum deserved to be happy again. Would her own broken heart ever begin to mend? She had her doubts about that, but at least she could start to pick up the pieces and carve out a new life for herself here in the land she had always loved.

With this in mind she went back into her parents' cottage and picked up the telephone to tell Alison that she would be putting the Cotswold flower business up for sale at once.

Victor's injured leg was throbbing with weariness as he made his way to the last of the four possible houses which were for sale in Rowanmore. He had parked his car in the free car park on the edge of the town so that he could explore on foot which would be the most convenient places for the local nurseries and schools. The first property had been too close to a busy road, the second had only a miniature garden all under crazy paving, the third was in a good position and had a large garden but needed a lot of work doing to the interior. So his hopes were not high as he drew near to the final house on his list.

Birch Cottage was set on the edge of Rowanmore, where the dwellings became fewer and the moor became closer. It was detached and set in a large untidy garden which had a swing hanging from one of the fruit trees. There was a big living room, a fairly large kitchen and two bedrooms plus a shower room and a utility room. Everything appeared to be in good order, he noted as the owner showed him round. As she did so she explained that it had been the family holiday home for several years but that her husband had now gone to work at a university in Canada so they had decided to sell it.

It would do for him and Robbie, Victor

decided. The nearest school was not too far away and the price was about right. He had no heart for house-hunting because no place would ever be a home without Shona, but at least when he and Robbie moved into Birch Cottage he would not have to face Shona's sister every time he went to pick up his son. He had always liked Isla and felt at ease with her, but since she had declared her love for him he was afraid of her.

He was also afraid that her determination to marry him instead of Fergus would cause problems for him at the Glen View Hotel, and perhaps even lose him the gardening work that he was enjoying. So the sooner he was installed in Birch Cottage with Robbie, the better. Before leaving the cottage he made an offer to buy it, and went away satisfied when his offer was accepted.

Nine

For days after she had posted her letter to
Paul, Grace found herself listening in the
early mornings for the sound of the postman dropping an answer through the letterbox of Faith's Cottage. She began to get up
very early so that she would be downstairs
when his reply came. It was so quiet at that
time of day. There was only the birdsong
and the ever-present murmur of the lambs
grazing on the other side of the back garden
hedge to be heard as she sipped her mug of
tea and waited for the sound of the postman
walking down the path..

In spite of her parents' absence there was
plenty of mail coming to Faith's Cottage. All
sizes and shapes of envelopes managed to
raise Grace's hopes, but always they were
addressed to the Rev G. or Mrs R. Hastie.
She wondered if Paul was still away, and was
tempted to phone his office to find out but
at the last minute, with the phone already in
her hand, she lost her courage. If he was still
away he would not have received her letter
yet. He would be sure to ring her as soon as

he returned. So, as time moved slowly on, she tortured herself with hopes which were raised one day and dashed the next.

While she waited, Grace tried to fill her days by keeping the cottage garden tidy and by going up to Glen View to help Isla do the flowers. Because the girl who had taken on the job of assistant receptionist was not very interested in flower-arranging Isla was glad of her help. Sometimes, if she could spare the time from her work in the kitchen, Laurel Appleby came to watch Grace and to learn so well that she soon became quite skilled herself. This was just as well because Grace had now signed the lease of The Flower Basket and would shortly be too busy to help out at the hotel.

'I'd like to help you with the move into your shop, Grace,' Laurel offered when she and Grace were sharing a long walk through the glen one early summer afternoon.

The two women had become firm friends already. Laurel did not often mention the reason she had wanted to put distance between herself and her friends in Yorkshire but she did express her anxiety about what her parents were enduring as the foot and mouth disease became more widespread and the threat to their farm animals increased.

Grace did not make the mistake of telling her not to worry. Laurel was an intelligent, caring girl who knew only too well that if the epidemic reached her parents' farm it would mean ruin for them. So she listened as Laurel spoke of the problems, such as record low prices at market for sheep, which had already affected her parents' livelihood.

'At least Mum and Dad won't have all the expense of my wedding,' Laurel said as they sat on a flat rock to take a breather before tackling the uphill walk back to Glen View.

Grace smiled. 'I expect they will have, one day, and they'll be delighted to do that when these bad times are behind all of you,' she said.

Laurel shook her head. 'I'll never be able to trust anyone else, after the way Daniel behaved.'

'Never is a long time, and you're a lovely girl, Laurel,' Grace tried to comfort her.

'At least I have my career to fall back on, and I love working at the Glen View.'

'It's good to have something satisfying to do when things start falling apart.' Grace gazed as she spoke at the remains of the buildings which had been burned so that sheep could be bred here to make profits for absentee landlords. 'Some of the folk who were forced to leave here during the Highland Clearances crossed the Atlantic and did very well for themselves in America,' she told the Yorkshire girl. 'Every now and then people come to visit here who are descendants of the crofters who once lived in this village.'

'Someone brings flowers too.' Laurel pointed to the faded posy of white roses. 'I think it's the gardener, Victor Thorpe.'

'Yes, it is. His wife loved this place. Shona was a history teacher, so it was of special interest to her.'

'It must have been really terrible for Victor to lose her so suddenly. He'll think he has nothing left to live for.' Laurel remembered the desolation she had glimpsed in Victor's face when she stopped to ask him the way while he was bringing the spray of flowers to place in the heart of the ruins. Those flowers had faded now but his grief would still be alive and painful.

'Victor has his son to live for. Some people would find that a very good reason for living, maybe the best reason of all,' Grace said thoughtfully as she rose to her feet.

Laurel also stood up and prepared to move on. 'Will your husband be coming up to help you with the move, Grace?'

Grace was startled by the unexpectedness of the words. Yet it was quite a natural thing for the girl to ask, since she had no idea that Grace's marriage was disintegrating. Laurel must have heard her fending off questions about it. Had she noticed how often Grace replied with excuses about the pressure Paul was under with his business? Or simply pretended she had not heard them? Since Laurel was so close to her Grace could not avoid answering.

'No, Paul won't be coming up here when I move, Laurel, so I'll be glad of your help if you can spare the time.'

They were walking back now, taking their time because of the steepness of the terrain. As they drew nearer to the hotel they could see Victor working in the front gardens. Or rather trying to work, in spite of the fact that Isla was leaning towards him, speaking urgently while he went on lifting out weeds from among the primula plants which edged the borders of the drive.

'Isla seems to be very fond of her brother-in-law, doesn't she?' Laurel murmured.

'What do you mean?' Grace was frowning as she stared at the pair, who seemed to be unaware of their approach.

'Well...' Laurel hesitated, then went on uncertainly, 'She seems to be always on the lookout for him; always trying to get him to talk to her even when he's busy.'

'I suppose she's wanting to know how her nephew is doing,' Grace said thoughtfully. 'Isla must be quite worried about him.'

'She'll know how he's doing, because Robbie is still living with Isla and her parents.'

'I thought Victor was going to look after him now.' Grace frowned as she remembered the day she had found Isla weeping in one of the guest bedrooms. Had her tears been because now that Victor was here Robbie would be going to live with him?

'Vic's going to move into a cottage he's buying in Rowanmore. He was telling me about it at lunchtime today. It's all settled and he's moving at the weekend,' Laurel said as they moved on.

'I suppose Isla and her parents will miss Robbie when he goes to live with his father. Though they'll only be three miles away so I suppose they'll see each other often.'

'Is Isla very much like her sister in looks? I mean, they were twins, weren't they, Grace?'

'Yes, but they weren't really all that much alike before Shona and Victor got married. Now Isla seems to have lost a lot of weight, and she's very nervy and on edge when she used to be quite lively and always laughing. I suppose the tragedy has changed her personality,' Grace ended.

They were back to Grace's car now and about to part company as Laurel went to change into her chef's gear ready to start on the evening meals. Victor's call made them both turn their heads in his direction. His strong face was flushed and wore a stormy expression as he strode towards them, limping quite markedly in his haste. Isla took a step or two after him then appeared to change her mind and hurried past them all straight into the back entrance of the hotel.

'What is it, Victor?' Grace wanted to know. He was breathing deeply, apparently struggling to regain his composure.

'Oh, it was Laurel I was speaking to, Grace,' he managed at last, wiping a hand across his forehead as though to clear something away from there. 'I wondered whether she could spare me a cup of tea. Can you, Laurel, please?'

'Of course, Vic! Are you all right? You look a bit...' the girl broke off, having decided not to go on and say just how angry and distressed Victor looked.

'I'll be fine, once I've had a drink and a rest,' he assured her.

'Why don't you come in and have some tea as well, Grace?' Laurel was looking at Grace with a plea in her eyes. She was not sure just how to cope with Victor in his present mood, Grace realised. So she changed her mind about going straight back to Faith's Cottage.

'Yes, that sounds like a good idea.'

Within minutes they were sitting at the window end of the staff-room with a big pot of tea and a plate of warm scones. Victor was beginning to relax and Grace was leading the talk with her plans for the move into the Rowanmore flower shop.

'Laurel has offered to help me,' Grace told

Victor as the other girl poured the tea into three mugs.

'Your husband won't be coming up then?'

'No. He can't get away just now.' Why didn't she tell them Paul wouldn't be coming at all? They must both be wondering why she was buying a business up here when her husband's office was nearly five hundred miles away in the Cotswolds. 'I wanted to be nearer to Mum and Dad now they're getting older,' she added on the spur of the moment.

'Are they not so well then?' Victor asked. 'I thought, with them going to New Zealand...'

'Oh, they're fine really, but I worry about them sometimes,' Grace put in hurriedly.

There was a long moment of silence during which she wondered whether she had managed to convince them that all was well with her marriage. All just might be well with her marriage, she argued silently. It could just be that Paul had extended his holiday and was not yet back home to find her letter. She was relieved when Laurel broke in to speak of her own anxiety about her parents.

'I keep feeling that I've let them down by moving so far away just when they needed me most.'

'You'll be able to keep in touch by phone, won't you?'

'Yes, of course, but...'

What ever Laurel had been going to say was never uttered because at that moment Fergus walked into the room. His eyes darkened when he saw Victor and the smile which had been about his mouth disappeared.

'What are you doing in here at this time of day?' The question was addressed to Victor. It was plainly an expression of disapproval.

'I would have thought that was obvious. I'm having some tea,' Victor replied mildly.

'You're supposed to be still on duty, I believe?'

'Yes. I'll stay on late and make up the time, if that's what's upsetting you.'

'You had your tea-break an hour ago as usual, I suppose?'

'Yes.'

'Then what's the idea?' Fergus demanded. 'We don't employ you to spend your time in here chatting up the women.'

Grace felt her heart thumping as the tension in the room rose sharply. What was it all about? Now Laurel was on her feet, her cheeks bright pink with embarrassment as she faced Fergus with her explanation. 'Victor wasn't feeling well, so I suggested he took a rest and had some tea.' Fergus ignored her and kept his stern gaze fixed on Victor. 'If you're not feeling well enough to do the work...' he began harshly.

166

Victor emptied his mug before replying. 'I am, for most of the time, but if you want to get rid of me I'll go as soon as you like. It's not my bloody fault that this damned leg let's me down sometimes.' He lifted his head, squared his broad shoulders and got to his feet. 'If you don't want me here I'll have no difficulty in finding employment elsewhere. Somewhere I don't have to put up with your nit-picking. I'm well qualified in man-management after my army career. Which is more than can be said for you!'

With that he stumbled across the room towards the door. Both women watched apprehensively as he drew nearer to Fergus, but when he was only a couple of strides away Calum's cousin did a swift about face and marched away. Victor turned back then to speak to Grace and Laurel. All the anger had left his features and there was only pain left.

'I'm sorry you had to witness that. Fergus can be such a prat when he's on a short fuse, and he seems to be permanently on one these days.'

'Perhaps because Isla and he don't seem to be getting on as well as they ought to be,' Laurel said quietly. 'Whenever they're to-gether the sparks seem to be flying.'

Victor halted on his way back to the garden. 'Is it really as bad as that?'

Laurel hesitated. 'Maybe I shouldn't have

said that, because I only see them when they're at work. I don't know how they are when they're away from here.'

Grace frowned. 'Perhaps it's time they set another date for their wedding?' she suggested.

'Oh, I didn't realise...' Laurel began. 'I thought they hadn't been engaged for long.'

'It's my fault they are not already married,' Victor halted and they saw the desolation in his eyes. 'At least, it's the fault of the maniac who put a bomb into a shopping centre and left my boy without a mother. I couldn't have coped, without the help Isla and her mother have given me by looking after Robbie. There won't be anything to delay the wedding now though, because I'll be moving into my own house next Saturday.'

'As soon as that?' Grace stared at him. 'How on earth have you managed it, Victor?'

He gave a harsh laugh. 'By playing on the seller's sympathy. There isn't anything to do to the place indoors, it's the garden that needs a lot of work, and the woman's eager to join her husband in Canada as soon as possible.'

Victor was certainly in a rush to set up on his own and take Robbie with him. Grace frowned as she remembered how she and Laurel had seen Isla leaning towards him out there in the garden, almost as if she had been pleading with him. Then Victor had seemed to be so agitated when he caught up with her and Laurel and asked if he could have some tea. Quite suddenly she found she could guess at why Fergus was in such a foul mood. His marriage to Isla had been postponed because of the sudden death of her sister, and now Isla seemed so often to be seeking to spend time with her brother-in-law. There was the way Isla had changed her hairstyle too and slimmed down so that she looked so much like Shona at times. Did Fergus believe Isla was setting her cap at Victor? That could be the reason for the irrational way he had spoken to Victor. Was Isla determined to marry Victor instead of Fergus? This thought became so worrying to Grace that she pushed it hurriedly to the back of her mind.

'Will you need any help with your move, Victor? I could look after Robbie for you at Faith's Cottage.' The words seemed to come out of her mouth without her realising what she was saying.

'Would you really, Grace?' Victor's face cleared. 'I don't want Isla to ask for time off to help me, as she suggested. Fergus is in no mood to agree to that. It would only cause more problems for me than I already have.'

'I'll be glad to help. Just let me know what time you'll drop him off at Faith's Cottage.'

'I could give you a hand in the afternoon when I'm off duty for a couple of hours, if it would help,' Laurel offered.

Victor's face softened as he turned his gaze on the younger girl. 'That's kind of you, Laurel, but won't you need your rest before you do the Highland Banquet for the coach party that's booked in for Saturday?'

Laurel laughed. 'If I'm not helping you, I'll probably be out walking Fergus's dog or going shopping in Rowanmore for my mother's birthday present. I can drive down instead of walking and buy the present first, then come and give you a hand if you tell me where I'll find you.'

'It's Birch Cottage, on West Braeside. That's on this side of Rowanmore. There are birch trees in the garden and a swing for Robbie. Now, I'd better get back to work and put in that extra hour.'

He hadn't taken an extra hour off, in fact it was barely half an hour since he had made his plea for some tea just to escape from Isla. What was he going to do about Isla? The girl really was becoming an embarrassment to him, and he was beginning to suspect that her pursuit of him was what was upsetting Fergus. It had to be, because they had got on well enough during the times he had come to Rowankirk when Shona was alive. If he didn't somehow manage to distance himself from Isla there would be more unpleasant scenes. And one of them could result in him throwing up his job at Glen View, because he was not going to be talked down to by bloody Fergus McLeod. Victor sighed as he pushed away futile regrets for the life he had once loved as an army officer. That sort of life was over now and he must adapt as well as he could to the way things were for him and Robbie.

Soon after Victor had gone back into the garden, Grace said she must also depart to get on with working out what she would need to stock The Flower Basket. Laurel made her way to her own cottage with her mind full of unanswered questions and bewildering feelings. What on earth had got into Fergus to make him speak to Victor like that? Something in the atmosphere had made her afraid that violence would erupt. Poor Victor, to be faced with such a situation when all he had needed was a bit of understanding. He was going to need all the help he could get over the next few weeks as he took on the care of his little son and tried to make a new home for him. She would do what she could to help him, Laurel decided, and not just on his moving day. If she were to watch out for the times when Isla was seeking his company and make an excuse to talk to Victor herself it might just calm things down between him and Fergus.

It had seemed like a good idea, she

thought ruefully a few days later, to interrupt whenever Isla was annexing Victor either in the staff dining room or outside in the hotel garden, but in practice it brought her another problem, one she had not anticipated. Sometimes she would get the impression that Calum was not too happy about her intervention. Not that he ever voiced his disapproval. Rather it was the expression on his face that gave her a clue as to his feelings.

'Don't you have things to do in the kitchen, Laurel?' Isla asked quite sharply when Laurel came to check with Victor about the time he would expect her at Birch Cottage the next day.

'Not right now. Everything's under control. I just wanted to catch Victor before he goes home, because it's his moving day tomorrow and I'm giving him a hand when I go into Rowanmore during the afternoon.'

'He'll have all the help he needs from us, from Mum and me, won't you, Victor? There won't be any need for you to give up your afternoon time off.' A heavy frown spoiled the beauty of Isla's face as she spoke.

'I'll be glad of Laurel's help...' Victor began, looking uncomfortably from one woman to the other and moving his dusty hands uneasily down the sides of his jeans.

'You'll need me to look after Robbie,

surely?' Surprise lifted Isla's dark eyebrows.

'Grace is having Robbie for the day at Faith's Cottage,' he told her.

'But he doesn't know Grace—'

'He does. I took him along to the cottage last night for a couple of hours and he loved it, so there won't be any problems there.'

'It's about time Grace went back to her husband,' Isla said sharply. 'That's if she still has a husband to go back to.'

Ten

There was a long moment of silence after Isla had uttered her harsh comment. Victor shifted his feet uneasily, wondering why she had sounded so unkind about Grace when he had thought them to be old friends. He was still perplexed about this when a new thought came to disturb him. Why didn't Grace ever mention her husband? Why did she always come up with exactly the same answer every time anyone asked why Paul was not with her? Was it true that his business was so successful that he could not get away from it to join her for a few days? Was he right in thinking that Grace always changed the subject when anyone spoke about her husband?

Laurel could feel hot colour creeping up from her neck to burn her cheeks. She knew beyond all doubt now that Isla was determined to have Victor and was not pleased that she and Grace were going to help him with his move into Birch Cottage. A swift glance up at Victor's scowling face indicated that he was probably as aware of the situation as she was. Pity for him stirred inside her. He was a nice guy who was obviously still grieving for his adored wife and was trying to set about making a new life for himself and his little son, and now he was having to cope with this sister-in-law who was set on becoming his new partner. No wonder he was looking distressed. No wonder too, that Fergus was in such a volatile state of mind that he seemed unable to encounter either Victor or Isla without allowing his rancour to boil over. All at once Laurel wanted to put distance between herself and these people whose emotions were starting to put them at odds with one another.

'I've left something behind in my cottage,' she muttered. 'I'll just go and get it.'

'I'll see you tomorrow, some time during the afternoon,' Victor said. 'You do know where to find Birch Cottage, don't you, Laurel?'

'Yes. Grace showed me,' Laurel replied before hurrying away towards Kingfisher Cottage.

Before she reached the cottage Fergus came out of the back door of the hotel and strode to where Isla was still urging Victor to let her help with his move. Victor had taken a couple of paces away from her, ready to make his escape, she guessed. When Laurel reached her front door she opened it hurriedly and went through to the back garden so she would not be tempted to watch what was happening. She was out of sight of Victor, Isla and Fergus here but not, she very soon discovered, too far away to miss hearing yet another series of angry exchanges. Why didn't Isla accept that Victor did not want her, or any other woman except her dead twin sister? Would she continue to harass him until Fergus was unable to control his jealousy and turfed Victor out of his job?

Could Fergus do that? Did he have the power to dismiss Victor? Or did that decision rest with Calum? Laurel could not be sure about that. What she was certain of was that she did not want Victor to be forced to leave his employment here. She felt sorry for him and had come to like him very much. To become fond of him, in a way. He had gone now, down the mountain side to the guest house that he would soon be leaving, so it was safe for her to go to her kitchen and get on with cooking the dinners for tonight's guests. Ben would be arriving in a few minutes and would need instructions from her about what he should be doing.

Before young Ben arrived from his home down in the village Fergus came into the kitchen and told her tersely that he had been looking for her.

'Where on earth were you when you

should have been here making a start on the dinners?' he demanded, running a hand through his auburn hair, a habit of his when he was on edge.

'I'd left something behind in my cottage so I went back for it.' Laurel felt uncomfortable as she made the excuse. It was obvious that Fergus was still in a foul mood.

'Didn't Isla tell you that a booking for twelve extra dinners came in while you were off duty?'

'I didn't see her until—'

'You were talking to her only a few minutes ago. I saw you,' Fergus cut in.

'It was only for a moment. She probably didn't have time to tell me.'

'Or perhaps her mind was on other things?' he suggested.

'I don't know...'

'Surely you can remember what you were talking about?'

'It was about Victor's move.'

'Victor Thorpe again! That bloody man's causing far too much distraction from what we are trying to do at Glen View these days. This place is a hotel, and we are all here to serve the guests who are our paying customers. It isn't a social club.'

Laurel's eyes widened as she listened. Her nervousness vanished and she began to resent the injustice of his accusation. 'I was still off duty. It's only five thirty now,' she pointed out. 'Surely Victor was finished for the day too?'

'Isla wasn't finished for the day...'

Laurel was on the point of remarking that what Isla was doing was really nothing to do with her when Calum entered the kitchen. He seemed instantly to pick up the atmosphere of tension. His eyes narrowed as he moved his glance from Laurel to Fergus, then back again to Laurel. It was to her that he spoke.

'Is anything wrong, Laurel? You look a bit uptight. I'm not used to seeing you in that sort of mood – you always seem so unflappable.' He smiled at her, but she saw that there was concern reflected in his eyes.

'No, there's nothing wrong, Calum. At least there's nothing wrong here. It's just that I'm a bit on edge now because I'm worried about Mum and Dad.'

'Why? Is one of them ill?'

'No, but the foot and mouth disease is affecting their farm. They can't move any of their sheep to get them to market so there's no money coming in, and because most of the public footpaths are closed there are a lot of cancellations for Mum's guest house. I'm quite worried about them.'

'Of course, you must be. I was afraid there might be something causing you concern here. Are you quite certain there isn't?'

Laurel managed a smile. 'Absolutely.

Everything here is just fine thanks, Calum.'

'I do want you to be happy here, and I'd like you to know that your work at Glen View is appreciated, Laurel,' Calum went on. 'You will let me know if you have any problems?'

'Yes, of course.' Her glance travelled briefly towards Fergus before moving back to Calum. 'Though I don't expect to have any that I can't handle myself,' she told him with a lift of her head and a firm set of her lips.

'Good for you! Now, can you spare me a few minutes, Fergus? I need to talk to you about the coach party we have coming from Devon tomorrow.'

A moment later the two McLeods were on their way to Calum's office and Laurel was left to reflect that what might have developed into a row between herself and Fergus had simmered down because she had shown Calum's cousin that she would not be intimidated by him. This had not been easy, but she had known instinctively that if she wanted to keep her job here she must gain the respect of both Fergus and Calum McLeod. Calum had shown his regard for her already, but with Fergus in the mood he was in right now she would need to be careful.

Soon the hotel was full of visitors and the buzz of activity all over the place meant that Laurel had little time for observing whether the atmosphere between Isla and Fergus had been restored. Since the weather was fine and sunny Laurel often took her meal breaks out in the back garden of the hotel. Sometimes Victor came to join her on the rough bench set close to the boundary wall of Glen View. By common, unspoken, consent they avoided any mention of either Isla or Fergus but Victor did voice his concern about whether he was doing the right thing in taking Robbie away from his grandparents so soon after the death of their daughter.

'It may appear to them that I've rushed things in getting my move going so quickly when they were willing to go on looking after Robbie full time,' he explained. 'I felt I ought to get on with it because Shona's mother is looking so tired. It isn't as if she has her husband there all day to help her with Robbie, because he's the green-keeper at the golf club.'

'I'm sure you've done the right thing. It'll all work out well for you and Robbie once you're settled in at Birch Cottage. Just give it time, Vic. That's what my dad always says about things that might cause problems.' Laurel smiled as she told him that.

'Your dad, and your mother, must have plenty of problems to cope with just now.' Victor knew from the television news that though there were no cases of foot and mouth disease within over a hundred miles of this part of Scotland there were many new cases being reported daily in the north of England.

'Yes. I can't help worrying about them, and feeling guilty about leaving them at a time like this.'

'You were not to know how bad things would be, and they wouldn't have wanted you to stay there if you had the chance of a better job here, would they?'

Laurel sighed. 'The foot and mouth outbreak had already started when I applied for the job here, and they did want me to stay on with them. Only my mind was so full of my own troubles that I hadn't taken on board what it was going to be like for them. It isn't just the farm that's at risk, it's the bed and breakfast my mum runs. Hardly any visitors are coming and she's had a lot of cancellations. I keep phoning them and they say they're fine but I don't know whether to believe that or not. I feel so guilty for running away.'

'Running away? It wasn't really like that, was it?' Victor stared at her intently as he asked the question.

She nodded. 'Yes, it was. I couldn't bear people feeling sorry for me because the guy I was engaged to was sharing a flat in London with another girl when he was supposed to be looking for a place we could share. I kept hearing them say what a rat Daniel was, and I knew they thought I was a bit naive not to have guessed what he was up to. So when I discovered there was a job going here I decided to try and get away from the gossip instead of staying and coming to terms with what had happened.'

'Has it worked for you, getting away from where it all happened?' Victor asked quietly.

Laurel took her time about answering. 'I'm not sure. Sometimes I think it has, then something comes to remind me that I should have been living in London now and married to Daniel.'

'It's best to leave thoughts like that behind,' he told her, 'and just concentrate on the future. There could be a great future for you, Laurel, once you manage to do that.'

She smiled at him as she rose to her feet. 'Your future could begin to take off tomorrow when you move into Birch Cottage with Robbie. I hope it will, Vic.'

Grace was up very early on the morning Vic and Robbie were to move into Birch Cottage. As she sipped her mug of tea she heard the sound of letters dropping through the door of Faith's Cottage. One of them was a thick packet of correspondence sent on by Paul from the Cotswold house. On opening it she found a collection of business correspondence plus a couple of postcards from her parents. So Paul was back in their home again. How long had he been back, and why had he not answered her letter offering him his freedom?

Among the correspondence was a formal letter from Alison Dale saying that she would like to buy the Cotswold flower shop. Grace was surprised – she had always been under the impression that as a single mother of two children, Alison found it hard to manage. There was no time for speculation about that right now though because Victor would be bringing Robbie to her soon. It was a bright morning so the little boy would be able to play in the garden, and later, when he had his afternoon sleep, she would prepare a meal for Victor and Robbie to share with her before they spent their first night in Birch Cottage.

Before they arrived she would telephone Paul and tell him about Alison's offer to buy her shop. It was more than time that they discussed their future. Her heart began to thud as she tapped out the familiar numbers and heard the ringing at the other end of the line. On and on went the ringing until she was forced to accept that Paul was not there to answer it. Being a Saturday, he would not be at his office, and it was too early for him to have already left for the golf club. When they had lived in the house together Paul had enjoyed staying in bed late on Saturdays while she rose early and went to her flower shop in good time for what was always the busiest day of the week. Frustration made her slam down the receiver when finally she gave up any hope of an answer.

From not wanting to speak to Paul at all she had now become determined to find out where he was and what was happening down there in the Cotswolds.

Afterwards, she could never be certain of what had made her ring Alison Dale at the shop. It was a random thought, triggered perhaps by the amazement she had felt at Alison's intention of purchasing her floristry business. Again she tapped out the keys automatically, as she had done several times in recent weeks, and waited for Alison, or Sandra, the young trainee florist, to speak.

'Good morning! Graceful Flowers.' The voice was masculine, educated, pleasing with the hint of warmth it contained.

Grace felt the breath catch in her throat and a tremor begin deep inside her.

'Graceful Flowers here. Can we help you?' the same voice poured into her ear.

Still Grace was unable to believe what she was hearing, and quite unable to answer. She waited, watching her hand shake as she hung on to the receiver. Reasons began to form in her mind about why Paul should be at her shop. Was Alison ill? If so, why had

Alison, or Paul, not informed her so that she could go down there and take over for a time? Paul knew where she was living now, so did Alison. In the seconds that passed she heard the familiar slam of the flower-shop door, and caught the sound of femimine heels walking swiftly across the tiled floor, before Alison Dale's voice cut straight into her reeling brain.

'Are there problems, darling? Shall I take over?' was what Alison said, quite clearly. Her tone was warm, sensual almost. Grace had never heard Alison speak to anyone in such a way before.

Instantly then she knew. The whole scene became revealed to her as though a theatre curtain had been raised on it. There were the meals Alison had invited Paul to share while she had been in hospital, meals shared with Alison Dale's small boy and girl. That would be when Paul began to realise what he was missing in not having children of his own. A feeling of sickness began to stir unpleasantly in the pit of Grace's stomach.

'Graceful Flowers, Alison Dale speaking. Can I help you?' Yes, that was Alison sounding so bright, so much in control. Certainly not the same woman Grace had felt so sorry for when she talked sadly of her own failed marriage. Had the children always been there when Paul shared those meals with Alison, or had they been spending time with

185

their father who lived in a nearby village?

'It must have been a wrong number, darling.' Again the voice belonged to Alison, so it would be Alison who put the phone down before Grace could manage to say anything.

What could she have said, anyway? What did she have to go on except the fact that Paul had been there at the shop with Alison, and that Alison had called him 'darling'. Some people were liberal in their use of endearments, but not Alison Dale. Even her two enchanting children were spoken to in a casual, jokey sort of way. As she stared down at the now silent telephone, Grace knew she would have to use it again soon to try and find out the truth. First, though, she must calm down, get rid of the shakes that were affecting her hands and the weakness which was making her legs feel like jelly. Fresh air would help, perhaps.

The air in the back garden was piercingly fresh in spite of the sunshine as she took in deep breaths to clear her head. From here the view was of mountains that were starkly beautiful with their lower slopes clad in the soft pink of heather. There was a psalm about mountains, a psalm her father was very fond of. How did it go? 'I will lift up my eyes to the hills: from whence cometh my help.' What help could come to her if she had lost Paul's love?

As the thought came to her she acknowledged to herself that throughout all her weeks here she had been pinning her hopes on Paul realising that he could not live without her, even though she was no longer able to give him children. It was for that reason she had kept secret from everyone why Paul was not with her, and would not be coming to help her move into The Flower Basket. It was for that reason she had only taken on the rental of the place rather than buying it at the advantageous sum it had been offered to her. It was the hope that Paul would want her back which had pulled her out of countless moments of despair during her weeks in Scotland. Now that hope was gone, because even though at this distance from Paul and Alison she had only guesswork to go on, instinct had extinguished hope.

There were no tears to be shed this time. They had all been used up in the long nights that were behind her. All that was left for her to do now was to try and find a way ahead, a means of holding on to her self-respect and building a new life for herself here. She must try to do that before her parents came back from New Zealand. Was The Flower Basket going to be enough for her in future?

It would have to be enough, because the help that might come to her from the distant hills was something she found hard to believe in right now. With that thought in her mind she turned back towards the cottage door, determined to pack a few things so that she could leave Rowankirk very early in the morning and drive to the Cotswolds to get at the truth.

Eleven

By the time Victor arrived at Faith's Cottage with his little son, Grace had packed the smallest of her travel bags with a change of clothes so that she could leave at the crack of dawn for her long drive. She would not stay at the Cotswold house overnight, only for long enough to collect more of the clothes and personal items she would need when she moved into the flat above The Flower Basket. The rest could be collected by a local furniture remover and follow at a later date. Before driving back to Scotland she would book into a motel and again make an early start so that she had a couple of days back in Rowankirk to prepare for her move.

'I hope Robbie won't be too much trouble,' Victor said when she opened the front door to him and the toddler. 'Shona's mother says he can be a wee imp of mischief when he has a mind!'

Grace laughed. 'I'll have to be right on the ball then, won't I?'

'Talking of which...' Victor took a brightly

coloured football out of the sports bag he had brought with him. 'Footer is his favourite game. Have you ever played, Grace?' There was a twinkle in his eyes as he asked this.

Grace shook her head. 'Not for a long time. Not since I played in the manse back garden, or in the Glen View garden with Calum and Fergus and the rest of the crowd. I expect Robbie'll put me right though.'

'He will! He's a smart wee boy.' There was pride in Victor's voice as he told her that.

Already Robbie was inside the cottage exploring some of the nooks and crannies to be found in the old building. A metallic crash warned them that he had found his way into the kitchen and upskittled the tall rack on which the saucepans were stored. Before they could reach him to find out if he was hurt he emerged clashing two saucepan lids together as he informed them that he was 'Band! Band! Robbie likes band!'

'I hope your ears are able to stand the racket, Grace, and I hope you know just what you've taken on,' Victor said when he could make himself heard.

Grace laughed. 'I'm finding out, aren't I? Maybe you'd better go before I change my mind!'

Victor's expression changed, became anxious. 'If you've any doubts I'll take him with me. I could be asking too much of you, because he's a regimental band all on his own, isn't he?'

Grace laughed again. 'You could say that! He's certainly got the idea,' she added as Robbie lifted the aluminium pan lids high above his head and banged them together enthusiastically. His chubby face was alight with his delight at the noise he was creating..

'Robbie loved it when there were regimental bands on parade over in Ireland. Shona used to bring him to see us whenever she could,' Victor explained.

At the mention of his mother's name Robbie stopped banging the lids together and stared at his father with puzzled eyes. Grace held her breath, waiting for the crying to begin.

'Mummy Shona,' he told Grace. 'Mummy's gone, but Mummy still loves me.' With that he took to lifting the lids high above his head again, lost in the magic of pretend while the man and the woman watching him were lost for words.

Grace bit her lip. Victor pressed his lips tightly together. 'I didn't know they had told him that,' he said at last.

'It was the right thing to tell him, because it's true. Isn't it?'

'Is it? I wouldn't know any more,' he whispered.

'Robbie's grandparents believe it's true, and she was their daughter.' As she spoke, Grace had in her mind memories of Ruth and Alexander Summers with their children sitting in the same seats every Sunday in the tiny church at Rowankirk waiting for her father to start the family service.

'I just wish...' Victor began in a troubled voice.

Grace reached out a hand to place on his arm. She did it instinctively, not realising that it was something she had seen her father do on countless occasions to comfort troubled people.

'You have to try and believe it's true, for his sake, Victor,' she murmured.

Victor lifted her other hand with his own sun-browned fingers, one of which bore the plain gold wedding ring placed there in Rowankirk Church when he married Shona, and carried it to his lips. His kiss was light and fleeting but it lingered there for long after Grace had moved a step or two away from him.

'You're quite a special person, Grace,' he said softly. 'Your Paul is a very lucky man.'

Grace turned away swiftly so that he would not glimpse the pain in her face. 'I've left something in the cooker. I must take a look at it,' she said hurriedly. 'I'll be back in a minute.'

In the kitchen she opened the oven door,

then closed it again a couple of minutes later with a bang that brought Robbie running to ask if the biscuits were ready.

'Robbie's hungry,' he said.

Grace reached for the biscuit tin and gave him a piece of shortbread. As she put the lid back on the tin she saw that Victor was standing in the doorway staring with puzzled eyes at the cooker from which neither heat nor aroma were emerging.

'Is there something wrong, Grace?' he asked quietly. 'Anything I can help with?'

Grace got a hold on her emotions and managed to smile at him. 'No, thanks all the same, Vic. I'm just a bit at odds with myself because of the after-effects of my operation.' That summed it up perfectly, she thought. The after-effects of her operation: not the weakness she sometimes felt but the loss of her husband to a woman she had thought was her friend.

She glanced up at the kitchen clock, the one which had hung on the wall of the manse for as long as she could remember, and said, 'I should take off now, Vic, while Robbie's busy emptying the peg bag.'

'I'll see you later, and thanks a lot, Grace, for everything.'

They spent the morning playing football and gathering small stones from the garden of Faith's Cottage to make a little cave that would provide shelter for the frog they had discovered while they were out there. Robbie had to be persuaded that the frog would be happier in the cave than it would indoors. When they had shared a picnic lunch the little boy was obviously sleepy so Grace put him to rest in her bed. He was asleep before she had drawn the curtains. As she stared down at him, one hand clutching his teddy, the other thrusting a thumb into his rosy mouth, Grace felt an aching sense of loss at her own failure to have a baby. Victor's child was so adorable. He was there because of the love Victor had shared with Shona, a reminder for all time of something very precious and worthwhile. For her there was no such reminder of the love she had shared with Paul, and for Paul no child to remind him of their ten happy years together. For the first time, she felt a glimmer of understanding of how Paul must be feeling. Then she pushed the thought away from her and set about preparing a chicken casserole for the evening meal to be shared with Victor and Robbie.

All went well for Victor until lunchtime. The woman who had cleaned Birch Cottage for the previous owner had been pleased to continue her service in the same house and had everything looking spotless ready for the arrival of Victor's furniture from the house in Ireland. There was some pain for

Victor in being reunited with items he and Shona had chosen together for their home but he made himself push this aside and lost himself in the hard physical work of laying floor coverings and moving things about till he found the right place for them. He was feeling fairly satisfied with the progress he had made, and had decided it was time to stop for a beer and a sandwich out in the garden, when the door knocker clattered and Isla walked in.

His spirits took a steep spiral downwards at the sight of her. He was sure he had made it clear to Isla yesterday that he had all the help he needed so she would not ask for time off to help him when the hotel was full to overflowing. Yet here she was, looking very pleased with herself. She was wearing a black and white cotton dress, tight in the bodice and flowing out from the hips towards her ankles. Victor was certain the dress had belonged to Shona. Anger began to boil over in him as he stared at her.

'What brings you here? I thought you had a full house up at the Glen View today?'

'I'm entitled to a lunch break, so I thought I'd have my lunch with you, Vic,' she told him with a dazzling smile.

'There isn't enough for two. I thought I'd be on my own.' Victor knew he must sound ungracious but he was unable to disguise the feelings of dismay her arrival had aroused in him.

Isla laughed as she pushed the curtain of heavy black hair to one side of her forehead with one hand before lifting the picnic bag she had brought with her. 'I came prepared. I guessed you wouldn't have anything much in the house yet so I asked Laurel to fix us a lunch.'

Victor fought to control his temper. 'Don't you think Laurel has enough to do when there's a hotel full of guests without putting extra work on to her?'

Isla's eyes narrowed, her voice became sharp as she responded, 'I am Fergus's fiancée, part of the family, almost.'

Victor sighed. 'I can't imagine Fergus taking kindly to you being down here with me when you might be needed up at the hotel. You know how easy it is for you to upset him these days.'

Isla set down the picnic bag, evidently determined to stay even though she knew he did not want her to.

'That's one reason why I'm not going to marry him.'

They were on dangerous ground now. Panic was beginning to rise inside Victor, bringing a cold sweat to his brow and a tremor to his hands. Then his many years spent dealing with every sort of crisis came to his aid. He straightened his shoulders, lifted his head and took a deep breath before he spoke.

'Shouldn't you be discussing this with Fergus, rather than with me, Isla? It's hardly fair to try and involve me in anything as personal as this.'

'But you are involved, Vic, whether you like it or not. Because you're the main reason why I can't marry Fergus. I told you that the other day, but I don't think you believed me then. So I'm telling you again.' She took a step towards him as she finished speaking and lifted her face upwards as though waiting for him to kiss her.

Victor stepped backwards so suddenly that he almost tripped over the rolled-up rugs that were just behind him in the space under the stairs.

'Don't be ridiculous!' he snapped.

'I'm not being ridiculous. I'm talking sense, if you'll only listen to me. You've lost Shona, so you need someone else to share your life and help you look after Robbie. You'll never find anyone who is more like Shona than I am.'

As she finished speaking, Isla crossed the distance between them so swiftly that Victor was caught off guard. Her body was leaning into his, her breath was warm on his chin as she stood on tiptoe and claimed his mouth to pour into him the sort of kiss that he had not experienced for many, many months. It was the sort of kiss he had last shared with

Shona in their bedroom early on that fateful day when they had gone together to the shopping precinct for the last time. Isla's kiss was choking him; bringing waves of revulsion surging up from his guts to make him lose control of himself momentarily.

'For God's sake, stop!' He pushed her away from him so violently that she staggered and had to grab the kitchen door frame to hold on to her balance.

It did not take her long to recover. 'You can't live without love, Vic! You know you can't. I can give you all the love you need—'

'No! No, you can't. Not you, Isla.'

'Why not? I'm Shona's twin. I can give you everything she gave you, even the other children Shona would have given you. Just give me the chance, Vic. Once you get used to the idea you'll enjoy having me in your home, and in your—'

He knew what she was about to say and the very thought of it filled him with rage. His hands clenched as he fought against his desire to hit out at her.

'Damn you, Isla! What do I have to say that will convince you I don't want you instead of Shona?'

Even as the words were coming out of his mouth and he was watching her face crumple, he knew what he would have to say. Only he just could not manage to get the words out fast enough.

'There's nothing you can say that will convince me of that. I just know I'm the right one for you. I've loved you ever since I first saw you, before you married Shona.'

'I can't believe that—' he began.

'It's true. Fergus was second best, once I'd met you, Vic.'

He had to do something; something that would put an end to a situation that was rapidly getting out of hand. So he voiced the idea that had leapt into his mind a few seconds ago.

'I've already found someone who will love me, and Robbie—'

'I don't believe you!'

'You will, once the official announcement is made. Now go back to Glen View and Fergus, and put all this out of your mind, as I intend to do.'

'You can't mean this!'

'I do. I intend to forget you even came here today, Isla, and I advise you to do the same.'

'Who is she? You haven't had time to meet anyone else...'

'I have.' Why didn't the bloody woman just go and leave him in peace? Without putting his hands on her to move her out of his way he was unable to walk away from her and make his escape into the garden.

'It's her, isn't it? The young girl from

Yorkshire. The chef. It's Laurel Appleby. No wonder you were cross with me for asking her to pack a lunch for us.' Hot colour rose in Isla's cheeks as she made the accusation. Her voice became loud and angry.

Victor opened his mouth to deny that Laurel was the woman he had in mind, but it was too late. Isla was forcing a mirthless laugh which ended in a sob. 'And I thought it was Calum who fancied her!' She paused, choked back the sob, then went on, 'I still think Calum does fancy her. So you could have problems with your job at Glen View when you announce your engagement, Victor.'

He knew he ought to tell Isla she was mistaken, that it was not Laurel Appleby he had fallen in love with, that he was not in love with anyone, but he did not do so. Afterwards, when Isla had gone back to her car and driven away from Birch Cottage, he wondered how he was going to get out of the position he now found himself in.

When Robbie woke from his sleep he looked around him at the strange bedroom and was afraid. Where was Grannie? Where was Grandpa? Then he remembered the lady called Grace; the lady who had played at footer with him out in the garden and who had helped him to find stones to make a cave for the frog. They hadn't decided on a name for the frog. It would have to have a name. Robbie had wanted to find some food for the frog but the lady called Grace had said that frogs found their own food. All at once Robbie thought it would be a good idea to see if he could find some food. Something like shortbread, or chocolate biscuits. Or maybe ice cream? Yes, ice cream would be best. This decision made, he slid off the bed and went in search of the kitchen.

He spoke to Grace from the open doorway. 'Robbie likes ice cream.'

Grace smiled as she spun round with water dripping from her hands. 'I like ice cream too, Robbie,' she told him as he advanced into the room and made a beeline for the fridge.

There was no ice cream in the fridge, but the village post office and store would have some. It would be something different to do if they walked there to buy some.

'Shall we go for a walk and find some ice cream, Robbie?' she suggested.

'Robbie likes walks. Eddie Bear likes walks.' Robbie dashed back into the bedroom to return a moment later with the stuffed chocolate-brown bear who had arrived at Faith's Cottage along with the football and a change of clothes for Victor's son.

Soon they were heading for the centre of

the village with Robbie holding on to Grace's hand and clutching Eddie Bear under his arm. When the ice creams had been purchased, and were being enjoyed, Grace decided that they would visit the children's play area which was behind the church and try out the swings and round-about. Robbie loved the roundabout, and so, he said, did Eddie Bear. Grace was on the point of saying it was time for them to begin the walk back to Faith's Cottage when Donald Muir came through the gate that led from the churchyard into the playing field. If they hurried away now it would look as if they were trying to avoid meeting him, so Grace said Robbie could have one more turn on the roundabout.

'Hello, Grace! I had a postcard from your father this morning. They seem to be having a great time in New Zealand, don't they?'

'Yes. I had a card myself this morning, but of course mine was sent on from the Cotswolds.'

'How are things with you?' Donald asked then. 'Any better?'

Grace averted her gaze, not wanting to share with him, or anyone, the rawness of the pain which had haunted her all day ever since she had heard Paul speaking over the telephone from Graceful Flowers, and heard Alison call him 'darling'.

'The divorce will go ahead, as quickly as

possible. I want to be free as soon as I can,' she said calmly, hoping to disguise the bitterness she was feeling.

'Are you quite certain that's what you really want? Have you considered that your husband may be having second thoughts by now about adopting a child? It could bring you so much joy,' he added as his eyes rested on Robbie. 'Don't do anything too final until you've talked it through with him. Talk to him!'

Grace turned her head and gazed into Donald Muir's perceptive eyes. 'I have talked to Paul. Or rather, he spoke to me this morning when I rang the friend who is running my floristry business near our home. Paul answered the telephone. I was so surprised that I couldn't say anything. Then I heard her, Alison, call him "darling". That's all I needed to know.'

Donald Muir remained silent while he took in what she had told him. It was his way, not to be intrusive but to give people time.

'I knew then why Paul had asked me for a separation. I remembered all the meals Alison had made for him while I was in hospital, and the presents he had bought for her children. In my innocence I had imagined that the children would be there at every meal, but it occurs to me now that they could have been with their father in the next village. Alison is young, and attractive, and she has two children already so...' Her voice tailed off. She had said too much; far more than she had intended to, because this man seemed ready to listen. This was a man who cared, but did he understand?

'I'm sorry,' she said as doubt set in. 'I shouldn't have off-loaded my problems on to you. I'm sure you have plenty of worries of your own.'

'We all need someone to share our worries with. I'm lucky, I have the best friend of all to share mine with.'

Grace was perplexed for a moment, then she caught the glance he threw over his shoulder at the little church of St Bride's, Rowankirk. Then she understood, and envied him.

'Thanks for listening,' she said. 'I'm going down to the Cotswolds early tomorrow to find out the truth, but I'll be back in a couple of days to open my flower shop here.'

'Make sure it is the truth you find, Grace. Don't spoil your life for a half-truth. It's so easy to do that, as I know only too well.'

She did not answer him but took Robbie by the hand and walked with him through the churchyard to Faith's Cottage.

Twelve

When Laurel's car stopped outside Birch Cottage and she rang his front door bell, Victor halted on his way through the hall to greet her. How he was going to face this lovely young girl after telling Isla that he was going to announce his engagement to her? He must have been out of his mind. Of course, that was exactly what he had been at the time he said it – out of his mind with anger at Isla's proposal that he should put her in Shona's place.

Laurel was on his doorstep now, waiting to help him unpack the boxes of tableware, kitchenware and linen that were piled up in the spacious kitchen of his new home. Embarrassment engulfed him and kept him rooted to the spot. Then Laurel knocked vigorously, and he knew he could not put off any longer coming face to face with her.

'I was getting worried,' Laurel said when he opened the door which he had closed so firmly when Isla stormed away with tears streaming down her cheeks. 'I thought perhaps your bell wasn't working.'

'I'm sorry you had to wait – I was putting rubbish out into the bin in the back garden so I didn't hear you ring.' He felt acutely uncomfortable as he invented the excuse, and quite unable to meet her eyes. She was such a straight-dealing, plain-speaking person that he was full of shame when he recalled how easily he had allowed her name to be used to get rid of Isla. 'Do come in. Would you like some tea or coffee before we start?'

'We could have it while we're working. I'll make it if you like.' She followed him through the hall to the back of the cottage, where she located the kettle, filled it at the sink and set it to boil. Then she looked around her. 'Where do you keep the mugs?' she asked.

'I haven't found them yet. They'll be in one of the boxes marked tableware, I think.'

'How did you manage at lunchtime when Isla came?' Laurel was already opening a box as she spoke, without looking round at him.

Victor's brain went into overdrive. 'Isla didn't stay, once she found that Robbie wasn't here. I think she had intended to look after him for a while.'

Laurel was puzzled as she straightened up with a couple of mugs in her hands. 'I wonder why she didn't ask me to put some orange juice and chocolate biscuits into the picnic for Robbie?'

It was getting too complicated for him, Victor decided. A swift change of subject was needed before it got any worse. 'Did you find a present for your mother?'

'Yes. It didn't take me long, so I wondered if Isla would still be here.'

'She was only here for a few minutes. What did you get for your mother?' Victor was determined not to talk about Isla's visit again.

'A small watercolour of the loch. She loves pictures, and she loves Scotland.'

'Will you be seeing her for her birthday, or will you have to risk posting it?'

'I don't know. I might drive down one day when we are quiet at Glen View, stay overnight and come back the following day. That's if Calum will let me take my days off together.'

'If your mother loves Scotland why don't you ask her to come up here for a few days?' he heard himself say.

Laurel considered this. 'I hadn't thought of doing that. Perhaps if things are quiet at the hotel Mum might be able to stay there. I'll have to see.'

'Your mother could always stay here, once I've got the place to rights.' What on earth had made him say that, he wondered, when it was too late to change his mind.

Laurel was surprised. 'Do you really mean

that, Victor?'

'Yes. It might do her good, after all the worry she's having about the foot and mouth outbreak.'

Laurel's eyes clouded. 'She might not want to leave Dad to cope on his own. They're really close, you know...'

'He's really lucky to have someone like her then, at a time like this.'

Really close, the way he and Shona had been close in the sort of bond that some people would never experience. How could Isla ever imagine that he would find that sort of relationship with her? He pushed the thought away from him hastily.

'The tea's ready.' As though able to guess where his thoughts were leading him Laurel put an end to his introspection and knelt on the floor to strip the sealing tape from a box which was labelled 'groceries'. Neatly, and quickly, she unpacked these and asked him where he would like her to put them.

Victor rubbed a hand across his forehead. 'I'm not sure. Where do you think?'

'Not too near the cooker if they are going in a high cupboard, which they'll need to do since you've got such a small child in your family.'

His puzzled expression led her to go on. 'Small children like to experiment with messy things, if they can get at them. So you need pans and other unbreakables at lower levels and china, glass and dry foods in the wall cupboards. That is if you don't want to find yourself walking into the kind of mess I once created when I tried to make my mum a birthday cake on the kitchen floor.' She laughed as she confessed to that, but there was an underlying sadness there.

'Are you homesick, Laurel?' he asked gently.

'Not often, just now and then. I suppose because of Mum's birthday being so near and me not being there to celebrate with her.'

'Then do ask her to come up and stay here.' It was the least he could do after allowing such unforgivable use of Laurel's name.

'I will,' she promised.

Gradually, imperceptibly, after that, Victor began to relax and forget how awkward he had felt when she first arrived. When it was time for her to drive back up the hillside to Glen View he tried to thank her.

'I can't tell you how grateful I am to you, Laurel. You've managed to do so much in such a short time. The kitchen is ready for use, and it was in chaos when you arrived. You're a real home-maker, as well as a superb cook. No wonder Calum was so pleased to bring you back up here with him from Yorkshire.'

'Oh, he didn't do that, Victor!' Laurel felt

compelled to put him right about that. 'I had no idea when I came to the Glen View that Calum owned it. In fact I was amazed when I found out. You see I wanted to get away from the Skellkirk Abbey Hotel when things went wrong between me and Daniel, and the job here was advertised in the *Yorkshire Post*. So I went for it.'

'Calum must have come to really like Yorkshire people if he advertised the job there rather than in a Scottish newspaper,' Victor said thoughtfully. Then it suddenly dawned on him that there could have been just this one Yorkshire person Calum was hoping to get. A moment later Laurel confirmed his suspicion.

'I think he did, and we all liked working with him. He was great!'

Laurel's hyacinth blue eyes sparkled as she told him that. A new thought came to him then. The girl was probably in love with Calum. He thanked her for helping him and watched her leave, with the hope in his mind that his rash words to Isla would not spoil things for her.

Mist was rising from the loch and the winding road was empty, as Grace began her long journey early the next morning. It could be the last time she made that journey, if her suspicions about Paul and Alison proved to be true. Following on that thought came a reminder of what Donald Muir had said to her yesterday afternoon.

'Make sure it is the truth you find, Grace. Don't spoil your life for a half-truth. It's so easy to do that, as I know only too well.'

Donald's face had been so sombre as he shared those words with her. Briefly, she began to wonder what had made him utter them, whether it was some experience he had been through in his last parish in inner city Manchester. Soon she reached a wider and straighter stretch of road where she was able to increase her speed and banish Donald Muir, and his advice to her, from her mind.

By early afternoon she was on the outskirts of the beautiful Cotswold market town which had been home to her for ten years. The tree-lined streets were awash with tourists peering into the windows of the small bow-fronted shops that sold clothes, confectionery, books and gifts. On the edge of the elegant market square was her own shop, also possessing a bow-window, and with a basket of trailing geraniums hanging from a bracket on either side of the door. The place looked spic and span, so Alison had been caring for it well during her absence. Had she also been caring for Grace's husband while they had been living apart?

With that thought haunting her, she drove

away from Graceful Flowers, crawling through the crowded streets that were so familiar to her and looking about her as though for the last time. Because maybe it was for the last time. If the truth about Alison and Paul was waiting for her here she would know she would be doing the right thing in starting to make a new life for herself in Scotland. If there was no truth in her suspicions, and if Paul still loved her, it would not take long to reverse her plans and let the flower shop in Rowanmore go.

Her heart was racing as she brought the Volvo to a halt in a quiet road not far from her house. She wanted to walk the remaining distance to her own home, though she could not have explained why. There were people cutting lawns and a few children playing at the far end of the road, but the house she was heading for looked deserted, with the blinds drawn and the front door closed. For a long moment Grace stood at the foot of the drive staring up at the bedroom windows. Then she turned her head to take a look at the garage, set back a few feet from the rear of the dwelling. With the door firmly in place it was not possible for her to tell whether Paul's car or any other vehicle was inside. So she would have to take a chance on who she would find occupying her home when she entered it.

Her fingers were trembling as she inserted

her key in the lock of the oak front door. Pausing to take a deep breath, she stepped inside, alert but apprehensive. There was nothing waiting for her except silence, an almost oppressive quietness which she found eerie.

'Paul!' she called urgently. 'Are you there, Paul?'

The grandmother clock in the corner of the hall startled her when it struck four times. She moved to the foot of the stairs before calling her husband's name again. Then, as there was still no response, she went slowly up the staircase holding on to the banister. If she held on to that she would not be tempted to run down those steps and out of the house because she was afraid of what she might find there.

At the top was a square landing with six doors opening off it. Six white-painted doors all with expensive hand-painted knobs which she must turn, one after the other, if she wanted to get at the truth. She ought to start with the master bedroom, but when her hand was on the rose-painted knob she lost her courage and almost ran to the opposite side of the landing to reach out for a knob which showed primroses and violets. This was a guest room they had never used. It would one day make a perfect nursery, they had decided before they both became too immersed in their respective

213

careers to remember what they had said. Now it held only a few unwanted gifts which were waiting to be given to charity. Grace closed the door on them.

A bluebell-decorated doorknob revealed a double guest room furnished in plain modern style with curtains and bedcovers that were hyacinth blue and pale green. The room had obviously been unused since her parents last visited her and Paul on their way to the airport and New Zealand. A wave of longing for her parents suddenly engulfed Grace. She needed her father – that serene, fair-minded man who could always see things from another's point of view – and her warm and loving mother. They were thousands of miles away, available to her only by letter or telephone, so all she could do was push the longing for them aside and move on to the guest bathroom.

Ferns and water lilies made the room look cool and fresh. The jars of bath oils and bars of soap were all as she had left them when she made her escape from the house all those weeks ago. It was like looking at a house which was for sale, everything too tidy. She shuddered and moved on.

Now it was time to look in Paul's study, after turning a knob painted with Oriental poppies. The room was much as it had always been, plainly furnished with a desk and chair, filing cabinets of pale wood and carpet and curtains of dark green. The desk was orderly because Paul was a man who liked things to be tidy, almost too tidy.

There was nothing for it now but to open the door of the master bedroom. It had to be done, if she were to find the truth. Her eyes wandered from the neatly made bed covered in a spotless white, rose-sprigged duvet and frilled pillows, on to the dressing table to search for the silver-backed brushes which had lain there alongside her own hair brushes and combs. There were no brushes to be seen. Her own were in the guest room at Faith's Cottage. Where were Paul's?

A few strides across the room and she was sliding open Paul's mirrored wardrobe. Yes, some of his clothes were to be seen but not as many as there ought to be. The dressing chest told the same story: neat piles of underwear and socks but plenty of space too. Where were Paul's clothes now?

The only upstairs room still to be looked at was the en-suite bathroom. Again, there was confirmation of what Grace had suspected: no shaver in sight and no toothbrushes or toiletries.

Downstairs there was the same unoccupied air evident in the large, light, unnaturally tidy living room and the dining room, which showed a thick layer of dust on the dining table and the dresser. The cloakroom off the hall showed the same pristine towel which Grace had placed there on the morning she should have flown to Italy with Paul. It was only necessary for her to take a look at the kitchen from the doorway to know that it was not being used.

On the hall table there were no letters to be found. Paul must be coming to collect them every day but it seemed he was no longer living here. So where was he living? Grace could make a guess, but how was she to find the truth of it? She must have the truth and not half-truth. Donald Muir had told her she must not spoil her life for a half-truth. So she must go now to the place where Alison lived with her children, the spacious Victorian terraced house on the far side of the town.

Again Grace felt compelled to park her car well away from that house and walk the remainder of the way. She moved at a slow pace on reluctant feet, staring into front gardens with unseeing eyes. By the time she reached Alison's home the temptation was strong inside her to turn about, get into her car and drive away to some place where she could pretend that all was well and that her marriage was not over.

There was a boy's bicycle leaning against the front fence of Alison's house; there was a dog gnawing away at a rubber bone in the front porch; there was the sound of laughter coming from the open window of the living room. Then Grace heard the singing. She listened as several young voices and a couple of older voices blended together to wish someone a happy birthday. There was a burst of laughter as someone blew out candles on a cake. That was when Grace knew she was not going to find the truth today because she could not spoil a child's birthday party. All she could do was drive back to her own house and wait there to see if Paul came home.

The hours passed slowly as she waited, even though she filled the time by finding suitcases and filling them with clothes from her wardrobes. When that was done she went out to a nearby garage where she bought a sandwich in a plastic pack and a carton of milk. It was quite dark now, after eleven o'clock, and she was feeling desperately tired but unwilling to go to bed in this house which had once been home to her. Instead, she curled up on the big sofa and drifted into an exhausted sleep almost at once.

Somewhere around midnight she woke as light flooded the room. She raised her head and saw Paul standing there with his hand still on the light switch, and with an almost comic look of astonishment on his handsome face. At first he did not know what to say to her, or she to him. He was the first to recover.

'Why didn't you let me know you were coming?'

There was no gladness in his greeting, no smile on his face.

'I thought I'd surprise you,' was all she could think of to say as she rose stiffly from the sofa to face him.

'You've certainly done that. I thought you'd gone up there for good.'

'It seemed the best thing to do; the only thing to do.'

'I thought your parents were in New Zealand still?' A heavy frown creased his high forehead as he spoke.

'They are.'

'Then why go up there?'

'Because you didn't want me to go to Italy, did you, Paul? You didn't want me here either. You didn't want me in your life at all. Your letter made that very clear,' she reminded him quietly.

'All I asked for was a period of separation so I could decide—'

'Whether you loved me enough to settle for having no children,' she broke in. 'Have you made your mind up about that yet?'

'You're making things very difficult for me, Grace,' he hedged as he shifted his weight from one foot to the other uneasily. He did not seem able to meet her challenging stare.

'You made things very difficult for *me*,

218

Paul, when you told me without any warning that I was not enough for you for my own sake, that there had to be a family too. There had never been any indication until then that you were so desperate to have children. If there had been, I'd have tried for a baby before I found I needed to have the operation.'

'I didn't know then. There always seemed to be plenty of time for us to start a family. It wasn't until I...' He broke off then, realising that he'd probably said too much.

'It wasn't until Alison started asking you to meals while I was in hospital? Is that what you were going to say, Paul?'

The dark flush which stained his cheeks was an answer in itself. 'They're lovely kids,' he began.

'And Alison is young enough to have more lovely kids. That's what it's all about, isn't it, Paul?'

He sighed. 'How did you guess?'

'I rang the shop from Faith's Cottage early yesterday morning, and you answered the phone.'

'That proves nothing. I was only there because—'

'I heard Alison call you "darling". That was when I began to wonder, and to start adding things up. So I decided to come down and find out the truth.'

'I'm not living with her – not staying overnight, I mean. That's why I'm back here now. There are the children to be considered.'

He was beginning to sound defensive, quite in a panic. Grace felt almost sorry for him. Yet she was angry with him too.

'You are not staying overnight but you're there at other times. This house tells me that you are living somewhere else, even if you are sleeping here.'

Suddenly he gave in. 'I don't know what to say to you, Grace. How to express my regret about the way things are going. All these weeks I've been torn two ways, between my loyalty to you and what I could share with Alison. When your letter came offering to let me go it was a relief to me. Because the way things are now I'll need to be free as soon as possible.'

'The way things are now? What do you mean?' Sickness stirred deep inside Grace as she waited for him to answer. Though she could guess at what his answer would be. Pain sqeezed her heart as she made that guess and waited to hear him confirm it.

'I mean that Alison is almost sure she's pregnant.'

Grace made a small sound that was half laugh, half sob. 'It didn't take long, did it? Did you want to be certain before you married her? Or was it her way of making sure she got you?'

'It wasn't like that. I really care about her...'

'You said you really cared about me.' Grace got to her feet and went to stand very close to him, close enough to be able to glimpse the shame in his eyes. 'It was what *you* wanted that came first with you, and that's not really love, is it? I won't be embarrassing either you or Alison by coming back to this town to live. I'll be buying a new home and a business in Rowanmore.'

With that she turned her back and walked away from him, out of the room, out of the house they had once shared, and out of his life.

Paul called her name before she reached the front gate, but she did not turn back even though her every instinct was to do so. There would be no point, because she had found the truth that she had come here to search for, and that truth had put an end to her marriage. Acceptance of that brought an unexpected feeling of relief to her as she walked along the quiet street to where she had left her car. Within minutes she was out of the town and on her way towards the motorway which would lead her back to Rowanmore.

221

Thirteen

Victor was not looking forward to Monday when he would have to come face to face with Isla in the course of his work at Glen View. His reluctance to be in the close company of his sister-in-law had already caused problems with her mother. Ruth Summers had called at Birch Cottage to invite Victor and Robbie to join the family for Sunday lunch, but unsure of whether or not Isla would also be at the table with them, Victor had decided he could not risk it.

'Och, it'll save you from having to cook for yourself and the wee boy,' Ruth had insisted.

Victor knew he was in a tight spot because Shona's mother had wanted to have Robbie with her the day he moved into the cottage, and had been hurt because the little boy was to spend the day with Grace. She had then suggested they have a meal with the family that evening and he had been forced to tell her that Grace had already promised to cook for them. When he refused her offer of Sunday lunch on the grounds that Grace was again making a meal for them her manner became very cool. Victor began to feel guilty then about the lie he had told her.

'You'll need to be very careful not to cause gossip, Victor, for either yourself or Grace,' Ruth had warned. 'A woman on her own, a woman whose husband has stayed away from her for so long, is often a target for wagging tongues.'

'Don't be ridiculous, Ruth!' Victor spoke more sharply than he had intended, and saw at once that he had hurt Shona's mother. 'I'm sorry, very sorry,' he hastened to add. 'There's nothing in my friendship with Grace that should cause any concern or gossip.'

'This is a small place, and Grace is the minister's daughter.' Ruth was still frowning as she tried to justify her warning to him.

'Mr Hastie is not the minister here now, and this is the year 2001.'

Victor answered more sharply than he had intended. He was beginning to wonder now, in his tired frame of mind, whether it might have been wiser for him to stay on in Ireland instead of moving to Rowankirk with Robbie. Only there was no family in Ireland for his wee boy to grow up with, as there was here. One member of that family was becoming more of a hindrance than a help though. How the devil had he managed to allow himself to drift into such a tricky and

223

totally unexpected situation? How was he to know that Isla would throw herself at him? There had never been any indication that Shona's sister fancied him until he had come here to live. Blast the woman! How was he going to get her to back off? If Isla's mother discovered what she was up to, Victor was certain she would be appalled and embarrassed.

In the meantime, Ruth was worrying about his friendship with Grace. He really was up to his neck in it, and could see no way out. He sighed, and rubbed at the place on his forehead where pain was beginning to nag remorselessly.

Ruth Summers bit her lip, and hurried to put things right. 'I should not have spoken to you as I did, Victor. You're a young man still and you'll need help with bringing up your wee boy, specially now I'm not so well as I'd like to be. I only called to bring a few scones and biscuits for the two of you, so I'll just say goodnight to Robbie then I'll be on my way again.'

Victor felt shame wash over him. He owed a great debt to Shona's mother for taking on the care of Robbie at a time when the sudden death of her daughter had taken such a heavy toll of her health. He was also fond of her and did not want to get at odds with her.

'Don't rush away, Ruth,' he urged. 'Stay

and have a sherry with me, or a wee dram.'

'You'll be busy, you'll have things to do, with just moving in here,' she objected. 'Unless I can help you with anything?'

Victor smiled as the tension inside him eased. 'I'm not planning on doing anything else tonight, Ruth. I've used up all my energy and enthusiasm for getting things straight. So I'll leave the rest for tomorrow.'

'You'll need to get your kitchen straight before you have to prepare breakfast tomorrow, won't you? I could help you with that.'

'Laurel from the hotel came in and gave me a hand with that during her off-duty time this afternoon.' As the words were coming out of his mouth Victor thought they might have been better unsaid, but it was too late now.

Ruth was frowning again. 'The young girl from Yorkshire? The chef?'

Victor nodded. 'Yes, she was coming down to the village anyway to buy a present for her mother's birthday.'

'Isla thinks that girl could be a trouble-maker. Though perhaps I shouldn't have said that if she's a friend of yours...' Ruth was looking uncomfortable now.

'I don't know Laurel very well, but she seems a nice enough girl to me.'

'She's very young, I believe?'

'Yes, and a long way from home for the first time. She's homesick, and very worried about the foot and mouth disease outbreak because her parents are farmers.'

Ruth's face softened. 'Aye, it's a dreadful thing to be happening, and at a bad time for the tourist trade as well. Some of the women at the Women's Rural meeting were saying they'd had bed and breakfast bookings cancelled, and there's no cases of the disease within a hundred and fifty miles of this area. No wonder the poor lassie's so worried.'

'How about that drink then, Ruth? What's it to be, sherry or a wee dram?'

'A wee dram, with plenty of ginger ale, please.'

So the awkward moments were left behind and the two of them spent a pleasant half hour on the subject of the small boy who slept peacefully in the room next door.

At the Glen View Hotel dinner was over and music was issuing from the reception hall where a three-piece group of local musicians, fiddler, accordian player and guitarist were already into the lively tunes which would open the Saturday evening ceilidh that was part of the package-holiday entertainment.

'Are you staying on for the ceilidh, Laurel?' Calum asked as his chef lifted the starched white cap from her piled-up mass of soft brown hair and glanced round at the spotlessly clean kitchen left behind by young Ben and Maggie Reid's daughter-in-law who came up to help at weekends from her home in the village.

Laurel sighed. 'I don't know, Calum. I'm tired, but if I go straight home to the cottage I'll be watching the television news and worrying so much about Mum and Dad that I won't be able to sleep when I go to bed.'

'Then you'll be better staying here with the music to help take your mind off things.'

'You could be right, but I'll need to go and have a shower and change first. I'll be back about nine.' Laurel hesitated, then went on, 'I was wondering whether I could take two of my days off together, after the coach party has gone, to go down and take my mother her birthday present? What do you think, Calum?'

He smiled down into her anxious blue eyes. 'I don't see why not, as long as you promise to come back.'

Her eyes were full of her astonishment. 'Of course I'll come back. What makes you think I might not?'

'The new manager at the Skellkirk Abbey Hotel will have heard all about your roast beef dinners from the regular customers, so he might try to tempt you back.'

Laurel laughed. 'He's probably got someone better than me by now. Someone more experienced, perhaps?'

'I doubt it. It's not just experience that makes a good cook, Laurel, it's enthusiasm and creativity as well. You've certainly got those qualities. Now, go and get ready, and don't forget to save your first dance for me.'

Calum was so kind to her, so understanding, Laurel reflected as she made her way through the garden to her cottage. He was a good man to work for. There was never the same hint of discord among the members of staff who gathered in their rest-room when Calum was present as there was when his cousin Fergus was around. Why was Fergus always so ready to find fault with Victor? It had happened again at staff lunch-time today. Isla had asked Laurel to pack a picnic lunch for two, then had put her head round the door of the staff-room to ask where the packed lunch was. Fergus had been furious when he discovered she intended to share the picnic with Victor at his new home. His language had been colourful, and explosive. Laurel had left the room hurriedly, unwilling to hear what Fergus had to say about Victor.

The ceilidh was already well under way by the time she made her way back into the hotel wearing a sleeveless dark blue top and a floaty green and blue patterned long skirt. She could hear the lively beat of the music as soon as she slipped in through the rear entrance. The guests were clapping in time to the beat and obviously enjoying the traditional entertainment. It was not until the burst of applause from the audience came to an end that Laurel was able to hear the voices coming from within the small office next to the staff-room. They belonged to Fergus and Isla, who were waiting in there until it was time for them to sing some of the lovely old Scots ballads that were popular with both the local people who came to Glen View for dinner and the tourists who came from much further afield.

Laurel's cheeks grew hot as she heard what was being said. It was impossible not to hear as she waited in the corridor to pass through the swing doors that were blocked by a group of guests all holding drinks and deep in conversation with one another.

'What the hell's got into you these days, Isla? Victor Thorpe can't make a move without you following him; throwing yourself at him in fact.' That was Fergus, past caring about keeping his voice down.

'I don't know what you're talking about, and I don't like your attitude either. If you don't stop shouting at me they'll be able to hear you all over the hotel,' Isla hurled back at him. 'I don't belong to you. You don't own me.'

'You do belong to me. That's why I can't stand by and let you go on chasing after your sister's husband,' Fergus broke in.

'I'm not! It's all in your imagination,' Isla hit back.

'If it's all in my imagination, why are we not getting married now as we planned before he came back here to live?' Fergus still did not attempt to speak quietly.

'Because I've changed my mind! I don't want to marry you at all.'

Isla sounded almost hysterical now, Laurel thought.

'You can't do this to me, Isla! I won't let you!'

'You can't stop me!'

'I can get rid of him. That'll put an end to it,' Fergus declared.

'You can't get rid of Victor unless Calum agrees,' Isla broke in. 'You know you can't.'

'I can put the sort of pressure on Calum that will force him to dismiss Victor Thorpe.'

Laurel knew she ought to make her escape before she heard any more of the argument. Go back along the corridor and out of the rear entrance, the way she had come into the hotel. Yet some instinct, of which she was not very proud, kept her feet glued to the ground.

Isla was speaking again. 'Don't be ridiculous! You can't make Calum get rid of Victor just because you are jealous of him.'

Fergus laughed. It was the sort of mirthless laugh which sent a cold shiver down Laurel's spine. She did not want to hear what was to come next..

'If I tell Calum that unless Thorpe goes I'll leave, because I'm fed up with the gossip that your stupid behaviour is causing, he won't hesitate to get rid of him. Family loyalty will make certain of that, I'm certain.'

'You wouldn't do that! I can't believe you'd do anything like that. It wouldn't be fair to Victor. It's not as if it's his fault.' Isla was worried now rather than angry.

'No, it's your fault. So if Thorpe goes, you'll be to blame.'

'I hate you, Fergus McLeod. I really hate you!'

As Isla uttered those words the crowd of people who were obstructing the swing doors began to move. Laurel was able then to rush through into the front reception hall. She moved through it at such a speed that Calum, who had been watching out for her arrival, put a question she was not prepared for.

'Is anything wrong, Laurel? You look rather upset.'

His words increased her agitation. She must think fast. 'I just caught my heel in the swing door and thought I was going to fall face first,' she managed to say on the spur of the moment.

'Do you want to sit down before we have that dance?'

'No, I'm fine. I'd like to dance first,' she insisted.

Calum was frowning as he led her on to the floor. 'I thought Fergus and Isla were going to be singing before now. I wonder what's happened to them?'

'They've probably lost track of the time.'

'They ought not to have done. It was arranged that they'd sing a couple of times before the interval dance. I think perhaps I should go and look for them.'

'No, don't do that...' Laurel realised too late that she had spoken without thinking.

Now Calum was staring at her with a puzzled expression. 'Why not?' he wanted to know.

What was she going to say? How was she going to answer his question? All Laurel knew was that she had to stop Calum, somehow or other, from going close enough to Fergus's office to overhear the words that could be still coming from there. She had to prevent Calum from hearing what his cousin might still be saying about Victor.

Inspiration came to her aid as she cast wildly about in her mind for ideas. 'I really do feel a bit grotty, Calum. It must be the way I wrenched my ankle when I tripped. Perhaps I ought to sit down after all. Could I have a glass of water, please?'

Already Calum was leading her to the nearest empty chair and bending over her with concern in his silvery grey eyes.

'I'll get some for you,' was all he said as he hurried away.

When he had gone Laurel allowed her shoulders to slump with relief. Perhaps while he was away Fergus and Isla would come and start their performance. She found herself praying that they would. A moment later the swing doors opened to admit them, both smiling as they took their places in front of the trio of musicians. Isla looked cool and in control, but Fergus had already lost his smile and was scowling as he answered something the group leader was saying.

There was tension in the air. It was almost tangible as Isla and Fergus lifted their voices to unite in song yet kept some distance between them. Usually Fergus would have his arm about Isla when they sang a love song, but not tonight, because Isla had quite deliberately moved away from him. Fear stirred again in Laurel as she watched the singers. Trouble between them meant that Fergus might go ahead with his threat to persuade Calum to dismiss Victor Thorpe. Would Calum be prepared to do that for his cousin? He was not the sort of man to behave so unfairly, but family loyalties could force him to. She would be disappointed in him if he did, because she had come to admire him so much: to enjoy his company;

to look forward to being with him; almost to wish... Hurriedly she pushed the thought away from her as the man who filled her thoughts put a glass of water into her hands.

Grace woke in the motel room to the sound of birds fighting over crumbs on the grass below her window. A glance at her watch showed her that it was still very early. Much too early for breakfast but not too early for some tea. She switched on the tea-maker and sat up, feeling suddenly wide awake and full of energy. Amazingly, she had slept from the moment her head had touched the pillow, in spite of the fact that she had gone to bed feeling so angry and upset with Paul and Alison for betraying her.

Now it did not seem to matter quite so much that her marriage was over. All that mattered to her was that the operation which had played havoc with her life and her marriage was behind her and she was feeling well again. Well enough to be glad that she had found the little flower shop to rent in Rowanmore, and well enough to look forward to making a new life for herself there.

She began to look round the room into which morning light was streaming. Only a few months ago, in a very similar room, she had thought she had nothing to live for and attempted to end her life. Thank God, she had not succeeded. Thank God for sending her back to a place where she had friends who cared about her. Friends like Calum and Victor and Laurel.

Fourteen

The glen had never looked more beautiful than it did on this summer morning. Grace drove the final few miles beside the shining water of the loch, then slowed down to a crawl when she reached Rowankirk so that she could enjoy the sight of the laburnum trees bending their blossom-laden boughs over each side of the main street. Behind the single-storey cottages and tiny shops were larger granite houses and hotels, and beyond them distant purple-covered mountains. The drive from the motel where she had spent the night had been a long motorway haul until the last twenty or so miles but it had been an uneventful journey and now she was home.

When she got out of the car on the drive of her parents' cottage it was good to stretch her legs and fill her lungs with the heady mountain air. The urge came to her then to walk away the stiffness in her legs and shoulders induced by the hours of driving, so as soon as she had washed her face and disposed of a mug of coffee she set off to walk briskly to the village newsagent to buy a paper and some fresh bread rolls.

The village was almost deserted on this Monday morning now that the children were all in school and most of the tourists were still in their hotels or guest houses. Grace was walking back towards Faith's Cottage carrying the folded newspaper and a bag of bread rolls when she caught a glimpse of Donald Muir locking the church door and making his way to the gate. He saw her at once and lifted a hand in greeting. It would seem churlish not to stop and speak to him, even though she was now ravenously hungry.

'I didn't expect to see you here today, Grace,' Donald said when they met at the gate. 'I thought you had gone back to your home for a few days.'

'This is my home now. I won't be going back to live in the Cotswolds. There's nothing for me down there now,' she told him.

'Are you sure about that? It isn't something you've decided in a hurry, without talking it over with your husband?' He was regarding her intently as he waited for her answer.

'I did go down there yesterday, and I did find out the truth. I waited in the home we used to share until Paul came back, very late, from Alison's house. He told me the truth, which is that he will have children

237

after all because Alison is pregnant already. So I told him I'd let the divorce go ahead as quickly as possible.'

'That can't have been an easy thing for you to do,' he said quietly.

'In a way, it was almost a relief to me. After all the weeks of waiting and hoping that Paul would change his mind and come back to me, I mean. The decision had been taken out of my hands because of the baby, and I just had to accept it. I was very angry, when he first told me. So angry that I had to work hard to control myself before I started to drive back. Then, after I'd stopped at a motel and had a few hours of sleep, I woke up feeling that I was lucky to be alive and well enough to put my mind to starting again somewhere else. Somewhere like the shop in Rowanmore.'

Donald smiled as he looked over his shoulder at the little church he had come here, so reluctantly, to serve. 'So my prayers were answered,' he said. 'Though not, perhaps, in the way I expected.'

Grace smiled back into the hazel eyes which had been so troubled when he first spoke to her. She found herself wondering what had brought Donald Muir to this quiet place after the challenge there must have been for him in an inner city parish. He did not seem to her to be the sort of man who would turn his back on a challenge without

238

a very good reason. Whatever the reason, she was glad he had been here when she needed someone to care about her.

'Thanks a lot for praying for me. I've got out of the habit of doing that myself since things went wrong with my marriage, though I found it easy enough to do when I was very ill,' she added honestly.

He laughed. 'We all find it easy to pray at times like that. Almost impossible at other times.'

'Even you?'

'Even me. Especially me.'

'I find that hard to believe.'

'Yet it's true. That's the reason why I'm here.'

Grace stared at him, unable to believe what she had just heard. 'Do you mean ... what I think you mean?'

He sighed. 'Yes, I'm afraid I do. At least, I did when I first came here. Now, I'm not so sure.'

Her eyes remained on his, intent, searching. 'You have to be sure, don't you? Otherwise...'

'Otherwise I've no right to be where I am.' He sighed again. 'The trouble is, I'm not sure I do have that right.' He stopped, then went on, 'I shouldn't be telling you this, should I? You, of all people, Grace.'

'Why not?'

'You're your father's daughter, so you

know how important it is that I don't have doubts.'

'But I shared my own doubts and fears with you, before I went to see Paul. So why shouldn't you share yours with me?'

'This isn't the time.'

There was a long moment of silence while Grace considered what he had just said. He seemed in a hurry to leave her now, but she did not want him to go. Not yet. So she leaned on the gate, and waited.

'I must be going, I've a meeting to prepare for.' His voice was brusque, almost harsh.

'If there is ever a time, you will let me know, won't you, Donald?' she found herself saying, and meaning it.

This brought warmth back to his face, and to his voice. 'Yes, I can promise you that. Thanks for the offer, Grace. It means a lot to me.'

He held out a hand to her across the shabby little iron gate and she put her own out to meet the firm pressure of his fingers. It was only a fleeting contact before he walked away from her and back towards the church.

Laurel was conscious of the hostile atmosphere as soon as Isla walked into the staff-room where the employees were gathered about the table to eat the late lunch she and Ben had served after all the guests had left

240

the hotel dining room. Isla glanced around the room before taking a seat as far away from Laurel as possible, and also as far away from Fergus as she could get.

Calum frowned as he noticed this, though he made no comment. His concern was all for his young chef, the girl who had gradually, imperceptibly, during the traumatic days immediately after his arrival at the Skellkirk Abbey Hotel, begun to push the nightmare events he had been forced to live with since the night of the fire into the furthest recesses of his mind. When Laurel had applied for the job here in his own hotel he could not believe his luck. He had been certain that she would stay close to her home in Yorkshire in the hope that Daniel Dailey would show up again one day and ask her to go back to him.

Instead, Laurel had shown that she had too much pride to hang around waiting for that to happen and suffering the unwanted sympathy of those who had known her lover better than she did. Which was why she was here in his home, sitting right next to him, and looking acutely uncomfortable because of the unfriendly vibes which were coming her way from Isla.

'I thought you'd have been down in Rowanmore cooking for Victor and Robbie today, Laurel.'

Isla's voice was sharp enough to make

Calum's own uneasiness deepen, and to bring a flush to Laurel's smooth ivory skin.

'What on earth made you think that?' the Yorkshire girl responded quietly.

'Well, you are more than friendly with the guy, aren't you?'

'I don't know what you mean...'

'Don't try to play the innocent. You were there at Birch Cottage with Victor while Grace was looking after Robbie, weren't you?'

Laurel's cheeks began to burn. She was conscious of Calum staring at her. 'I was only there for a couple of hours in the afternoon, helping Victor to get the kitchen straight—' she began.

'You'll be moving in with him soon, I suppose? As soon as you can, I imagine.' Isla glared at Laurel as she hurled the words across the table at her.

'I don't know what you're talking about. Going to give Victor a hand with his moving doesn't mean I'm ready to go and live with him.' Laurel was pushing away her meal as she spoke.

'That isn't what he said.'

'You must have misunderstood what he said.'

'I didn't. He made it plain enough to me...'

'Victor wouldn't say anything like that. I know he wouldn't!' Laurel was angry and upset now.

'I'm telling you, he did!'

'I'm not going to listen to any more of your lies.' As she finished speaking, Laurel was on her feet and making for the door.

Instantly, Calum was preparing to follow her. First, though, he turned to Isla. 'I'd like a word with you in my office at five o'clock, Isla.'

'But I'm—' she began.

'Be there, it's important,' he snapped before he walked out of the room.

First he made his way to the kitchen, but Laurel was not there. Then he went out by the back door into the rear garden and the car park. She was not there either. Without hesitation, he strode through the grounds until he came to the row of three cottages and rang the doorbell at Kingfisher Cottage. At first there was no answer, but he stood his ground and pressed the bell harder this time. At last the dark blue door opened and Laurel was facing him.

'I'm sorry I kept you waiting, Calum. I was in the back garden,' she said.

He knew that was not so. Her face was still marked with her distress and her voice was shaky.

'I came to say how sorry I am for what happened,' he began.

'It wasn't your fault,' she whispered.

'I feel as though I am partly to blame.

243

When I saw the mood Isla was in I should have stopped her before she could upset you.'

'Why does she dislike me? I haven't done anything to her...'

Calum hesitated, wondering whether to tell her the truth, then decided against it. After all, he might be wrong in what he suspected, in which case it would be far better to keep Laurel in ignorance. Isla must certainly be wrong in believing that Victor would be attracted to this young girl when he was still grieving for Shona.

'The trouble with Isla these days,' he began carefully, 'is that she and Fergus have put off their marriage for far too long and now the stress is getting to both of them.'

Laurel frowned. 'I still don't see why she has to take it out on me.' She rubbed a hand across her eyes as she moved further back into the tiny hall and opened the door wider so he could step inside.

'You mustn't let it upset you, Laurel. I don't suppose it'll happen again.'

'It isn't the first time she's picked on me, and in front of other people too. I'm beginning to wish I had stayed in Yorkshire.' She bit hard on her lips to stop them from trembling.

Alarm bells began to sound for Calum. 'Don't say that! I'm going to have a word with Isla in my office later this afternoon, so

I'll make sure it doesn't happen again.'

'She won't like that, especially as I'm the newcomer here and she is engaged to your cousin.'

'That doesn't give her the right to make false accusations against you,' he argued.

'She'll dislike me more than ever if you tick her off. It might be better if you started to look for another chef, one Isla is able to get on with—'

'No, it damn well wouldn't!' he broke in fiercely. 'I'm not going to lose you because of Isla. It's time she came to terms with what happened to Shona, and time she settled down with Fergus. Time she accepted that Victor has to make a new life for himself, too.'

Laurel's eyes widened when she heard him say that. So Calum was aware that Isla was chasing after her brother in-law. He also seemed to know that Isla was so jealous of her own friendship with Victor that she was trying to make trouble for her. Laurel still thought it would be best if she left the Glen View rather than cause problems for Calum.

Calum did not agree. 'You're still upset, aren't you?' Calum spoke tenderly as he put an arm about her shoulders. 'You mustn't be, my darling. Please don't let's have any more talk of me replacing you. Because no one could ever replace you in my life.'

The concern in his voice and the comfort of his firm hold on her shoulder brought the tears Laurel had pushed away earlier rushing back into her eyes. She tried to blink them away but was unable to stop a couple from escaping. When Calum saw them, emotion flooded him and before he was aware of what he was about to do he had lifted her face up so that he could kiss the tears away from her cheeks. Then, since she did not draw away from him, he took possession of her mouth in a long searing kiss that left them both breathless.

'Don't leave me, my love,' he begged as he stroked her hair. 'Please don't leave me now that I've found you.'

Laurel leaned against him and kissed him back. Her worries about Isla's jealousy were forgotten as she enjoyed the strength and the warmth and the kindness of him. The loneliness and homesickness she had been experiencing earlier were left behind as she gave herself up to the powerful attraction that came to life between herself and Calum. No longer did she regard Calum as her employer, the owner of the hotel where she worked, a boss she both liked and respected. Instead, he was a handsome man with a seductive accent and a warm person-ality. He was a man she was falling in love with; he was a man who had already fallen in love with her.

'I've been longing for months to hold you like this, Laurel,' he was murmuring as his mouth moved over her face and his arms pulled her close enough to feel the beat of his heart and the strength of his desire for her. 'Tell me you feel the same; tell me you love me as much as I love you, my darling girl.'

Laurel looked deeply into grey eyes that were widely set beneath his arched dark brows. She saw a blaze of desire reflected there that lifted her suddenly and amazingly out of her mood of unhappiness and made her feel exhilarated, on the very edge of excitement, hardly able to wait for what would happen next. Nothing mattered to her now except that sense of exhilaration, that heady excitement, that longing to be loved by Calum McLeod, which filled her whole being. As if in a dream, she moved backwards as he released her only for long enough to close the cottage door.

In the seconds that passed while she waited there in the tiny hall for him to engulf her again in his embrace she heard the murmuring of sheep grazing on the other side of her garden wall and the sweet song of a bird drifting in through the open window. Then the mood was shattered by the urgent summons delivered by Calum's mobile phone. Startled, Laurel stepped away from him while he spoke briefly.

Smiling ruefully, he kissed the tip of her nose. 'I have to go, my love, which might not be a bad thing for you. You'll have time to think before you commit yourself. Because that's what I'll want from you. Commitment!'

Throughout his first Sunday in Birch Cottage as he did more unpacking, played with Robbie and prepared easy meals for the two of them, Victor had found his thoughts returning to the scene he had been forced to endure with Isla during her visit the day before. Guilt plagued him every time he recalled the way he had allowed Isla to assume that he had a romantic interest in Laurel Appleby. He must have been mad to even start to travel along that particular road – it would almost certainly cause problems at the hotel for Laurel. It might even result in her losing her job, since Isla seemed hell bent on causing trouble if she did not get what she wanted.

The fact that what Isla wanted was *him* brought a hot wave of embarrassment washing over Victor. There was something almost obscene about the idea of him sharing a home, or worse still a bed, with Isla. It was because he had felt trapped, and appalled by her determination to force her way into the most intimate places in his life, that he had jumped at the chance to let Isla think that he cared for Laurel Appleby. Now he had got himself, and Laurel, into a situation that was fraught with difficulties, if not disasters. He had also got himself into Ruth's bad books, he soon discovered when his mother-in-law telephoned to ask him if he was going to drop Robbie off at her home as usual the next morning on his way to work at the Glen View.

'Yes, I'd like to do that, if you're feeling up to coping with the wee rascal,' he told her.

'I had to ring and find out because you seem to be avoiding us just now.' Ruth's voice held more than a hint of censure.

Victor sighed. He had been sure he'd sorted everything out satisfactorily with her last night over the shared dram of whisky, and now there was that hint of grievance in her voice again.

'Of course I'm not avoiding you, Ruth. What ever gave you that idea?'

'Well, you wouldn't let me help you move, and Isla says you sent her away with a flea in her ear when she brought some lunch down for you during her break. Then you told me you were having a meal with Grace today, when you must have known she was going down to see her husband.'

Oh God, he really had landed himself in it now. Why hadn't he remembered that Grace had told him she was going on a brief visit to her Cotswold house this weekend? He was losing his marbles! He must be, to have got himself into such a situation. How was he going to get out of this one? It would have to be another lie, there was no other way to deal with it.

'Grace must have made her mind up quite suddenly to go and see Paul, and forgotten to tell me,' he improvised.

'You've been snubbing Isla too,' Ruth went on.

'Why would I do that, Ruth?' he asked.

'Because you're carrying on with that young lassie who cooks up at Glen View, aren't you?'

'No!' He found himself almost shouting as he voiced his denial. 'No, I'm not.'

'Isla says you admitted that you were.'

'Then Isla must have misunderstood me. Laurel is just a friend. A very good friend,' he added.

'You'd best see it stays that way, if you want to keep your gardening job at Glen View,' his mother-in-law said then.

'What do you mean by that?'

'I'm only trying to warn you that Calum McLeod is head over heels with the girl, according to my Isla.'

'Why should you need to warn me about that?' Victor asked, even though he could make a guess at what the answer would be.

'Because if Calum thinks you have a fancy for the girl he'll send you packing and you'll need to find work elsewhere. You might have to take wee Robbie miles away from us then. I couldna' bear that, Victor. You know I couldn't, now I've lost my Shona.' Ruth's voice ended on a sigh that was almost a sob.

Victor felt a rush of pity for her that wiped out the irritation he had been feeling moments ago.

'I'll not be taking Robbie away from you, Ruth,' he told her gently. 'I want what's best for him, and what is best for him is here. If I can't have Shona I don't want anyone else.'

He had said goodnight to her then and replaced the telephone, but for some time afterwards he remained staring down at it while he wondered if what he had just said to Shona's mother was still true.

Fifteen

The mid-summer days were passing quickly at the Glen View, with the sort of events that were so attractive to tourists and locals alike bringing plenty of work to those who were employed at the hotel. Ceilidhs were arranged for mid-week evenings as well as Saturday nights, there were festivals of music and art taking place in small towns or large villages within easy reach of Rowan-kirk and Rowanmore, and there were the famous Highland Games to be enjoyed in other places. Yet even at this busiest time of the year the hotel was not as full as Calum had expected, or hoped for.

'I suppose some people are staying away because they are afraid the public footpaths will all be closed here like in parts of England because of foot and mouth disease,' Calum said thoughtfully as he discussed the menu changes for the current week with Laurel.

'At least there seem to be plenty of foreign visitors coming here: people from Germany, Italy, Holland and Belgium,' Laurel tried to console him. 'Where Mum and Dad live no one is going on holiday, or even for week-ends, Mum says. She doesn't know what they are going to do, with the mortgage they have to pay on the barn conversion for the walkers to stay in. I'm really worried about them. Maybe I'll feel better after I've been to see them. Are you sure you can manage without me, Calum?'

'Yes. I've already asked Mrs Reid and her daughter if they'll put in some extra time while you are away, and they've agreed. You'd better take three days, as it's such a long journey. I won't be so worried about you going now that I know you are certain to come back to me,' he added. Laurel felt warm colour creep up into her cheeks then spread downwards into her neck as she saw the expression in his luminous grey eyes. They had been very careful during these last few days not to allow their love for each other to become obvious to anyone else. Both knew this would be unwise and could lead to complications that they were not yet ready for. The atmosphere in the staff-room was difficult enough for Laurel to cope with already, even though, since Calum's blunt warning to her, Isla had made no further accusations against her. Instead she treated her with an icy politeness that seemed almost insulting to Laurel.

'Why don't you go down to Yorkshire

tomorrow, and come back on Friday in time for the next coach party to arrive?' Calum suggested.

'If you're sure you can manage...' Laurel did not want to take advantage of Calum's newly declared feelings for her.

'Yes, I'll manage, but I will miss you,' he told her quietly.

Would Calum still feel the same about her when she was not here to stir him to tenderness and passion, Laurel found herself wondering as she set about preparing frozen desserts to make life easier for Mrs Reid during her absence. Once, Daniel had told her he loved her and could not live without her. Once, Daniel had given her a ring to prove his love for her. Yet when he was away from her he had proved that he did not love her enough to be faithful to her. She would only be away from Calum for a few days though. That would not be long enough to put his love to the test, would it?

For Grace the time was also racing by now she had taken possession of the shabby little shop in the heart of Rowanmore and set about transforming it into something more closely resembling the business she had built up so successfully in the Cotswolds. She had given long and careful thought to the naming of this shop, even though she knew from her years of experience that it was not the name of the business that brought in custom but the quality of the service provided there. In the end she decided to change The Flower Basket to Grace's Flower Basket in order to put her own signature on the place right from the start.

A local signwriter changed the faded blue and white lettering above the front window into a rich green and gold, and painted doors and window-frames to match while Grace set about refreshing the interior of the premises with a shade of ivory which would make the right background for the flowers and foliage.

'You're really in a rush to get on with it, aren't you, Grace?' Victor said when he brought Robbie in to see her while they were out for a walk on a beautiful late June evening.

'Yes, I suppose I am.' She glanced around her at the almost completed main area of the shop where the first tall green metal vases were awaiting the arrival of the first flowers. 'There's nothing to wait for, now.'

The remark puzzled Victor. 'What were you waiting for, Grace? Or would you rather I didn't ask that?'

She took her time about answering. 'I suppose I was waiting for things to come right for me. Only they didn't. So I'm having to make a fresh start, and it might as well be here as anywhere else. At least here I'll have someone of my own, when Mum and Dad come back from New Zealand.'

Victor moved closer to her while Robbie sat down on the tiled floor and began to slide his fingers experimentally up and down one of the empty metal flower holders.

'Do you mean ... what I think you mean, Grace? Or have I got the wrong end of the stick and everything is fine with you and Paul?' His eyes were searching her face, looking for answers she might not be ready yet to give. He had been curious about why Grace did not often mention her husband. At times he had been puzzled by the way she avoided answering questions about Paul's prolonged absence. Now he was even more perplexed by what she had just said.

'Yes.' She sighed, and moved her glance to where Robbie was now hugging the green vase to his chest. 'I suppose I do mean what you think, and you haven't got the wrong end of the stick.'

'I'm sorry, Grace. So sorry. I wondered why you didn't talk about him. I mean, people do when they love someone, don't they?'

'I do still love Paul, but he's found some-one else to love. Someone who can give him children, now that I'm unable to do that.' Her voice broke as she told him that. Her glance, which had been resting on Robbie, moved to Victor's face as she went on with a rush. 'We left it too late to have our family because we were both so busy building up our careers. Then I became very ill and had to have a serious operation...'

'So you came here to recover.' He spoke very carefully, wanting to hear the rest but not to be intrusive if Grace was not ready to tell him any more. There was a long silence, except for the sound of Robbie humming happily to himself as he hugged the vase.

'I came here to give Paul enough time to decide whether he could go on with our marriage once he knew I wouldn't ever be able to have children,' she said at last, in such a low voice that he could scarcely hear her.

'Perhaps he will want to go on with your marriage, when he's had plenty of time to miss having you around,' was all Victor could manage to say that might comfort her.

'No!' She spoke so sharply that Robbie dropped the vase with a clatter and scrambled to his feet to come and clutch at his father's legs. 'He won't be missing me, because he's already found someone else who can give him a family.'

'Oh Grace, are you quite certain about that?' Victor looked away from her and down at his son. He was unable to bear the sight of the anguish reflected in her face.

Grace didn't deserve this, any more than he had deserved to be robbed of his darling wife by the terrorist bomb. You didn't always get what you deserved though. You had to make the best of what was left for you. What was left for him was wee Robbie, to look after as Shona had begged him to do. For Grace there was no such blessing, so she must try to build a new life for herself with this shop, so far away from where her life had fallen apart. He must try to help her, but how?

'Yes, I'm absolutely certain,' she answered. 'Paul admitted it. That's why I came back so soon from my trip to our old home. Because there was no point in me staying. The woman friend who helped me in my shop down there asked Paul in for meals during the weeks while I was in hospital. She already had two children, and now there's going to be a third. So Paul wants to marry her.' The words were said quietly but with undeniable bitterness.

'Do your parents know?' was Victor's next question. If they did, they would surely want to be back here with Grace.

'Not yet. I don't want them to cut their holiday short because of me. They've waited so long to go out there to see my sisters. So I don't want them to know yet, or they might feel they ought to come rushing back. By the time they do come back, in the autumn, I'll have proved I can manage on my own.'

'Will you? It's not easy, Grace. There's so much emptiness, so much loneliness to be lived with.' He spoke gently, trying to prepare her for the long nights when sleep would not come because of the empty place beside you in a bed which had once been shared with your love.

'It's different for you, Victor. Your love was still whole and beautiful right to the end. Mine has been ruined by deceit and unfaithfulness. So the only thing I can do is to put it behind me and get on with the rest of my life.'

There were no words that Victor could think of to answer that. It was too soon to tell her that she was a lovely, intelligent, kind woman who would surely meet someone else one day. All he could do was answer the urgent cry of Robbie for 'Eddie Bear! Want Eddie Bear, Daddy!'

'We forgot to bring him with us,' Victor remembered then. 'We usually can't go anywhere without Eddie, but there was the piper playing in the square for the visitors tonight. When Robbie heard the sound of the bagpipes he forgot all about his bear.' He scooped up the handsome dark-haired child under his arm and prepared to leave before Robbie became upset.

'We'll need to go, Grace, because it's his

bedtime and when he's tired he's easily upset. Will you let me make a meal for you on your moving-in day, as you did for me? I'd like to do that.'

The sorrow left her lips but did not leave her eyes as she smiled at him. 'Thanks, Victor, but I don't think I'll be living in the flat until some of my furniture comes up from the Cotswolds. I think I'll stay on in Faith's Cottage until nearer the time for Mum and Dad to come home.'

'Want Eddie!' Robbie cried.

'I expect he'll be waiting for you, so you can both go to bed,' Grace told him as she lifted one of his grubby little hands and kissed it before Victor walked away with his son.

She smiled and waved to them through the shop window. When they were out of sight she walked up the stairs into the flat with tears pouring down her face.

With Laurel away down in Yorkshire the atmosphere in the staff-room at the Glen View was calmer and more relaxed. Ever since Calum had warned Isla not to discuss the young chef's private life in front of his other employees, he had become aware that whenever he was present a state of icy politeness existed between the two of them. If any more references had been made by Isla to Laurel about her friendship with

Victor it must have been done without his knowledge.

Laurel had shown her love for him now by sharing her bed with him. Calum was certain she was not someone who would do that without feeling real commitment. It was too soon to ask her to marry him, because he had to be sure they would be right for each other. He did not want another long-term relationship to fall apart, as his engagement to Katharine had done after the fire. One was more than enough. He must take his time with Laurel even though he longed to declare to all who would listen that she belonged to him and he intended to love and care for her for the rest of his life.

Fergus, too, was easier in his mind now that Laurel was away. With Isla more relaxed he felt the time was right to press for an immediate rearrangement of their wedding. It was more than time they settled down together in the Coach House where they had once been so happy. He had been tolerant about Isla going back to live with her parents after her sister's death but now his patience had worn thin and he was eager for them to start a family of their own. The problems in Isla's family were sorted now, so the time was right. Fergus felt certain of that.

He chose the moment to talk to Isla after

261

they had finished singing several old Scottish ballads at the mid-week ceilidh and carried their drinks out into the summer-house at the rear of the hotel to cool off. It seemed the right moment because, as they had sung their final song, a well-known Robert Burns' love song, Isla had leaned against him and melted into him as she used to do so often. There had been, just for a few seconds, that spark of passion which had been absent from their relationship in recent weeks. So the time was right.

'When are you moving back into the Coach House with me, darling?' he asked as she laid her head back against the wicker sofa with a sigh, after taking a long drink of her white wine..

The words were enough to bring her upright so suddenly that liquid splashed from the glass on to the hand he was about to use to draw her mouth to his. 'Never! I told you it was all over.'

'You're still wearing my ring,' he reminded her.

'Only because you wouldn't take it back.'

'I wouldn't take it back because I knew you didn't mean what you said.'

'I did mean it. You know I did!'

'I don't know anything of the sort. All I know is that you haven't got over what happened to Shona yet. That the shock of it just got too much for you to cope with. I've

262

made allowances for that, but now I think it's time we got our own act together and got married.'

'I can't marry you, Fergus. I've already told you that, so there's no point in going all over it again, is there?'

'You were upset at the time, so we had a bit of a row. I knew you didn't mean it...'

'I *did* mean it!' she insisted. 'I'm not going to move back into the Coach House with you and I'm not going to marry you. That's final!'

'Why? There's nothing to stop us now...'

'There's the fact that I don't love you now. I love someone else. Surely that's a good enough reason?' She was on her feet, pushing away his hands, as she made for the open door.

Fergus was there before her, blocking her escape. 'You only think you love him. I've seen the way you follow him around, trying to convince him that you're the right woman to share his home and bring up his child. You've even grown your hair like Shona's, and started dressing like Shona to try and make him want you, but he doesn't, does he? Because you'll never be like Shona was inside, like the way Victor knew her. So you're wasting your time. Worse still, you're so jealous of the girl you think he really likes, that you've upset her and made Calum furious with you.'

'You're talking rubbish,' she gasped.

'I'm not. You're making yourself, and me, the subject of gossip. Calum doesn't like it, and neither do I.'

'Calum doesn't like it because he fancies her himself.'

'Calum hasn't got over Katharine, yet.'

'I think he has. That's why he brought Laurel up here from Yorkshire.'

'You're wrong. Just as wrong as you are in thinking I'll ever marry you. It's over, Fergus, and you have to accept that. If you don't, if you keep on pestering me, I'll find myself another job and leave here.'

'You won't do that while he's still here. While you still think you've got a chance with Victor. I can wait until it comes home to you that he really doesn't want you,' Fergus said before he spun round and marched out of the door, away from the summer-house and through the garden till he reached the Coach House.

Isla dragged the emerald engagement ring from her finger and thrust it into the pocket of her long skirt. There was a burning sensation behind her eyes and a threat of tears, but she would not give way to them. She was sorry about the way the long friendship she had shared with Fergus had been shattered, sorry she no longer cared for him as once she had done, but what filled her mind to overflowing was the way she felt about Victor. The compulsion she felt to take her sister's place in his life and to care for Robbie, the small boy she had loved since first she had set eyes on him. It was what Shona would have wanted. Isla was quite sure of that.

Now that her engagement to Fergus was at an end there must be a chance that Victor would be able to think of her differently. Not as Shona's twin sister, but as a beautiful woman who could bring love back into his life. She would go to Birch Cottage tomorrow evening and take a present for her adorable little nephew. Victor would not be able to send her away then, would he?

Sixteen

Calum had spent a couple of hours with Laurel on the evening before she was to drive down to Yorkshire to see her parents. The latest cases of foot and mouth disease were only a dozen or so miles away from their farm now so she was getting terribly worried. He urged her to invite them to come up to the hotel for a few days later in the summer.

'I don't think Dad will leave the farm,' she told him with distress plain to see on her face. 'Mum might come when my brother finishes his year at agricultural college. She'll be happier when Dad has someone to keep him company while she's away.'

Calum frowned. 'Don't leave it till August, my love. We'll be full up then because of the Highland Games at Rowanmore.'

'Victor said she could stay at his place if we were too busy here.'

His frown deepened. 'When did he say that?'

'When I helped him to move into his cottage.'

'It would be better if your mother stayed here.'

'I'll see what she says. Whether she's willing to come at all, I mean.' Laurel was anxious to leave the subject now. 'I just don't know what to expect, now there are foot and mouth cases so close to them.'

'I wish I could go with you, to be there if you need any help.' He pulled her close to him again as he prepared to leave. 'You will ring me, let me know you are safely there?'

'Yes, of course. I'll be fine.' She laughed. 'I managed to get myself here quite safely back in March, didn't I?'

'I only worry because I love you so much.' He kissed her again, and again, until neither of them wanted him to go back to his apartment in the hotel. 'You must get some sleep now, I don't want you to fall asleep at the wheel. I want you to come back soon, and safely, because you are more precious to me than anyone else has ever been in all my life.'

Laurel had felt a small frisson of uneasiness stir in her as he said the words. Was she more important to him than Katharine had been? The woman who had been his partner until the fire had devastated the Glen View Hotel and sent him down to Yorkshire to manage the Skellkirk Abbey Hotel? Calum had told Laurel about her and said he had realised she was the wrong woman for him, even before she left him. Yet for long after Calum had gone Laurel was unable to banish the woman called Katharine from her mind.

Victor found, once he had tucked Robbie and Eddie Bear into bed, that his thoughts went back to worrying about Grace. There had been something in her eyes, when she told him her husband had found someone who could give him the family she was unable to supply, that seemed to be haunting him. It was an expression of anguish so deep that he had been forced to look away from her and down at his own wonderful little son, that most precious gift left to him by Shona. There had also been the moment when Grace lifted the boy's grubby little hand and kissed it. A huge lump had swelled up in his throat and he had felt an urge to run away from her before his own grief came spilling out.

That small gesture had taken him back to the morning when they had left Robbie with the wife of one of his fellow officers, to play with her own two small children while he and Shona went to choose his birthday present. Shona had done exactly the same thing as she said, 'Bye, Robbie! We won't be long, sweetie.' Robbie had been holding a spadeful of sand in one hand when she had taken his other hand to press a kiss into it.

There had still been a speck of sand on her lips as she begged him to look after Robbie, in the moments before she died.

'It was different for you, Victor, your love was whole and beautiful right to the end,' Grace had said when he tried to warn her of the times of loneliness and emptiness which she would experience if she went ahead and divorced Paul. She had been right. There certainly had not been any deceit or unfaithfulness to ruin his own memories. Those memories were still good and perfect. At odd times now he was able to take comfort from them.

What was he going to do about Grace, though? How was he going to help her? It did not occur to Victor to wonder why it should be so important to him that he helped this woman whom he had not known very well until a few weeks ago. What a fool Grace's husband must be to throw away the love of such a kind, intelligent and beautiful woman. Victor's knowledge of men, gained over the years of dealing with all sorts of people while serving in the army, made him suspect that Paul Hardy would probably have settled quite happily for life with Grace, with or without children, if he had not become infatuated with her friend while Grace was in hospital.

It was a tragedy, in more ways than one, because Grace would have made such a lovely mother. Perhaps, his thoughts rambled on as he poured himself a measure of whisky and picked up his copy of *The Scotsman*, she would meet someone else before too long. Someone whose children were in need of a mother. Someone like himself. The thought, as it came to him, gave him such a jolt that he swallowed the whisky too quickly and made himself cough.

Yet the thought, once in his mind, would not seem to leave him. Robbie would have a happier life if he had a mother as well as a father to care for him, and already Robbie was becoming fond of Grace. As for himself, no one would ever be able to inspire in him again the sort of love he had felt for Shona: that mixture of passion and tenderness which had made her the most important person in his life from the time he had first met her. He had a great liking for Grace, though. They were friends and they cared about each other. It was only the passion which was missing.

Another advantage to considering partnership with Grace was that it would surely free him of Isla's obssession for him. He just had to free himself of that. Already the way Isla was pursuing him was causing friction between himself and Fergus. It was also bringing problems to Laurel Appleby because he had been stupid enough to allow Isla to think he had his mind set on her.

With Laurel away from the hotel for a few days he would be spared the embarrassment of hearing Isla speak to her with the icy politeness which had replaced her earlier antagonism, but once she was back it might all begin again. He ought to think seriously about how he might prevent that. Was it fair though to even consider a partnership with Grace, always providing she would have him, when he was still missing Shona so much? Surely the safest thing to do was to put the idea right out of his mind. He opened the newspaper and began to read.

Isla drove into Fort William especially to find the right sort of present for Robbie. In order to have time to do that she was forced to ask her deputy, Carrie Brown, to stand in for her on the reception desk. Carrie was not too happy about it. 'I was going to help Grace do the flowers when she comes up today,' she objected.

'I might be back before Grace arrives,' Isla said quickly.

Carrie was still not happy about the arrangement but since Isla was engaged to Fergus and Fergus was the hotel owner's cousin, she felt it best to give way. She was annoyed though, because she had come to enjoy watching Grace do the hotel flower arrangements and at the same time learn how to do this herself.

Isla was delighted with the hand puppet she found in a Fort William shop and could not wait to tell Victor about it when she returned to the hotel later that afternoon. Her eagerness abated when she found Victor talking to Grace in the car park as Grace packed away her spare flowers, greenery, oasis and tools. She was annoyed to see a frown come to Victor's face when she appeared at his side.

'Hello, Isla, did you have a good shop in Fort William? Carrie said you'd gone there. Did you buy something special?' Grace asked as she caught sight of Victor's frown.

'Yes. I bought a present for Robbie.' Isla spoke to Victor, not to Grace.

'It's ages to his next birthday.' Victor did not smile as he reminded her of that.

'It doesn't have to be his birthday for me to buy darling Robbie a present. I thought I'd bring it round for him tonight.'

'Won't you be on duty then, if you've had the afternoon off?'

Plainly, Victor did not want this visit from his sister in-law. Grace looked at him with sympathy. Carrie had mentioned to her, less than an hour ago, that there was talk among the hotel staff that Isla was always chasing Victor, and that she was no longer wearing her engagement ring. Grace felt worried when she heard that. She had noticed that Isla seemed very fond of her brother-in-law and was always ready to leave whatever she was doing to go and speak to him, but she had not thought this to be of any real significance until Carrie spoke of it. Now, as Isla gazed at Victor intensely from long-lashed violet eyes, there was little doubt left in Grace's mind that there was certainly far more than affection in her glances.

'Oh, no! Carrie volunteered to work my shift this afternoon so I can do hers another day,' she said in answer to his question.

Grace was surprised to hear that. It did not tie in with what Carrie had told her. She frowned as she closed the hatchback of her car and moved to open the driver's door.

'So I'll bring the present down to your cottage before Robbie goes to bed,' Isla declared with a dazzling smile. 'I can't wait to see Robbie's face. He'll love it!'

Victor was looking acutely uncomfortable now, shifting his weight from one foot to the other as if ready to set off at speed any moment to make his escape. As Grace watched him she noticed a slight twitch, of nervousness she was certain, bring a ripple to the muscle beneath his khaki T-shirt. A wave of pity for him invaded her. So what Carrie had hinted at was true – Isla was trying to take her sister's place in Victor's life, and Victor was becoming aware of it. Grace hesitated with her fingers on the handle of the driver's door. Her glance met that of Victor across the yards of gravel which separated them and she responded to the appeal that she recognised in his dark eyes.

'I'll see you at seven, Victor, and I'll bring some wine with me,' she said on the spur of the moment, and saw a swift blaze of relief wipe the strain from his face. She dropped into the seat and switched on the engine. A moment later she was turning her vehicle round and heading for the open gates and the road that went downhill to Rowanmore.

Victor watched her go with his heart full of gratitude. Grace had guessed what an awkward situation he found himself in with Isla. It was almost as though he had cried out to her for help and she had responded before the words left his lips. The weight of embarrassment which had been all about him, making him feel trapped and desperate to escape, lifted because of Grace's timely intervention. She would never know how grateful he was. But his troubles were not over yet, because Isla was not going to let him go without an explanation.

'What was all that about?' Anger brought hot colour to her cheeks and sharpness to her voice.

Victor was beginning to relax. 'Oh, it was about Grace coming for a meal with us tonight.'

'Why? Why should she come for a meal

with you?'

'Because I asked her, of course.' Friday was the evening he had invited Grace to eat with him, after she had moved her things into the flat above her shop, but Isla was not to know that.

'I meant, why did you ask her?'

He sighed, his patience growing thin again. 'Because Grace is a friend.'

'You hardly know her. You've only seen her on the odd occasions that you and Shona were on leave at the same time as she came up to see her parents.'

'I've got to know her better, and to like her, since she's been doing the flowers here for Calum,' he said curtly.

'She'll be too busy to do them when she opens her shop.'

'I think she's going to do them in the evening after the shop closes.'

'Why is she opening a shop up here when her other business is so far away, and her husband is so far away too? There's something strange about that, isn't there?'

'You'd better ask Grace about it yourself, since you're so interested. I'm going now to collect Robbie from your mother. Goodbye, Isla!' He spoke firmly as he walked away from her to put the tools he had been using back into the shed.

'I'll come tomorrow with Robbie's present,' she called after him.

'We won't be in. Why don't you leave it at your mother's for him,' he suggested.

There was no reply to that.

Grace telephoned him soon after he returned to Birch Cottage with Robbie, after picking the boy up from his grandmother's house. Robbie now went to a local playgroup several times a week and Ruth collected him from there to spend an hour or so with her before Victor finished work at Glen View.

'You must have thought I'd got mixed up about my night to come and have a meal with you,' she began hesitantly, 'so I thought I'd ring and put your mind at rest. It's Friday, of course.'

Victor laughed softly. 'It's tonight as well, Grace,' he said firmly. 'Don't let me down now, please! And thanks a lot for coming to my rescue like you did.'

Now Grace began to chuckle. 'I did it on the spur of the moment, and afterwards I was shocked at myself for jumping to conclusions. Especially that sort of conclusion,' she added wryly.

'It was the right one. I don't know what I'm going to do about it.' He broke off, not knowing how to go on without getting into waters that could be too deep for either of them.

'You don't need to ask me tonight, Victor,' she broke in. 'I'm planning on having a take-away from the Chinese place. I haven't tried it yet.'

'Then we'll both try it tonight, after I've got Robbie to bed. He's beginning to get grisly now he's tired. So I'll see you at seven, without wine, please.'

'I'll see you at seven, with wine as promised,' she insisted before she ended the call.

Fergus had been waiting for Isla to go back into the hotel after her encounter with Victor and Grace out in the car park. 'Isn't it time you took over reception from Carrie and let her go off duty for a while? She was supposed to be off duty for the whole afternoon, wasn't she?' The anger inside him had been simmering all the time he had watched from his office window as Isla stood too close to Victor, holding up the package from the toy shop in Fort William. He had seen the way Victor took a couple of steps backward, as though anxious to put distance between them.

'She doesn't mind. I'll do the same for her one day,' Isla retorted airily.

'One day when you're not too busy chasing after Victor Thorpe? Is that what you mean?'

'Don't be ridiculous! You've got a fixation about him,' she snapped.

'You're the one with the fixation about

him, and you can't seem to take on board the fact that he doesn't want you. That he doesn't want anyone except your sister.'

'I'm not going to listen to this. You've no right now to tell me what I can or can't do.' Her hand was on the door ready to walk out on him. 'We're not engaged any more.'

'It's nothing to do with whether we are engaged or not. It's all to do with the smooth running of this hotel, which is down to me,' Fergus broke in. 'You are causing friction among the staff here with your behaviour and it has to stop.'

'It isn't down to you. Glen View belongs to Calum. You just work here like the rest of us.'

'I told you before, if I ask Calum to get rid of Victor because his presence here is causing problems, he'll do that.'

'Victor isn't causing problems...'

'Not intentionally, but your chasing him is. Calum had to speak to you about the way you were treating Laurel, because you were jealous of her friendship with Victor, didn't he?'

Isla laughed scornfully. 'It wasn't because of that. He was worried Laurel might move in with Victor, and he didn't want that because he fancies her himself. As soon as Laurel's out of the way, down in Yorkshire, Grace is after Victor, and she's got a husband somewhere who might be interested in what she's up to right now.'

'Don't talk such rubbish, Isla!'

'I'm not! I was there when Grace told Victor she was going round to his place tonight with some wine. Victor said she was going for a meal, after Robbie was in bed.'

'No wonder you're in a black mood! Snap out of it, Isla, and let Victor get on with his life in his own way. He's had a bad time...'

'He'll have a worse time if Grace's husband finds out.'

'Leave it, Isla, for God's sake! If you don't, I'll get rid of Victor before either of you can stir up any more trouble. Understand?'

Isla did not reply. Instead she made her way to the front reception desk and told Carrie that she would take over her duty there immediately.

Calum, hearing the raised voices as he came back from an early evening walk with Fergus's dog, felt his spirits sink. Somewhere at the heart of the discord which kept surfacing among his staff was an element of jealousy involving Fergus, Isla and Victor, and of course Laurel when she was here. He knew he was going to have to do something about it, yet he was reluctant to take the obvious step. Fergus belonged here because he had been part of Glen View since his boyhood holidays with the family. In the days immediately after the fire, when the smoke he himself had inhaled had put him in hospital for some time, Fergus had been a tower of strength.

Isla too had been part of the Glen View family because of her long friendship, and later her engagement, to Fergus. So she must stay. It was unthinkable that Laurel should go, as she had suggested, to ease the situation. He simply could not let her go, he wanted her here with him for the rest of his life.

Having eliminated all except one, Calum came to his decision, though with reluctance. He could not allow the atmosphere at Glen View to deteriorate any further. If it did not improve very soon he would have to dispense with the services of Victor Thorpe, even though he felt such sympathy for him and was so pleased with his work in restoring the gardens to their former beauty. Yes, it would have to be Victor who left Glen View...

Seventeen

Laurel was weary by the time she neared her home in Skellthwaite, and more than a little apprehensive about what she would find there. Would her father's animals already be affected by the terrible disease which was devastating the farming community? When she reached the village, almost the first thing she encountered was a thick mat soaked in disinfectant which she must drive over to reach the farm. Then she saw the warning notices posted on gates to keep unauthorised people out of fields and footpaths. Fear took a firm hold on her and she could feel her heart pounding and a faint sweat breaking out on her brow. How were her mum and dad coping? She could not wait to find out.

After the warm hugs had been exchanged, the big mug of tea which came almost at the same time had been emptied and her father had told Laurel he was glad to see her, he was called to the telephone by her mother.

'Joe Ribston,' she said. 'He sounds bad too.'

Mary Appleby put a hand out to touch her husband's shoulder when she told him that. His face was sombre as he moved slowly out of the farmhouse kitchen to pick up the phone.

Mary shook her head sadly as she resumed her seat at the table opposite Laurel. 'Too much bad news about,' she murmured. 'It's putting such a strain on your dad. I'm worried about him, but he won't go to the doctor. Maybe you can persuade him to, love?'

'I'll try,' Laurel promised, but without much hope because her father could be a very stubborn man where his own health was concerned. When it came to the health of his animals things were very different. 'How far away is the foot and mouth now?'

'Not far enough. We can't take any of our animals to market, so there's no money coming in.'

'I can help there,' Laurel said eagerly. 'You can use my savings. There's about five thousand pounds in my account that I was planning to use when I got married. You and Dad must have that. I'll go to the bank tomorrow morning.'

Mary grasped her daughter's hand across the table. 'Thanks, love, but you might be needing it yourself for that, after all.'

Laurel shook her head. 'I won't. You and Dad can have it.'

Mary smiled. 'I meant what I said. You might be needing it yourself for your wedding. Daniel rang last night, wanting to speak to you. When I told him you were coming home today he said he'd get time off and come up to see you tomorrow.'

'Why? Why should he want to do that?' Laurel stared across the table at her mother.

Mary was puzzled by her expression. There was no delight there. Rather, there was annoyance to be seen in her daughter's beautiful blue eyes and a frown spoiling the ivory skin above them.

'He could be coming to say he's sorry,' she suggested.

'He's left it a bit late for that.'

'He's had time to miss you now,' Mary pointed out.

'So he thinks I'll be ready to take him back! Not likely!'

This sharp comment made Mary Appleby smile. 'Perhaps you ought to wait and see how you feel when you've talked to him before you say that.'

Laurel shook her head vigorously. 'No, I'm not even going to meet him. There's no point. I came to see you and Dad, not Daniel. He'll be wasting his time coming all the way from London.'

'He won't be coming from London. He's working in Manchester now.'

'It makes no difference. I don't want him.

There's someone else, Mum.' She hadn't meant to say that, it just sort of came out because she had always found it easy to talk to her mother. Now she was not sure whether to go on or not.

'Someone else?' Mary was smiling again. 'Is it serious?'

Laurel hesitated. 'I think so, but I'm not quite sure. I really like him, but it's early days. Too soon to be certain,' she confessed.

'Tell me more! Is it someone you've just met? Someone from the hotel? A guest, or one of the workers?' Mary was intrigued, and pleased that her daughter had now recovered from the trauma of being let down by Daniel so close to their wedding.

Laurel laughed. 'I'm not going to tell you any more yet. You'll have to wait till later. Dad's finished his phone call, I want to hear about that.'

Her father's face as he came back into the kitchen gave warning of what was to come. 'It's on Joe's farm now,' he said as he dropped into the chair nearest to the Aga and put his head into his hands. His shoulders shook silently as he grieved for his friend's tragedy.

Mary's glance met that of her daughter. Laurel rose to her feet, wanting to comfort him, but Mary shook her head. 'Come and see what I've been doing to the bunkhouse while you've been away,' she said as she took a firm hold on Laurel's arm and almost forced her out of the room and out of the back door. Once out in the bracing moorland air she sighed as she relaxed her hold and spoke again. 'There's nothing you can say to your dad that will help just now. He's best to have a little time on his own to think about what he's just heard from Joe.'

'I thought ... I just wanted to try and comfort him.'

'He's pleased to see you, and he'll be fine again in a few minutes. You'll have helped him a lot just by coming to see us.'

'I want to help in a more practical way, Mum. You must let me do that,' Laurel begged.

'We'll see, when we've talked it over with him. Now, come and see what I've done while things have been quiet.'

As they crossed the yard the border collie, Fern, greeted them. 'She's got pups. Four, all like her. I don't know what we're going to do with them because no one wants to take on a new dog when they haven't got the work for them to do.' Mary hated having to say that, but it was not the time to try and hide the truth from her daughter.

Laurel felt a lump start to form inside her throat when she heard that. Fern was a good mother, and a really good working dog. The idea of her pups having to be put to sleep if they could not be found homes distressed her deeply.

'Perhaps the RSPCA or the Canine Defence League will be able to find homes for them,' she suggested hopefully.

'They'd be happier going where they can work with sheep and cows. It's in their breeding,' Mary reminded her as they reached the converted barn, which had been turned into a bunkhouse to provide long-distance walkers with the sort of basic but clean accommodation that they preferred to hotels or guest houses. Fern had walked beside them, wagging her plumed, white-tipped tail. Now Mary spoke to her. 'Go back to your pups, Fern. There's a good lass.'

'Don't get rid of the pups, Mum, please. I can't bear the thought of that. Let me leave some money to pay for their feed, please!' Laurel begged.

Mary sighed. 'We'll see. Now come and look at what I've been doing to stop myself from sitting around and worrying.'

She pushed open the door and allowed light to flood into the high-ceilinged building. Laurel stared about her, silently taking in the changes which had been made. When she had left home a few months ago, the central area which served as a common room where the walkers could congregate in the evenings to compare notes about routes and experiences had possessed stark white

286

walls and bare unpolished board flooring with sturdy wooden seating that had well-washed covers. It had been spotlessly clean but basic, with curtained sleeping areas at one end and a small kitchen and showers at the other.

Now the place glowed with the colour Mary Appleby had splashed on to the walls to form a giant rainbow, with the gold of gorse bushes and the purple of heather reaching up to meet pale blue sky beneath the arc of the rainbow. Underfoot the bare boards had been painted a rich green. The chair covers had been dyed to match – green and purple and bright yellow.

'Oh, Mum! It's gorgeous!' Laurel gasped. 'Who did the painting for you?'

'I did!' There was such an air of pride and satisfaction in her mother's voice that Laurel could only shake her head in disbelief.

'But you can't even paint a door. Dad wouldn't ever let you loose with a paint brush after what you did to my bedroom when I was little.'

Mary laughed. 'He didn't even know I was doing this until I had it finished. Every time he went off to a meeting about the foot and mouth I came in here and slapped on some more paint to stop myself from going crazy with worry. You see, with no visitors coming I had too much time on my hands. At first I spring-cleaned the house from top to bottom, thinking things would improve as soon as the bad weather and the floods were behind us. Only things didn't improve and I began to be afraid I might not be able to cope with being isolated here on my own.'

Laurel was still lost in wonder, gazing around her in delight. 'Where did you get the idea from?' she wanted to know.

Mary laughed. 'It was one of those crazy TV programmes where you let somebody have a go at transforming your home.'

'I thought you didn't like that sort of programme?'

'I don't, but the mobile library couldn't get round because of the restrictions on movements in this area, and I'd run out of sewing and baking, so I watched them do a bedroom-cum-playroom for a country guest house and it looked so easy that I decided to have a go myself.'

'What does Dad think to it?'

Mary's face sobered. 'He didn't say much. Just asked me whether I thought we'd still be here at this time next year.'

'Oh, Mum!' Laurel took a couple of swift steps across the barn floor to put her arms about her mother as she saw her trying to blink away a few tears. 'Things will get better later in the year.'

'Will they?' Mary shook her head and a tear splashed Laurel's face. 'Sometimes I wonder about that. We seem to have got things wrong, somewhere and somehow, and now no one can stop this awful disease from spreading.'

'It hasn't spread to the north of Scotland, where I'm working. Why don't you come up and spend a week or two with me?'

'Your cottage isn't big enough, is it?'

Laurel thought of the tiny, pretty cottage which went with her job. Calum had suggested her mother should stay in the hotel because Kingfisher Cottage was so small. Or was it because he wanted her to be alone in the cottage when he came to see her after she finished her work in the kitchen cooking for his guests? The thought brought a flush to her cheeks, and reminded her that she had promised to telephone Calum and let him know that she had arrived home safely.

'Calum says you can stay in the hotel if you come when we don't have a coach party in,' she said, and was pleased to see her mother's face brighten.

'It would be nice to do that, when Craig finishes at college and can be here with your dad.'

'I must ring Calum now and let him know that I managed to get here safely.'

'Is he...?' Mary stopped as she saw her daughter's expression close up.

'He's my boss. He owns the hotel.'

'Why on earth was he working as manager

at the Skellkirk Abbey Hotel if he has a hotel of his own?' Mary wanted to know.

'There was a serious fire, a couple of years ago. Calum inhaled smoke and had to go into hospital. He left his cousin Fergus in charge of the renovation while he came down here to work.'

Mary frowned. 'Is he a lot older than you?'

'I expect so. Mid-thirties, I think. I'll go and ring him now on my mobile.' Laurel escaped to her own bedroom before there were any more questions.

'Thanks a lot for coming to my rescue, Grace,' Victor said as he opened the door of Birch Cottage to her soon after he had got Robbie bathed and into bed.

Grace smiled. 'I'm just glad I was there to help out. If I hadn't stopped to talk to Carrie I'd have been away before then.' She handed over a bottle of wine and followed him into the kitchen.

'I thought we'd have a drink before I go for the take away,' he told her. 'I did think about ordering it in advance but I wasn't sure what you'd like.'

Grace laughed, and he was struck by the way her silvery grey eyes became luminous. Her skin was pale and clear, her face oval with a pointed chin and a dimple, her hair short-cut, black and shining. 'I'm so hungry that I could eat almost anything,'

290

she confessed.

'I'll cook a proper meal for you on Friday,' he promised. 'For now, we'll eat Chinese. I'll find their menu and you can make your choice. Then you can sit and drink your wine while I go and collect it.'

When he had gone, on foot so as not to wake Robbie by starting up the car, Grace sat with her glass of wine in the big, pleasant living room looking out through the picture window at the front garden. There was a thrush perched on the wall sending his sweet song into the long Highland twilight. It was all so peaceful, the comfortable, sparsely furnished room, the beautiful cottage garden and the singing bird, that Grace relaxed enough to close her eyes and enjoy it. Until a sudden sound from the other side of the wall broke in and disturbed her. Instantly, she was on her feet and hurrying to Robbie's room.

'Daddy! Daddy! Eddie's gone!' The little boy had pushed back his duvet and was searching frenziedly for his teddy bear.

'It's all right, Robbie, we'll find him.'

Grace picked up the child and held him against her shoulder, but already he was struggling to free himself and get back to his bed.

'Eddie's gone! Eddie's gone!' He was in a panic, red faced and beginning to sob out his anguish. 'Mummy gone! Daddy gone!

Eddie gone! Want Eddie!' he wailed.

'Hush, Robbie, we'll find him in a minute,' Grace told him. She felt his terror, understood his fear, but was not sure how to deal with it. Her eyes searched the small room. There were stuffed toys, toys on wheels, books, balls and bats, but no sight of the beloved bear as the screams of the little boy increased in intensity. She had to do something, but what? It was then that an idea came to her.

'I wonder if Eddie's hiding from us, Robbie?' she guessed. 'I wonder if he's playing hide and seek and waiting for us to find him?'

Leaving Robbie where he was, in the centre of his bed, she began to move about the room so that she could open the door of the built-in wardrobe that revealed tiny red wellingtons and mini-trainers. 'He's not there,' she said, shaking her head. 'He must be hiding somewhere else.'

Robbie hiccupped and rubbed his eyes. Then he slid off the bed, which moved as he did so on smooth-running casters. Grace went to move it back, and found the bear. She held it up. 'Look what I found, Robbie. Eddie was hiding under your bed. Now he wants to go back into bed with you because he's feeling very tired after his adventure.'

She laid the bear on the pillow and watched as Robbie climbed back into bed to clutch Eddie tightly in his arms. 'Eddie tired. Eddie go to sleep. Robbie go to sleep now,' he murmured.

'Goodnight, darling,' Grace whispered as she tucked the duvet round him and dropped a light kiss on his forehead.

'Kiss Eddie,' Robbie ordered sleepily.

'Goodnight, Eddie,' she murmured as she bent her mouth to the brown furry head of the bear.

There was a huge lump in her throat as she went out of the room, leaving the door slightly ajar. Before she reached the living room Victor was back, standing in the hall, the parcel of Chinese food in his arms and a question in his dark eyes. Grace did not speak. Instead she put a finger to her lips and made her way to the kitchen at the back of the cottage. He followed her and closed the door behind him.

'What was all that about?' he wanted to know as he put down the bag of food. 'You look a bit upset, Grace. Was Robbie being naughty?'

'Oh no, it was nothing like that.' She spoke quickly to reassure him. 'He woke up and couldn't find his teddy bear, so he got into a panic.'

Victor sighed. 'Yes, he would. Ever since Shona died he's clung to Eddie. The bear was the last thing she gave him, and now he won't be parted from it.'

'He was terribly upset until I managed to locate Eddie underneath his bed.'

'He's quiet enough now, so you obviously managed to calm him down. Thanks a lot.'

'I told him Eddie was playing hide and seek, and that he was so tired after I found him that he wanted to go to sleep.' She laughed. 'I had to kiss both of them good-night then.'

'Grace, you're an absolute treasure. You ought to have...' He stopped himself in time from saying what he had so thoughtlessly been about to utter. 'Sorry, how stupid of me. Forgive me?'

Her face sobered. 'There's nothing to forgive.' She sighed. 'I couldn't help wishing, when I saw Robbie there, cuddled up with Eddie in his arms, that I hadn't put my business first for so many years. Until it was too late,' she added.

Victor touched her shoulder lightly. 'There could be better times to come for you, Grace,' he said. 'You've got to believe that.'

She sighed as she moved away from him to take the hot plates from the oven. 'I've got my new shop to live for, but it can't compare with what you have in Robbie.'

There was nothing he could say in answer to that. It was too soon to speak of the hope that was strengthening in his mind.

Eighteen

By the time Laurel had been home with her parents for a few hours she was certain she had done the right thing in coming back. It was alarming to discover in that short time how much the foot and mouth crisis had affected her father. He had always been an even-tempered, jovial-natured man who could cope with the ups and downs of his life as a sheep and dairy farmer. Bad weather over the winter and spring had brought the first set of problems for him to solve but he had been through such times before and survived. The outbreak of foot and mouth disease which had begun to cause anxiety early in the year was something totally different.

At first it had seemed that the measures taken by the Ministry of Agriculture would isolate the affected farms and prevent the spread of the disease, so life went on as normal in areas well away from where there were cases. Then it gradually became apparent that cases were breaking out far away from the original quarantined areas. The situation changed then. Every day fresh outbreaks were reported, the cull of affected animals grew widespread, cattle markets were closed and the movement of sheep was banned.

The days when Mary was able to bring comfort to him by saying that at least they had the bed and breakfast business and the bunkhouse to bring in enough money to tide them over for a while were over now because almost all the public footpaths had been closed and those who would have come to enjoy walking in the countryside or driving through it stayed away. George Appleby could, for once in his life, find nothing to be optimistic about.

'They're ringing the passing bell at the parish church every Monday until the auction mart opens again, and the people there are saying prayers for us,' his wife told him when she came back from her shopping trip to the nearest market town.

'We'll need more than prayers to see us through this lot,' he had replied morosely.

Laurel tried to get him interested in hearing about her new life at the Glen View Hotel, but it was a losing battle. All he was interested in were the radio and television news bulletins which kept him up to date on the progress of the epidemic, and waiting for the postman to bring fresh information from the government about what he was or was not allowed to do with his own animals on his own land. There was very little information coming that was of any help to him, which only added to his frustration. He was not eating properly now and losing weight fast.

'Perhaps he'll be better when Craig gets home from college and he has another man to talk to,' Laurel tried to comfort her mother.

'That won't be until next week. I don't know how much longer he can go on as he is. He can't seem to relax any more and he seems to be unsteady at times. Almost as if he's been drinking, but there's no alcohol left in the house. I just wish he'd agree to see the doctor.'

'Perhaps if I ask him to—' Laurel began.

'I wouldn't! He'll bite your head off,' her mother broke in.

That evening there was a phone call for Laurel. Believing it to be from Calum, who had promised to call her tonight, she hurried to answer it with a smile on her lips.

'Hi, Laurel, darling!' The voice that came back to her did not belong to Calum.

Laurel frowned. 'Who is it?'

'Have you forgotten me already?' Daniel teased.

Now she was angry. 'Surely you didn't expect me to go on waiting for you to ring me again after the way you treated me?'

'I'm really sorry about that. I didn't mean

to hurt you. It was just that I was lonely down there in London and I just sort of...'

'Sort of forgot all about me? Is that what you're trying to say?'

'Can't we put it all behind us now and start again? I've got this job in Manchester and we—'

'No! We can't do anything together now because it's over.'

'I don't believe you. We were so good together.'

'Not good enough to keep you faithful,' she reminded him.

'I've said I'm sorry, and I've got the day off tomorrow so I can come and see you.'

'You'll be wasting your time, so I shouldn't bother!' She hung up on him

Simmering with annoyance, she wandered out into the farmyard, needing to take deep breaths of the fresh moorland air to help her calm down. Fern came busily to meet her, circling happily round her with her white-tipped tail waving madly.

'Good lass, Fern!' Laurel said when, at a single word of command, the border collie lay prone on the cobbled surface of the yard with her head resting on her outstretched paws. 'Shall we go and see your pups?'

As though she understood exactly what had been said, Fern uttered a single joyful bark and led the way to the hay shed where the four little dogs were enclosed in a cosy corner built of bales of straw. For a few minutes Laurel watched them rolling and jostling one another, four gorgeous little creatures who had the bright eyes and sharp intelligent faces of their mother. They would probably prove to be good working dogs, since their father was a dog who performed well in the county sheepdog trials.

Would these puppies be able to train for work when they were old enough, though? Would there be any animals left for them to fetch down from the fells? Or would their young lives come to an end too soon, as the lives of so many animals were doing now that the cull of livestock was moving closer to the family farm every day? Laurel shivered as the enormity of the catastrophe flooded her mind once again. She had to do something to save these pups and their mother, and she had to do something to help her parents, but it was not going to be easy because so far they were simply refusing to accept any cash help from her.

Her introspective thoughts were scattered by the amplified sound of the house telephone. It could be Calum, this time. She moved towards the door of the shed as her mother's voice called her name. Then she crossed the yard at speed and burst into the house.

'He's got a nice voice,' her mother teased. 'A lovely accent.'

'He's a nice man.'

Laurel sped through the kitchen and into the hall to pick up the phone. 'Hi!' she greeted Calum breathlessly as she listened to the bumping of her heart.

'Are you missing me, darling girl?' he wanted to know.

'Oh yes, all the time!' she confessed.

'I'm wishing now that I hadn't told you to take the extra day, but that's selfish of me. How are things with your parents?'

She sighed. 'Awful, absolutely awful, and there's nothing I can do to help them. They won't let me help with my savings.'

'Is there anything I can do to make things easier? Anything at all? You only have to say...'

A wave of love for him washed over her. Calum was such a good man. She had not realised just how wonderful he was until she had gone to work in his Scottish hotel. The feeling she had for him was still so new that she could not be sure it would last, but for now she would just enjoy loving and being loved by Calum.

'You've helped by giving me time off now, instead of me having to wait until autumn for my holiday, Calum,' she told him softly. 'I'm so grateful to you for that.'

'I'd like you to go away with me in the autumn, darling. What do you think to the idea?'

'It's brilliant, but I thought we had a lot of coach parties booked for September and early October. Will we be able to get away then?'

'We certainly will in October. I'll ask Fergus to stand in for me then. I want it to be a special holiday for us, but I'll talk to you about that when you come back. In the meantime, take care of yourself, and remember I love you.'

Smiling as she replaced the phone, Laurel went to join her mother, who was preparing their supper in the spacious kitchen which had windows giving spectacular views of the heather-covered moors glowing purple beneath the dying sunlight. Mary saw the radiance still reflected on her daughter's face, brought there by the words spoken by Calum over the four hundred miles which at this time kept them apart. She saw this and was afraid for her daughter. Laurel had been badly hurt a few months ago, so devastated that she had made her escape to Scotland. Would this new man, who had encouraged her daughter to make the move so that she would still be working for him in his own hotel, also bring her heartache one day? She shivered, and tried to push the worrying thoughts away from her.

Laurel frowned. 'What's wrong, Mum? You can't be cold on such a warm night...'

Mary shook her head. 'No. It was just

someone walking over my grave. I was wondering about your new man. What sort of person he is, I mean.'

'You'll meet him when you come up to stay, and you'll like him,' Laurel promised.

'What age is he?'

'He's in his mid-thirties.'

'So he could have been married before? Or maybe still be married to someone? Be careful, love! Don't get hurt again, and don't hurt anyone else,' Mary begged.

'There's no one else in Calum's life, I'm certain,' Laurel answered, too quickly. The thought came to her even as she said the words that there had been someone called Katharine in Calum's life before he met her, someone who'd been his partner for several years. Since the memory of this brought uneasiness to her mind she pushed the thought away from her.

'Don't fuss, please, Mum. You've got enough problems without starting to worry about me.'

'There's nothing as important to us as your happiness. Always remember that,' were her mother's final words on the subject.

Early the next day she told her mother that she was going to meet a friend in Skellkirk for coffee and asked if she could get any shopping for her. After some thought, Mary asked Laurel to buy some whisky for her

302

father. 'It seems to help him to relax in the evening when the news has been bad, as it so often is now,' she said.

'Any particular sort?'

'The cheapest,' came the answer very quickly. 'He never was much of a drinker, but now...'

'I'll see what I can find at the supermarket.'

'I'll get some money for you.' Mary went out of the kitchen to find her purse.

As soon as she had gone, Laurel went out to her car and started the engine. She was not going to wait to argue it out with her mother about who should pay for the drink. If a tot or two of whisky helped her father to cope with the trauma of the foot and mouth outbreak she was ready to buy a gallon of it if necessary. By the time Mary came back downstairs with her purse her daughter was speeding over the moor in the direction of the little cathedral city of Skellkirk.

It was usually quite difficult to find a place to park a car in Skellkirk on Thursday, that being the day an open market was held in the square where the ancient market cross stood. Not so today. There were plenty of parking spaces standing empty. Laurel glanced about her at the stalls which were piled high with fruit and vegetables, at the paperback book stalls, the sweet stalls, the cheese stalls and the many stalls selling

303

colourful cotton skirts, shirts and tops. Usually there were people thronging the spaces between them, local folk and tourists alike all hoping to find bargains. On this day the customers were few and far between. She found this puzzling, until she went into the shop that sold newspapers and magazines and was greeted by the woman who remembered her from her days working at the Skellkirk Abbey Hotel.

'Hello, it's a long time since you were last in here. You were going to get married and move away, weren't you? So you'll just be here on a visit?'

'Yes, I'm just here on a visit. I work in Scotland now, and I didn't get married after all,' Laurel said all in a rush. 'Where is everyone? I thought the place would have been heaving with people on such a lovely day yet there's almost no one about. I didn't even have a problem finding a place to park the car.'

The smile was wiped from the woman's face as she answered. 'You wouldn't have, these days. The place is empty all the time, except for locals coming in to do their shopping, and they're not spending like they used to. The visitors aren't coming any more to stay in the hotels and guest houses, and even some of the day coach trips are half-empty. It's a disaster for the traders.'

'I've been so worried about my parents

304

that I came to see how things were. I was hoping things wouldn't be quite so bad by now,' Laurel told her.

'We all thought that, and we were all wrong. It's only a few miles away now and spreading fast and there's just nothing we can do about it. If trade doesn't improve soon we'll be ruined,' the woman added with a despairing sigh.

Laurel was shocked. Although she had been aware of how disastrous the foot and mouth crisis was for her parents and other farmers she had not realised how seriously other people in the Dales villages and market towns who relied on the tourist industry for their living were affected by it. In a burst of sympathy for the shopkeeper she spent recklessly on chocolates and magazines for her mother before going to the supermarket to buy a couple of bottles of whisky for her father. On then to the bank where she drew a few hundred pounds from her account in the hope that she would find a way of making her parents accept her help. She was glad to return to her car then, to drive through the quiet streets and back over the moor to her home.

There was another vehicle parked in the yard alongside her father's Range Rover and her mother's little car. The sight of it gave Laurel a jolt. She had seen it last just after Christmas when Daniel left to go to his new job in London, and to look for a flat for them to share. A wave of annoyance, hot and piercing, washed over her. Angry words gathered inside her throat as she hurried in through the back door.

'What are you doing here?' she demanded the minute she saw Daniel sitting on the shabby, comfortable sofa that stood underneath the kitchen window.

Daniel's thick blonde eyebrows that matched his corn coloured hair rose in surprise as he got to his feet and came towards her. 'I told you I'd got today off so I could come and see you,' he said, as though they had met only a few days ago and were on the best of terms.

'And I told you not to bother!' Laurel answered sharply. 'You're wasting your time, and mine as well!'

'Don't be cross with me, sweetheart. I've said I'm sorry about what happened.'

There was that deep, caressing note in Daniel's voice that she had once found so exciting. It did nothing to her now. She looked at him with scorn in her gaze and wondered how she could get rid of him before her mother invited him to stay for a meal. That was if she had not already done so. Her glance went to her mother, who had already poured him a mug of tea and was now filling another for her without asking if she wanted it. Having handed the drink over to her, Mary went out of the room and left Laurel alone with Daniel.

Laurel drank deeply of the tea, which was so hot that her throat stung. When she had recovered from the pain she spoke again, voicing her anger. 'Do you really think all you have to do is say you're sorry and I'll be ready to come back to you? Hasn't it occurred to you that after all these months I might have met someone else?'

'Not someone who'll be as good for you as I am,' he said confidently. 'We had such great times together, and we could do again. There's a vacancy for a chef in the hotel where I'm working now. I mentioned you to chef, told him how good you are, and he said I could take you over there to see him. So, what do you say?'

Laurel was too stunned to say anything at first. Then she told him exactly what she thought of the idea. 'I say you'd better get in your car and go back to Manchester right now before I throw one of the copper pans at you!'

'Your mother thought you might like the idea because you'd be able to come home more often,' he said as he moved closer to her.

'That's because she didn't know I was in love with someone at the Glen View,' she retorted crisply. 'So you'd better be on your way, because as I said before you are wasting your time here.' To prove the point she walked to the door that led into the farmyard and held it open for him.

'So you went to the Glen View, the place Calum McLeod owns?' Daniel stood only a foot or so away from her as he asked the question.

Laurel did not answer. All she wanted was for him to leave, and not bother her again.

'I wonder why he came down here to work at the Skellkirk Abbey when he owned a place like that? Did he ever tell you? Wasn't there some mystery about a fire after a New Year party?'

'I don't know, and I don't really care,' Laurel declared. 'All I know is that I like my job there and don't intend to leave it and come back down here to work.'

'Not even to be here for your parents when they need you? You could change your mind about that if things don't get better for them soon. Your mother was telling me—'

'If I came back to help them, I wouldn't be coming back to you, Daniel. Not now or ever!'

He shrugged. 'Well, it was worth a try.' He was halfway through the door when he turned back and pulled her to him so that he could give her a long hard kiss that she fought against with all her strength. 'Certainly well worth a try. I fancy you more than ever now.'

Laurel wiped her mouth on her sleeve. 'Well I don't fancy you, so don't come back!'

Victor was doing some serious thinking as he worked that day planting daffodil bulbs beneath the trees and shrubs in the front and side gardens of Glen View. By the time they flowered next spring Shona would have been dead for nearly two years; two years during which he had plumbed the depths of grief and despair as he tried to be both mother and father to Robbie. There had been loneliness too during the long nights when Robbie was in bed.

It had been different on the couple of evenings when Grace had come to share a meal with him. There had been someone to talk over his problems with then, and someone he could help too, at a time when things had gone wrong for her. That was a good feeling, being there for Grace when she was feeling anxious and depressed. Would it work if they were together every evening?

He sighed, as he thought of what would inevitably come after the evenings, or even during them, if he allowed their friendship to move on to a different stage. It was not that he thought Shona would not have wanted him to share his home and his love with someone else. Rather it was that in spite of his liking for Grace, and in spite of the fact that she was a warm and lovely woman, he felt no spark of passion ready to ignite between them. Would it be fair to Grace to expect her to be willing to share his home and his life, and Robbie, when he was aware that he did not ache and burn to possess her body as well as her friendship?

It had come to him recently that if he did not find himself another partner before long he was in danger of losing his job at Glen View, because not only had Isla's pursuit of him caused her to break her engagement to Fergus McLeod, it had also put Fergus always on the lookout for faults with his work, even reminding him that it might be cheaper for them to hire a firm of landscape gardeners to care for the hotel grounds. Lately he had noticed the way Calum seemed to be uneasy about the situation Isla had created between himself and Fergus.

He could not afford to lose his job at Glen View, especially now he had bought Birch Cottage. His army pension and savings would not be sufficient to provide Robbie with the sort of good education that he and Shona had planned for their wee boy. So he must come to a decision soon about whether to ask Grace if she would take on Robbie, whom she already adored, and himself when she was free to marry again. It would not be easy.

Nineteen

Isla was becoming quite desperate now to step into her sister's shoes; to become wife to Victor and stepmother to wee Robbie. She had believed that once Victor came out of the army and moved to Scotland to take over the upbringing of Robbie from his grandmother it would not be too long before she managed to do that. Especially as she had always got on so well with her sister's husband when he and Shona came to spend their army leaves in Rowankirk, or when she had gone to visit them in their home in Ireland.

They had been drawn even closer, Isla was certain, after the terrorist bomb had robbed her of her twin sister, and Victor of his wife. There had been times when, in the private hospital room where Victor was recovering from his injuries, they had cried together. Once, they had embraced each other on the narrow hospital bed, seeking comfort in their shared world of shock and grief.

Perhaps it was then that Isla experienced a reawakening of the strong physical attraction she had felt for Victor soon after their first meeting. She had been devastated by it then and fought hard against it because Victor belonged to Shona, and Isla loved her twin sister. Since they were soon to be married so that Shona could accompany Victor on his overseas posting, it had been easy for Isla to believe that she would soon get over it, as she had managed to recover from other strong physical attractions.

Only it hadn't happened like that at all. Instead, every new man who invited her out was compared with Victor and found wanting in looks, personality, and everything else. Her only steady friendship was with Fergus, who had always been there to share school holiday outings and to partner her at village dances. When Fergus's melodic baritone voice began to bring requests for him to sing at ceilidhs and family celebrations he started asking her to go with him. When he discovered that she was the possessor of a sweet, expressive singing voice herself, he persuaded her to join with him in a duet one night.

At first the idea filled her with terror, but the prolonged applause which soon became a regular feature of their appearances helped Isla to conquer her nerves. She began to enjoy wearing a glamorous evening dress while Fergus wore a kilt of the McLeod clan tartan, and to rise to the challenge of blending her smaller, sweeter voice with that of Fergus.

The adrenalin generated by the applause, together with the buzz brought about by the wine which flowed during the evenings, brought a state of euphoria to their shared journeys back to Rowankirk in the early hours of the mornings following their performances. So it seemed natural, at times when they stopped to get a breath or two of mountain air on the way home, to find that their kisses could so easily lead to shared lovemaking.

It was the way things were when you were a single girl in your late twenties without a permanent partner, Isla convinced herself, and it didn't have to mean that you were seriously involved with one another. All it meant was that you were two individuals who worked together, sang together, and sometimes felt like making love together. So it gave her something of a shock when Fergus told her he thought it was time she moved into the Coach House behind Glen View with him and they began to make plans for their wedding.

'I didn't know you were thinking of anything like that,' she told him, when she got her breath back.

'Of course I am!' he declared. 'Surely that's what it's all about? It's not some casual fling for me, and I can't believe it is for you, Isla. It's time we were settling down, like Shona and Victor have done, with a home and family of our own. I'm going to buy you a ring and we'll celebrate our engagement on New Year's Eve. Then we'll get married in the summer, when we've had time to plan everything together. By this time next year we could be expecting our own wee boy or girl. That'd be great, wouldn't it?'

It was that final sentence which had silenced the words of protest Isla had been about to utter. Because from the moment she had first set eyes on Robbie, Isla had adored him and longed for a child of her own. So she had gone with Fergus to Fort William to choose a ruby and diamond ring. Then she had moved into the Coach House with him and they had begun to plan their wedding. Their plans had been put on hold when the fire brought extensive damage to Glen View and put Calum into hospital.

Shortly after that came the devastating news that Shona had been killed. Everything else was forgotten as Isla and her parents travelled to Ireland and brought Robbie back to Rowankirk with them. Isla moved out of the Coach House and went back to live with her parents so she could help her mother to care for Robbie, who was fretting for his mummy and daddy. Fergus had been very understanding about this at first, until Victor was released from the army because of his injuries and came to make a new life for himself and his son in Rowankirk. His attitude changed then and he began to resent the time Isla spent trying to help her brother-in-law.

'Victor doesn't need you fussing round him now. He's well enough to cope with looking after Robbie without your interference,' he had snapped at her only that morning, when she was waiting for Victor to arrive so she could ask when it would be convenient for her to take the owl glove puppet to Robbie.

'I'm not interfering. I'm just wanting to give my little nephew the present I've bought him!' she had snapped back.

'Then why don't you just give it to Victor and let him give it to Robbie?'

'Because I want to give it to Robbie myself, to see his face, that's why!'

'It's his father's face you are really interested in, isn't it?'

'If I am, it's no business of yours. I'm not engaged to you now so you've no right to...' Isla knew that the anger was leaving her as she said that and tears were threatening.

'When will you get it into your head that Victor doesn't want you; that he doesn't want anyone else yet because he's still grieving for your sister?'

'He's not! He's getting involved with Grace.'

'Of course he isn't. She's only been helping him and Robbie to settle into the cottage. Grace has a husband, and she isn't the sort of woman to play around just because Paul isn't here.'

Isla did not wait to hear any more. Instead she went behind the reception desk to answer the phone, and to make up her mind that in spite of what Fergus had said she would call at Birch Cottage tonight when she finished her spell of duty at Glen View and take the owl puppet to Robbie. If she went before Robbie's bedtime Victor wouldn't send her away, would he?

Laurel's mother was pleased with the gifts she brought back from Skellkirk for her, though she shook her head at the size of the box of chocolates and the number of expensive magazines she found in the carrier bag beside them.

'My, you've been having a good spend!' she exclaimed. 'It feels a bit like Christmas!' Her face sobered then. 'We never realised last Christmas, when you bought me continental chocolates like these, what we'd be facing so soon afterwards. What was it like in Skellkirk today? Were there many people about?'

Laurel shook her head. 'No. The place was deserted. It wasn't busy at all, like it should be in the middle of the tourist season. I felt so sorry for the shopkeeper that I spent as though it *was* Christmas. There's some whisky for Dad too. I got that at the super-market.'

'Two bottles! He will be pleased.when he comes in from milking.' She paused. 'He wasn't too pleased when he saw Daniel here this morning. I don't think he ever really took to Daniel.'

Laurel frowned. 'He didn't tell me that at the time.'

'It was more a case of hoping he was wrong and you were right about Daniel being the one for you. That's why, when Daniel phoned and asked if he could come and see you, I agreed. I wanted you to have the chance to see him again before you got too involved with anyone else.'

Laurel smiled. 'He actually had an inter-view lined up for me with the head chef at the big hotel in Manchester where he's working now. So I told him he was too late, that there's someone else.'

'Will I be meeting the someone when I come up to see you?' Mary wanted to know.

'I hope so.'

'I wish you were staying a bit longer. It's so good to have you here to talk to just now when I'm worried out of my wits about your dad,' Mary confessed. 'It's not so easy to talk to other farming wives because some of them are having a worse time than we are, not able to leave their farms even to get their own shopping.'

'I'm sorry I've only got until tomorrow, but we have a coach party coming for a week and a wedding reception booked for Saturday afternoon.'

'Perhaps you'll get down to see us in the autumn. You'll probably be due for some holiday then instead of just an extra day or two, won't you?'

Laurel didn't know what to say in answer to that. Of course she would be due for some time off by then, but Calum had spoken in his phone call about them going away together in late autumn. She felt guilty about even considering spending her time anywhere other than here with her parents when they were going through such an awful time, but she longed for the chance to be with Calum in a place where they could openly show their love for one another. Maybe the foot and mouth crisis would be over by the autumn...

'I hope you and Dad will be able to come up to Rowankirk before the autumn. You could come when Craig is here to look after the stock,' she suggested. 'You'll love Rowankirk. It's so beautiful, with the mountains and the loch and all the wild flowers.'

'We'll see how things go.' Mary Appleby would not commit herself to promising anything that she might not be able to carry out.

Apart from the frightening way their bank account was dwindling now that there was almost no money coming into it, she was increasingly afraid for George's health. He was looking so haggard about his face and so painfully thin about his body. There was a grey tinge taking over his usually ruddy skin, and there were those times when she would notice the way he put a hand on his chest as though to soothe an ache he was experiencing. When she had remarked on this he had brushed off her concern with the sort of sharp words that he did not often use to her. So she had stopped mentioning her concern, and gone on worrying about him. Now she wondered whether she ought to share that particular worry with Laurel. Even as the thought came into her mind, George was coming into the kitchen for his tea and the opportunity was lost.

'Whisky? Can we afford it?' he asked bluntly when he caught sight of the two bottles Laurel had placed on the tall oak dresser.

'It's a present for you, from Laurel,' Mary told him. 'Something to help you sleep at night.'

'Thanks, love, but you'll need your money if you're going to take up with that Daniel again and get married.' There was no smile on her father's face as he said that.

'I'm not going back to Daniel again, Dad.

I told you so last night.'

'So you did! I'd forgotten. I must be losing my marbles!' he laughed, but there was no joy in the sound.

Fear stirred inside Laurel as she studied him closely. This could not really be her dad, could it? Her dad was not yet fifty years old, and he had been a fit, handsome, good-natured man with a great sense of humour when she left home in early March to go to her new job at the Glen View. Now, his face was deeply lined and haggard, his eyes were dull and sombre. He couldn't have gone downhill so rapidly in only five months, could he?

'You're not losing your marbles, Dad,' she said with forced cheerfulness. 'You just need to take a break, have a holiday. Why don't you let Craig take over from you for a few days and come up to Scotland with Mum?'

George shook his head. 'I couldn't leave the lad on his own to cope with the stock, in case the foot and mouth comes any closer to us.'

'It might be over by the autumn.' Laurel knew there was little chance of that but she had to say the words if only to convince herself that it might be so.

'Pigs might fly!' her father responded bitterly.

She had heard him use the expression countless times since she was a child. In fact she had, when very young, sometimes searched the sky above the farm hoping to see a flying pig. Now she forced a laugh. 'You've been saying that for as long as I can remember,' she told him. 'I used to look up sometimes, when I was little, to see if any pigs really had taken to the air.'

'They could do with taking to the air over at Jeff Harper's place right now. Since he's been told he can't move his pigs they're living in overcrowded conditions. It's not right! It's just not right to be forced to treat your animals that way!' George banged his fist on the kitchen table as he almost shouted the words, knocking over a mug, which shattered on the tiled floor. A wave of hot colour wiped the greyness from his face momentarily. Then he dropped into his chair and his chin fell forward on to his chest.

Both women were on their feet at the same time. Both bent over him with fear in their hearts. 'He's breathing, thank God!' Mary whispered as she lifted his chin and felt his pulse. 'Ring 999 and tell them we need an emergency ambulance at once.'

While they waited they held his hands, one each side, praying silently that they would not have long to wait. It seemed to them to go on for ever, although when they reached the hospital in Laurel's car shortly after the paramedics delivered him there they discovered that it had only been several minutes. They were shown into a small, hot, waiting room and told that someone would be with them shortly. While they were waiting cups of tea were brought, which they drank silently as they listened to the hospital noises of trolleys being wheeled, bleepers sounding, and flat-heeled shoes moving briskly over vinyl floor covering.

At last there was the door opening to allow a senior nurse to enter. She was calm, smiling and kind. 'Mrs Appleby, your husband is much better. He's fairly comfortable now, but Dr Clark thinks he should stay for a couple of days and have some tests done. He's not too happy about it – says he has to be back on his farm – but I think you ought to persuade him to stay with us.'

'What is it? What's wrong with him?' Mary asked, while Laurel held her breath and waited for the nurse to answer.

'He's had an angina attack, quite a bad one.'

'But he doesn't have angina...'

'He does now, I'm afraid. He's very stressed, but you did the right thing in calling the ambulance quickly.'

'Can we see him?' Laurel asked.

'In a little while. He's in the ITU but we'll move him out of there as soon as possible. Now there are one or two forms to be filled in...'

'There's the milking to be done too,' Mary remembered with a shock.

'Your husband was worrying about that but I told him you'd make arrangements for it to be done.' The nurse smiled. 'Or are you able to do it yourself, Mrs Appleby?'

Mary straightened her shoulders. 'Yes, if I have to. It's no good being married to a farmer if you can't cope in a crisis.'

'You'll be able to come back and see your husband tonight after you've seen to your cows. The visiting is open until eight. Now I'll get someone to take you to see him for five minutes.'

Driving back to the farm half an hour later Laurel was amazed by her mother's calmness. It had been a terrifying experience, first seeing her father collapse, waiting for the ambulance to arrive and then watching while the paramedics gave him emergency treatment, yet her mother had not given way to panic at any time. Even when, while they were in the waiting room, she had suggested using the pay-phone there to call her brother at his college to tell him they needed him, Mary would not give way.

'We'll ring Craig when we have some definite news to give him. He'll be better able to make his arrangements then to come home,' was all she would say.

So it was home to do the milking, collect the eggs and shut up the hens for the night, and catch up on all the things her father would have been doing if he had not been lying in a hospital bed. No time for a proper evening meal, just a cup of tea and a sandwich that neither of them really wanted before they drove back over the moor road to spend the last hour of visiting time with her father. He was wired up and attached to a machine that monitored his condition, and was not inclined to make conversation with them. It was all very worrying, even though the senior nurse assured them that he was fairly comfortable now. How could her dad be fairly comfortable when he was imprisoned in a hospital bed worrying himself to death about the threat of foot and mouth disease?

When they left the hospital at the end of visiting time Laurel knew she could not go back to Scotland tomorrow and leave her parents to get through this latest crisis without her. She was needed here, and she would stay.

Twenty

Calum began to be uneasy when he failed to contact Laurel the third time he tried. She had told him she would be in all the evening, so why couldn't he speak to her? Why did the loud ringing on the other end of the line go on and on without bringing an answer? He was being a fool, he told himself, to get into such a state just because Laurel was not there when he needed to speak to her. It must be because he was still not sure of her; not really certain that she belonged to him and would not reject his love as Katharine had done.

Why was he still not sure of Laurel, even now that she was his lover as well as his friend? Was it because of what he had overheard Fergus saying to Isla? He had not meant to eavesdrop, such a thing was abhorrent to him. It was just that Fergus was shouting when he told Isla that she was wasting her time in chasing after Victor because Victor had a fancy for the girl from Yorkshire.

'Why else do you think Victor had Laurel

helping him to move into his cottage when he didn't want you there?' had been the final thing he had heard Fergus say before he hurried out of earshot and made his way up to his private apartment on the top floor of Glen View, doubt and dismay crowding into his mind.

Pacing the floor of his spacious living room, he was oblivious tonight to the beauty of the purple heather which clothed the lower slopes of the mountains and the glory of the sunset which poured scarlet and gold light over the distant peaks. Fear and jealousy had complete possession of him now and would not be pushed aside by common sense. So lost was he to anything else that when the telephone on his desk began to ring he was at first startled by the sound. Then relief washed over him. It would be Laurel calling! He felt certain of that as he strode across the room and snatched up the receiver.

The words waiting to be uttered were imprisoned in his throat as a male voice spoke his name. It was a voice he did not at first recognise; a voice which held something he did not like. Who was it? Surely not someone trying to sell him something he did not want at this late hour?

'Calum Mcleod?'

'Yes, speaking!'

'You'll be missing your little chef from

Yorkshire, won't you?' There was a sneer in the voice which brought a rush of fury to Calum.

'Who the hell are you? Why are you wasting my time like this?' He ought to hang up on this guy, who was obviously a nutter, yet curiosity stopped him from doing that.

'Daniel Dailey. Remember me? From Skellkirk Abbey Hotel? Remember Laurel and me? Just thought I'd put you in the picture...'

Yes, of course he knew the voice now! He'd always disliked the overload of self-confidence in Dailey's voice, even though he could find no fault with his work at the Skellkirk Abbey Hotel. 'Yes, I do remember you. How are things going with you?' He had to pretend an interest he did not feel. Perhaps the guy was ringing to ask him to provide a reference for a new job?

'Things are going very well for me. I've got a great job now in Manchester.' Daniel Dailey went on to name one of the most prestigious hotels in the city.

There it was again, that boastful note that he could not stand. How on earth had Laurel ever come to get engaged to someone like Daniel Dailey? That was something he'd never be able to understand. While he was still puzzling over this Dailey spoke again.

'I've got an interview lined up there for

Laurel with the head chef—'

'Why? Why should you do that?' Calum broke in harshly.

'Because she'll want to be closer to her family while they're caught up in this foot and mouth business, won't she?'

'She hasn't said anything about it to me,' Calum broke in again.

'But she's down there with them right now, isn't she?'

Hearing him say that gave Calum a jolt. 'How do you know that? She only went down there a couple of days ago...'

'I know because I went over to see her yesterday.'

There it was again, that boastful tone that made Calum want to knock his head off. He'd soon take the wind out of the guy's sails. Then he could get him off the line and ring Laurel again. She wouldn't mind that it was so late.

'Laurel will be back here tomorrow,' he snapped.

'I wouldn't be too sure about that.'

'What the hell are you talking about? Of course she's coming back tomorrow. She wouldn't let me down. You ought to know her better than that.'

Daniel laughed. 'Well, I certainly know Laurel better than you do, and I've certainly seen her since you have.'

'I don't believe you,' Calum cut in yet

328

again. 'She'll be back tomorrow, as planned. Now I suggest you shove off and don't ring me again. I can't think why you bothered to do so in the first place.'

'Can't you? I thought that would have been obvious, since I was engaged to Laurel at the start of this year, and might be engaged to her again before long.'

'Get lost!' Calum snapped as he slammed down the phone.

In the silence that followed, he punched his right fist into his left palm and gave voice to a few choice words that he would not have uttered in Laurel's company. Then he turned back to his desk and tapped out the number of her parents' phone again. It was almost ten o'clock now and he hoped her parents, being farmers, did not go to bed as early as this, but he had to speak to her so that he could banish the disquiet from his mind.

For what seemed to be a very long time he listened to the ringing, loud and insistent, that must surely be penetrating every corner of the farmhouse and probably the out-buildings beyond it. Why did he go on waiting when plainly no one was going to answer? When he put down the phone at last he was forced to admit to himself that it was because he was not yet certain of Laurel's love for him. How could he be when Fergus had hinted that she was more than friendly with Victor, and when Daniel Dailey had insisted that Laurel would not come back to Glen View tomorrow?

'I'm sure we ought to ring Craig now and tell him about Dad,' Laurel said as the car came to a stop and she got out to open the farm gates. 'He'll want to come home as soon as he can.'

Her mother sighed. 'Craig's got important exams or tests or something just now. That's why I didn't want to worry him.'

'He'll have to know, and he won't like it that we haven't told him right away.' Laurel closed the gates again. Fern had heard their arrival and was barking a greeting from the hay shed.

'All right, you win, love! I'll give him a ring as soon as I've put the car away.'

Would she have time to make a quick call to Calum before then, Laurel wondered. Things would have quietened down at Glen View by this time in the evening, with the dinners all finished in the dining room and the guests either out for a late evening stroll in the hotel garden or enjoying leisurely drinks in the lounge bar. Calum would probably be in his top-floor apartment catching up on the news while he enjoyed a dram of whisky. She hurried ahead of her mother and unlocked the back door so she could be first to reach the phone in the hall.

It was cool in the hall, where the last rosy colours of sunset poured through the long narrow windows which were set on either side of the front door that was hardly ever used. There was the spicy scent of chrysanthemums in the air from the tall gold and white sprays she had purchased in Skellkirk that morning, which her mother had placed in an earthenware coffee pot on the old oak chest where the telephone stood. Laurel reached out to pick it up at the very moment the ringing began. Her heart raced. It was probably Calum, who would have been trying to get in touch with her earlier while she had been at the hospital.

'Hello!' she said breathlessly, listening to the bumping of her heart as she pictured Calum's face, long, lean and handsome, with firm lips and grey eyes. He would be smiling as he heard her speak, that smile which could turn her bones to water and her blood to fire. Even to think of him at this distance made her feel weak with longing.

'Mrs Appleby?' There was a note of enquiry in the voice which belonged not to Calum McLeod but to a woman.

'That's my mother. I'll get her for you if you'll hang on for a minute.'

Laurel sped through the kitchen and met her mother as she came into the house by the back hall. 'There's a call for you, Mum,' she said.

'Who is it?' Mary frowned. She was feeling drained now after what she had been through in the last few hours, and more than a little frightened.

'I don't know. She didn't say.'

Mary shrugged. 'Could be something to do with the WI, I suppose. Will you make us some tea love, please?'

There was a kettle already singing softly on the Aga. Laurel took the big brown pot which was always near to hand and warmed it before tossing in a couple of Yorkshire tea bags and adding boiling water. She had put milk into two mugs and was about to pour the tea when her mother came back into the room.

'That was quick!' Laurel said. It wouldn't be long now before she could make that call to Calum. She lifted the big brown pot. Before she could pour from it her mother spoke.

'There's no time for tea. We have to go back to the hospital right away.'

'Why?' A cold wave of fear engulfed Laurel as she asked the question.

'Because he's had another attack. A worse one. I'll get the car.'

'No. We'll take mine. I'll drive.'

Her mother did not argue. She was still calm, but ashen faced and trembling inside. Already Laurel was fishing in the bottom of her shoulder bag for her car keys as she hurried out to the yard where her own small car waited. There were no warning words coming from her mother on this journey about keeping her speed down. There were no words spoken at all as they traversed the narrow, winding moorland road, slowing down only when the sheep that grazed there left the heather to meander on to the road. For both women it seemed an endless journey during which they were oblivious of the dying sun that brought such glory to the sky, of the splendidly plumaged pheasants which strutted and pecked about in the glowing purple of the heather and of the white stone arches of the abbey ruins to be glimpsed as they neared the little cathedral city. All they were conscious of on that journey was fear, and silent intense prayer.

Grace had looked up with a smile earlier that day when she heard the sound of Robbie's voice as he came through the door of her shop with Victor. Robbie wore jeans which were a miniature edition of the ones worn by his dad, and a T-shirt with the word 'Scotland' and the national flag printed on it. Under his arm he carried Eddie Bear.

'You're out early this morning, Robbie,' she greeted him.

'Playgroup. Eddie Bear likes playgroup.' Robbie held up the bear to show Grace, then tucked it under his arm again.

'Yes, we're on our way to playgroup in the church hall,' Victor replied. 'I came to order some flowers. I thought you might have them ready for me to pick up later.'

'I could deliver them, if you don't have time to pick them up,' she offered

Victor hesitated. 'I'll collect them later in the morning, while Robbie's still in playgroup. I want to take them on my own. White roses and white heather, a small posy with white ribbons. A bridal posy kind of thing if you can manage it.'

Grace knew then what it was about, why Victor wanted to be alone when he took the flowers to the chosen place; the site of the Highland Clearances.

'I can manage that. There are roses fresh in, and the white heather we always have.'

'Our wedding anniversary.' Victor swallowed and bit his lip as he explained.

Grace felt moisture threaten her eyes. The pain in his face hurt her too. 'I'll do them at once. Everything else can wait. Come straight back from the church hall,' she murmured.

She watched through the shop window as they walked away, the tall upright man with his straight shoulders and military haircut and the small boy trying to match his stride. Life was so cruel to rob a small child of his mother, and to rob *her* of her husband.

Where was the sense in it?

Calum rose earlier than usual the next day, feeling irritable and restless still after his sleepless night. There had been plenty of opportunity for him to think during that long night. To think deeply and seriously and come to decisions. He did not like all of the decisions he had arrived at, but he would stick by them and act on them. It was too soon to do that as yet though. Much too early in the morning to do anything except take a shower, drink black coffee and go in search of fresh air and exercise down in the glen.

He followed a rocky footpath which went downhill to the ruins of the old village. As he walked, he went over and over in his mind what he would say to Victor Thorpe later in the morning. It would have to be done then, while Laurel was still in Yorkshire. Because he needed it to be a *fait accompli* by the time she returned so that she could not talk him out of dismissing Victor.

All the same, he was not easy in his mind about what he had decided to do during the small hours of that morning. He did not dislike Victor Thorpe. In fact he admired the man for taking on the role of hotel gardener so that he could support and educate his motherless son, after being accustomed during his years in the army to be in command of other men. He was also well pleased with the way Victor had restored and improved the grounds of Glen View.

Yet Calum knew he could not allow the strained atmosphere he had been aware of for some time whenever Fergus, Isla and Laurel were in the same room, to continue. If he did not put a stop to it soon Laurel might decide she had had enough of it and find herself another job. Maybe she was already doing that, down there in Yorkshire, if what Daniel Dailey had said to him over the phone was true. The thought was hardly bearable, so he pushed it to the back of his mind, certain now that his best course was to tell Victor that his services were no longer required.

By the time he reached the site of the Highland Clearances he had almost convinced himself that he would be doing the right thing, the only thing possible, in getting rid of Victor.

Next month most of the Glen View rooms were booked for a clan reunion which would bring guests from Canada and North America who were descendants of the folk who had once lived in these tiny croft houses and tended their crops and animals on the land which surrounded the loch. Two of those people were to marry here. Maybe he would ask Laurel to marry him here, or in the little village church of St Bride's if she would rather. He would ask her when they were away on the late October holiday he was planning for them.

With marriage in his mind, and a vision in his heart of Laurel wearing a long white dress and a lace veil, it gave him a jolt to catch sight of what appeared to be bridal flowers, white roses, white heather and white ribbons, resting on the worn stones of one of the empty windows. He moved slowly between the grazing sheep, crushing the amethyst heather under his feet, until he was close enough to be able to see the writing on the card which was visible on the edge of the floral tribute. The words were few and simple. 'Shona, remembered always, loved always.'

Did those words mean what they said? Or was Victor already thinking of putting another woman in Shona's place? If only he knew. Because he did not know, Calum knew that he would have to dismiss Victor from his employment that day, but he knew that in doing so he would be carrying out an injustice and losing his own self-respect.

Victor parked his car and went to the shed where he kept the tools he would need for the work he planned to do in the gardens of Glen View that morning. He felt more at peace with himself this morning than he had done for a long time. Robbie had

337

settled well into the playgroup, he had got the most urgent jobs at Birch Cottage attended to, and now there was only the problem of whether he had finally got through to Isla that he did not intend to allow her to take Shona's place in his life, his home, and his bed.

Last night, after he had bathed Robbie and got him into his pyjamas ready for an early bedtime, Isla had arrived at Birch Cottage. This time she had not rung the front doorbell but had gone round to the back door and walked into the kitchen as he was making a mug of hot chocolate for the boy. Since she had been wearing soft shoes he had not heard her approach. In fact he had been startled when she suddenly stepped close enough to place her hands over his eyes and say 'Guess who!'

Robbie had screamed with delight from his high chair, clapped his hands and shouted, 'Isla auntie!' while Victor slopped the milky liquid over the microwave and his hands. It had been all he could do not to turn about and swear at her, so angry was he at her intrusion. While he was still fighting his fury silently, Isla dived into her bag and brought out the owl puppet she had bought for Robbie.

'For darling Robbie. Have you got a kiss for Auntie Isla, my wee boy?'

It was her last three words which sent

Victor over the top. Shona had so often used them for their little son. That Isla should do so on the very anniversary of his marriage to her sister hit him hard. It was something he could not take, any more than he could bear the sight of Isla lifting Robbie from his chair and up to her shoulder to shower kisses on him. Swiftly he had moved.

'It's his bedtime, Isla, and he's overtired already.' He reached out for his son, who by then had had enough of the kisses and was struggling to escape from having to endure any more.

'Let me put him to bed. It's ages since I've done that.'

Victor ignored the request and carried the boy, who was now rubbing his eyes, into his bedroom. The milky drink was forgotten, the bedtime story was forgotten, as Robbie was tucked into bed, already half-asleep. Eddie Bear was in his arms. Isla tucked the owl puppet in beside them before following Victor out of the room and into the kitchen.

'Aren't you going to ask me to have a drink, Vic?' she murmured.

Panic was mingling now with the remains of his anger. He had to think of something, fast. There were dishes on the draining board waiting to be washed, dishes which had accumulated during the day. One of them belonged to Grace, who had given him an apple crumble a few days ago. With his eyes fixed on this he had spoken, the words coming out too fast, before his brain was fully into gear.

'I have to clear up a bit before Grace comes. She's bringing a meal for the two of us.'

'Again! What's going on?' Animosity blazed from Isla's eyes.

Victor swallowed. 'What do you think? Grace is good company, and a lovely woman.'

'She has a husband, and her father's a minister! What do you think the gossips will make of that?' Isla's face was ugly when masked by spite.

'Grace's father is a retired minister, and Grace is in the middle of divorce proceedings,' he had said, adding quietly, 'Robbie loves her.'

There had been no need to say any more. Isla had turned away from him and rushed out of the house. Would what he had implied be enough to keep her at a distance in future? Victor could not be sure. He was not even sure that he had been fair to Grace in allowing her friendship to come to his aid in this way.

One thing he was certain of was that Calum was walking briskly towards him, and that his employer was wearing a heavy frown rather than his normally pleasant expression.

Twenty-One

Grace was working in the shop making up the pew-end posies of pink spray carnations and feathery green fern with trailing pink ribbons to go into St Bride's Church for tomorrow's wedding. Almost the entire floor of Grace's Flower Basket had been lost beneath the carpet of scented blooms. In one corner a basket of containers stood beside the tall metal vases which held the stems of alstroamaria, star-burst lilies and huge, dark pink single carnations which she would require for the pedestals on either side of the altar and the one just inside the church porch. It had been a really splendid order for her, set in motion by Donald Muir, the minister who was to conduct the wedding service.

There had been an air of suppressed excitement about Donald when he came in to buy mixed flowers for the dining room of the manse, something she guessed he did not often do. When he had mentioned that the couple to be married would be calling to consult her about their floral requirements, his face had been as she had not seen it before on any of their chance meetings. He was a different man these days. His face was alight with ... Grace was not able to make a guess about what had banished the forlorn expression from his eyes and the careworn lines on his cheeks, but she was glad things seemed to be improving for him.

Things were on the up for her too these days. The shop was already making a profit. She was certain she had done the right thing in coming to live and work in Rowanmore, and her divorce from Paul was going ahead relatively smoothly. Only one thing was causing her some concern, the fact that as yet her parents and sisters were not aware that her marriage was over. Her mum and dad would be coming home to Rowanmore in six weeks. It would be time enough to tell them then.

There was lingering pain still because Paul had not loved her enough, and a much stronger pain because she would never have a child of her own. What had mattered very little to her during the years when she had been building up her exclusive floristry business in the town where Paul was in practice seemed to matter enormously now. It was a sort of grieving process that was hard to come to terms with, and it was made worse by the love she had come to feel for Robbie. She tried not to show that love to anyone except Robbie. It gnawed away at her so frequently that at times it was almost frightening. For the first time in her life she was able to understand and identify with those women who snatched a child from an unattended pram. So, as Victor ironed out his problems at Birch Cottage and she got busier with her flower shop, she must distance herself from Victor and Robbie before it was too late.

Thinking of Victor brought a picture of him sharply to mind as he had been when he came into the shop with Robbie to order the anniversary flowers. He had looked so bereft, so unbearably sad. When he came back to collect them he had been determinedly cheerful, which was almost worse. She had given him hot coffee and they had drunk it together in the workroom at the back of the shop, with the air all about them full of the smell of damp moss and the cloying scent of lilies. When they had emptied their mugs he had placed his on the work bench and prepared to depart with his posy of white flowers. Grace had not known what to say as he picked up the flowers and made for the door. He had turned back then, plainly embarrassed about something.

'Sorry, Grace,' he said with a rueful grin. 'I forgot to pay you. How much?'

She had shaken her head and told him to leave it until later.

'I won't run away from you,' he told her. 'You know that, don't you?'

A moment later he had gone, walking to his car, ready to drive to the place Shona had loved, to leave the flowers and the card Grace had watched him write.

'Remembered always, loved always', Victor had written in his bold, flowing hand. Quite suddenly, Grace had realised that she envied Shona, whose life had been ended by a terrorist's bomb but whose love lived on in the heart of Victor. Acknowledging her envy gave Grace a sense of shock. Taking a final long look at Victor as he lifted his head from unlocking his car door and gazed straight at her through her shop window gave her an even more profound shock.

During that long moment when their eyes met she discovered that she loved Victor Thorpe in a way she had never thought to love again, wholly and completely. She loved the way he looked: tall, straight and athletic in build with a square, quite plain face which lit up at odd times with humour and became extraordinarily handsome. She loved the way he spoke: so crisp, and self-assured. She loved the way he was: kind, caring, affectionate, a good friend, and maybe a wonderful lover. Though she would never know about that.

Grace was still lost in thought, surrounded by the flowers for the wedding, alight with the wonder of being in love with Victor, when the shop door opened to admit his sister-in-law, Isla Summers. Her inside was still trembling with emotion as Isla slammed the door and swung round to face her. The other woman did not give her time to speak but launched straight into what had brought her here.

'Is it true that Paul is divorcing you?' she demanded. Her set face and clenched hands betrayed her state of mind quite plainly.

'Not quite, it's rather that I'm divorcing him,' Grace responded coolly, even though it was in her mind to ask Isla what business it was of hers. 'I didn't realise it was common knowledge. I haven't even told my parents yet.'

'But you told Victor, didn't you?'

'How do you know that?'

'Because Victor told me.'

'Why should he do that?'

Isla's already flushed face took on a deeper hue still. 'He wouldn't let me stay when I went to see him last night. He said you were going there for a meal, again! I told him it would cause gossip, with you being the old minister's daughter and a married woman. So he said it wouldn't matter because you were getting a divorce. I didn't know whether it was true. Or if Vic was just saying it to get rid of me.'

'As I said, it's true, though I can't think

why you should be so interested.' Why
didn't the woman just go and let her get on
with her work?

'Can't you? Don't you think it's time Vic
found a new partner, and a new mum for
wee Robbie?'

'Perhaps he's not ready for that yet?
Perhaps he never will be. He loved your
sister very much.'

'He might come to love me, if you weren't
always in and out of his home fussing round
him and Robbie. You *were* there again last
night, weren't you?'

Grace opened her mouth to deny it, to say
that she had been here in her shop catching
up on paperwork. Then she changed her
mind and swallowed the words that were
waiting to be uttered. Victor must have been
feeling so desperate to escape from Isla's
pursuit of him that he had been forced to
conjure up an implied date with her to get
rid of the woman. She couldn't let him
down, could she?

'Yes, I was there,' she lied cheerfully. 'We
had a great time! Now I've got work to do,
so unless you want me to sell you something
I'll have to ask you to excuse me.'

Isla compressed her lips tightly, as though
attempting to bite back words that might be
better left unsaid, then walked out, leaving
the door wide open this time.

'Whew! Victor, what have you let me in

for!' Grace let go of a long, audible sigh, and went back to arranging the wedding posies.

'I'd like a few words with you, Victor, before you start work this morning. Will you come to my office, please.'

It was not a request, it was a command, Victor knew, as he closed the door of the tool shed and followed Calum through the back entrance to the hotel. There was something afoot that made him uneasy. Though it could not be anything worse than some of the things he'd been forced to endure during the last couple of years. He flexed his shoulders, and prepared to face up to whatever it was. Possibly some complaint about the vegetables or the soft fruit he was supplying for the kitchen. Laurel had not found any fault with them but the agency chef who was standing in for her this week might have done.

'Sit down, Victor.' Calum indicated a chair on the opposite side of his desk and Victor dropped into it.

'Is there something wrong, Calum?' To go directly to the root of any problem was the way Victor had always gone about things. It had worked in the army, and it had worked in his marriage to Shona.

'I'm afraid there is.' Calum appeared to be acutely uncomfortable. He was picking up the letter-opener from his desk and putting it down again and in between times staring out of the window into the gardens as if in search of inspiration.

'Does it concern my work here?' Victor asked bluntly.

Calum hesitated. 'Only indirectly,' he said at last.

'I'm not sure what you are trying to say...' Victor wanted this sorted, fast, so that he could get on with the work he had allotted for this day.

Calum sighed. 'I'm trying to say that even though I'm very satisfied with your work I'm not going to be able to go on employing you.'

'Why the hell not!' The question shot out of Victor with the velocity of a bullet leaving a rifle.

Calum flinched, then came to the point. 'Because your presence here is causing an intolerable atmosphere.'

Victor was on his feet, and back in army officer mood. 'What the hell are you talking about? Explain yourself, man!'

Calum sighed again. 'Calm down, Victor,' he said quietly. 'There's nothing personal about this. You must have been aware of the friction there is in the air every time Fergus, Isla and you are all in the same room at the same time. I can't allow that to continue, because if it does something drastic will happen.'

Into the pause that came then, Victor spoke, quietly but with authority. 'So my position here is to be dispensed with so that Fergus and Isla can remain? To go on fighting with one another, I presume?'

'Sit down again, Victor, and let's get to the heart of the matter. I'm going to be blunt. Maybe too blunt for you. As I see it, Fergus is at odds with you because he blames you for the ending of his engagement to Isla.'

'I had nothing to do with it.'

'It wouldn't have happened if you hadn't come back here with your little son; back to a place where your wife's twin sister is in a hurry to take over her sister's place in your home. You can't be blind to that, Victor. Isla is insanely jealous of the women friends in your life, Grace Hardy and Laurel Appleby in particular. Her jealousy surfaces too often for my taste and causes a most unpleasant atmosphere when it does. It's only a matter of time before Laurel decides she has had enough of it and is leaving. That's something I'm not prepared to allow. So—'

'So you're getting rid of me first?'

'I don't feel I've any alternative.'

'Don't you think that's unfair, illogical? To sack someone whose work is more than satisfactory because someone else is making a nuisance of herself?'

Calum sighed again. 'It isn't just Isla, it's Fergus as well, making complaints. They're family, I owe Fergus for the way he took over here while I was still in hospital.'

Victor's spirits sank as he listened. His own new start, made with such difficulty and distress, in Birch Cottage with Robbie was at risk now. How was he going to save it? How was he going to make certain that he kept the reasonably well-paid work that he enjoyed at Glen View and that Robbie remained close to him in Birch Cottage? As he scoured his brain for answers he saw a familiar vehicle enter the Glen View car park and come to a halt. He watched as Grace slid out of the front seat and went round to open the back doors of her van. His eyes remained on her as she unloaded several flat flower boxes, unhurriedly, gracefully, and carried them towards the back door of the hotel. There was a huge lurch in the region of his heart as he made his decision. He was not sure if it was the right decision but he had to take a chance on it. He spun round from the window and took a step closer to Calum before he spoke.

'Would you have still dismissed me if I had told you I intended to share my life with Grace?' he asked.

Calum was taken aback, visibly so. 'What about her husband?' he asked.

'There is no husband, now. He found someone else while Grace was recovering from her operation. They are in the middle of a divorce.'

Calum whistled his surprise. 'I'd no idea. No one mentioned it.'

'No one knew, except me.'

'What about your friendship with Laurel? Where does she fit into the picture?'

Victor laughed quietly. So that was what it was all about! Calum had a fancy for the little chef from Yorkshire and he was afraid of losing her.

'It doesn't fit into my picture at all, Calum.' He chose his words carefully. 'We're just friends. I've an idea Laurel has someone she's more than friends with, though she keeps his identity under wraps.'

Calum was on his feet, the interview at an end. Suddenly, inexplicably, he seemed to have thrown off his earlier troubled mood.

'You'll not be wanting to leave here if you are looking at a future which includes Grace, will you, Victor?' he said thoughtfully. 'So shall we put the discussion we've just had into the waste bin? I've got to admit that I'd be sorry to lose you, and I'd like you to accept my apology for getting things wrong. Can you do that?'

'Yes, of course. I'd better get to work now before the showers they are forecasting begin.'

Victor hurried out of the office, intent on having a quick word with Grace. He'd better ask her to have supper with him tonight so that he could at least attempt to explain to her how he had managed to save his job, at her expense. It would not be easy.

The phone rang as Laurel struggled to open her eyes after only three hours of sleep. She leapt out of bed and ran downstairs to reach it before her mother did. It might be the hospital calling again, but it also might be Calum. A wave of relief washed over her when she heard his voice.

'Where were you when I called last night, Laurel?' he wanted to know before she could say anything. 'I kept ringing until quite late but I couldn't get an answer.'

'I wasn't here. I was...' Laurel was dismayed to find herself choking back tears as she tried to explain the trauma of that urgent phone call asking them to go back to the hospital, of the journey over the moorland road and the long nightmare hours spent waiting as they fought for her dad's life. Words would not come, all that would issue from her throat were the dry sobs which were all that remained at the end of it. She fought hard to regain her composure so she could tell Calum all about it.

Only Calum did not seem disposed to listen. All he wanted to do was talk. 'I had a call from Daniel Dailey. He said he'd been to see you and that he'd arranged an interview for you with the head chef at the hotel in Manchester where he's working. Is that true?'

Still Laurel struggled to find words; the right words. But all she could find inside her head was confusion. 'Yes, Daniel came to see me. I told him not to bother, but he still came.'

'And you went out with him? Was that why I didn't get an answer to my calls?'

'No! No, No! We weren't here because we had to go back to the hospital. My dad had another attack, so they sent for us.' Laurel almost shouted in her eagerness to explain.

Calum was mystified. 'Another attack? What do you mean? Is he ill?'

'Of course he's ill! Very ill, but not as ill as he was last night when they sent for us. Did you say Daniel had phoned you? Why should he do that?'

'You tell me! He talked about you wanting to stay closer to your parents because of the foot and mouth crisis, but he never mentioned your dad being ill.'

Laurel sighed. 'He wasn't ill when Daniel was here, although he was not well either. The worry had brought on a bad angina attack. I can't come back until I've seen them through this crisis, Calum. You do see that, don't you?'

'Yes,' he agreed, reluctantly.

'I'm sorry. I know it will make things very difficult for you this weekend but I must stay with Mum until Dad is over the worst. I'll be back just as soon as I can.'

'Is that a promise, darling?' he wanted to know.

'Yes, it's a promise,' she answered shakily, because the tears were threatening again.

'And you won't go for that interview in Manchester?'

'Of course not. It was his idea, not mine.'

'And you will marry me, before the year is out?'

'What did you say?' Laurel's head was spinning. She must be hearing things; wonderful things that she could hardly believe.

Calum laughed. 'You'll have to come back, if you want to know the answer to that,' was all he would tell her before he brought the call to an end.

Twenty-Two

As she placed the pedestal flower arrangements on either side of the altar before fixing the posies on the ends of the oak pews in the little church of St Bride's, Grace found her thoughts going back to the words she had shared with Isla. Had she really done the right thing in telling Isla that she had been to Birch Cottage to share a meal with Victor when in truth she had been working in her shop until late in the evening?

She had said it on the spur of the moment, without stopping to think where it might lead in the mind of a woman like Isla Summers. All she had been able to think about when faced with Isla's jealousy was that Victor might be harmed by Isla's relentless pursuit of him. When he was ready; if ever he *was* ready, to share his life with another partner, Grace was certain it would not be Isla. Until he met someone, Grace knew she would go on helping him by providing him with company when he felt like it, by ironing and mending Robbie's clothes, and by making a meal for the two of them some-times. She also knew that she would go on loving him.

The fact that she had uttered that deliber-ate lie made her feel particularly uncomfort-able when she recalled it here in the little church where Victor had married Shona, and where her own father had until recently been the minister. It was a relief to hear the church door open and footsteps draw near to where she was at work securing the last scented pink posy to the end of the pew where her box of equipment was resting.

'Good morning, Donald,' she said with a smile.

'Good morning, Grace. How beautiful the place looks. You're very clever with your flowers.'

'I love preparing for weddings,' she told him. 'I enjoy sharing in the joy and the excitement of it all.'

That caused him to raise his eyebrows. 'Even now? In spite of what happened to your own marriage?'

She hesitated only for a moment. 'Yes. My sisters are both happily married, and my parents still adore one another.'

'Do your parents know yet about your divorce?' His eyes searched her face as he asked the question.

Grace did not answer immediately. She would like to have told another lie and said yes, but she could not do it here, in this building. 'No,' she said at last with a sigh.

'Are you sure you're doing the right thing in keeping the news from them, Grace? This is a small place and they are on the other side of the world, but with air travel and telephones the world isn't a very big place these days. They would be very hurt if they heard about it from someone else.'

'How could they do that? No one up here knows, except you and...' She stopped, remembering that Isla and Victor knew about her divorce. Victor would not spread the news, but how long would Isla keep it a secret from her own parents, who were friends of Grace's parents? Dismay began to grow inside her.

'Me and...?' Donald Muir prompted.

Curiosity stirred her into asking a question rather than answering the one he had just put to her. 'Why does it matter so much to you? It isn't as if I come to your church...'

He surveyed her gravely, concerned for both her and her parents. 'If it had been your father giving the advice to someone else that I've given to you, would it have mattered to him whether that person was a church-goer or not?'

She shook her head, able to recall in that moment her dad as she had so often seen him in this building, listening to someone, sharing a trouble, offering his help. All at once she felt an almost overwhelming need to talk to her dad, a longing to dash out of the church and run to Faith's Cottage so she might telephone him.

'If I tell them now, they might feel they have to cut their holiday short and come back. I don't want that to happen,' she declared.

'It won't, if you can convince them that you are coping well on your own. You are coping well, aren't you, Grace?'

She nodded. 'Yes, for most of the time. I'm over the worst, now.'

'They're certain to be shocked, but telling them now will mean they've had time to come to terms with the situation before they arrive home,' he pointed out.

Suddenly it was all clear in her mind. 'Yes, of course. I hadn't thought about it like that. My mind, and my emotions, were in such a muddle that I couldn't think straight. I'm glad you were here to advise me.'

'I didn't want you to make the same mistake as I made. The mistake that almost ruined my life, and brought me here,' he said quietly.

Grace had been about to gather up her bits and pieces and leave the church so that Donald could check that all was ready for the wedding. Now she lingered, delayed by her curiosity about the man.

'What do you mean? Or would you rather

not say?'

He smiled. 'I don't mind, now that it's all behind me. My wife wanted me to leave our inner city church two years ago because the workload left us too little time together. I wouldn't do that, because – as a result of being so stressed – I'd lost sight of the fact that I had a responsibility to Jane as well as to the folk of my parish. So she left me. I soon found I couldn't cope without her, but I was too pig-headed to admit it and say I had been wrong and I was sorry. To cut a long story short, I came here to recover from a breakdown. I didn't tell Jane about it. She was injured in an accident, and didn't let me know. So we nearly lost one another.'

Donald paused to shake his head, then smiled again as he went on: 'The young couple who are getting married here today knew me when I was at the city church. They came here on holiday and met me when they came to look round this church. They told me about Jane's accident, so I went to visit her in hospital. She's coming to their wedding, and to stay on here with me.'

'I'm so glad!'

'Your father will be too when he hears. Will you tell him, when you ring him, please?'

'Yes, of course. I'd better go and do the flowers for the reception, and leave you to

359

your work.'

Grace made her escape, feeling too emotional to remain in the church. She would ring her father later and tell him Donald's good news, and her own not so good news, after she had dressed the hotel tables with the low dishes of pink and white spray carnations which were already in the back of her van.

Victor was impatient to finish his work that day. There was a restlessness inside him which even the work of planting out bulbs beneath the trees which bordered the long front drive of the hotel could not banish. He worked on determinedly through a couple of heavy showers and got so wet that he was in need of the spare pullover he always kept in the back of his car. When he went to get this before going to the staff-room for his lunch break he found it was not there. With water trickling down his back, it was easy to make the decision to miss out on the meal break shared with other staff and to drive down to his home to dry himself off and change his clothes.

He was not hungry anyway. Food could wait until tonight, when he hoped to share it with Grace. On his way through the village he would call in at the butcher's shop and buy steak. Then, before coming back to Glen View, he would telephone Grace and invite her to share the steak with him after Robbie was in bed. He would need to confess to her then what he had been forced to tell Calum in order to save his job. The thought of what Grace would say to him brought a hot wave of embarrassment flooding over him. He must have been mad to tell Calum he and Grace were to become partners! Grace would be disgusted with him when she heard. He was so nervous of telling her that when he lifted his phone to speak to her, still wearing his soaking wet clothes, he almost blurted out his confession at once. The sound of her shop bell ringing was the only thing that stopped him from doing so.

'Just a quick word, Grace. Can you come to supper tonight? I need to talk to you,' he began.

Her answer was brief. 'Yes. I'll get in touch later about time. I have a customer waiting.'

Victor stepped out of the pool of water which had dripped from his clothes on to the floor of the hall. He ought to have changed first, only he had been in too much of a hurry to fix the supper date with Grace. His life was in a state of confusion, he reflected wryly as he towelled himself dry after taking a hasty shower. It would be worse still when he told Grace what he had done. She would probably walk out on him and that would be the end of their friendship. What a bloody fool he had been to mention Grace as his future partner. Why hadn't he played for time with Calum, invented some fictional woman who was going to move in with him and Robbie?

Victor was still asking himself these same pointless questions when Grace rang him late that afternoon. He had just got back from Glen View after picking Robbie up from his grandmother's, and was giving him his tea, when the phone disturbed him.

'Grace here, Victor. You asked me to come over tonight, said you needed to talk...'

'Yes, I do, after we've got Robbie to bed and had our meal.' In the short silence that followed the thought came to Victor that it was the sort of dialogue he once would have shared with Shona. The pain he experienced then was not, as it would have been a few months ago, razor sharp but more of a deeply felt ache. He straightened his shoulders and spoke again. 'I've got some steak, and new potatoes, and salad. Will that be all right for you?'

Grace laughed. 'What's the alternative? Jam sandwiches with Robbie? Of course it's all right. What time shall I come?'

'Any time after seven thirty. Robbie'll be in bed by then.'

'I'll see you then.' Grace hung up. Usually when she went to Birch Cottage for a meal she went before Robbie was in bed, so they could all eat together. That it was not to be so tonight left her feeling vaguely disappointed, until she set about bringing in the flower vases from outside the shop, checked the orders for the next day when there was to be a big funeral at Rowanmore Church, and counted the money from the till ready to drop it off at the bank safe on her way home to Faith's Cottage. She did not hang about tonight, as she did on some evenings, in case some of the people sauntering through the little town decided to come in to make late purchases. With the phone call to be made to her parents weighing heavily on her mind, she wanted to get this over with in the privacy of Faith's Cottage.

It was her father's voice which travelled so clearly over the thousands of miles from her sister's home in Wellington. He made things easier for her by asking, immediately after whether she was well and not overdoing things, how Paul was.

'You don't seem to mention Paul during your calls these days, Grace. We were wondering about that. If you were having any problems, I mean. Though I expect we are feeling rather over-anxious with being so far away from you. I'm sure Paul is looking after you, making sure you don't do too much before you are really fit again. So how is he? Perhaps I could have a word with him, if he's at home.'

Grace took a deep breath, then began to speak slowly, hesitantly, tracing as she did so the shape of Paul's face in the family photo which hung in the hall of the cottage. 'I'm not speaking from the house I shared with Paul, Dad, I'm at Faith's Cottage.'

'Why? Are you taking another holiday? Was the one in Italy not very good? We didn't get a postcard, so we wondered...'

'We didn't go to Italy, Dad.' There was no way of telling him except by the plain truth. 'Paul left me a letter, just before I was to meet him at the airport, telling me he couldn't settle for a childless marriage.'

'It took him a long time to realise that!' her father said indignantly. 'You've been married for ten years.'

'We're not together any more, Dad. I've agreed to a divorce and it's going ahead.'

She gave him a few moments to take this in before going on. 'I've bought a small flower shop in Rowanmore with a flat up above it,' she went on hurriedly.

'Why didn't you tell us before?' Her father sounded perplexed, maybe a little hurt too. Grace felt guilty when she realised that.

'I didn't want to worry you,' she began.

'We should have been there to support you instead of all these miles away. Your mother will be so upset. We'll see how soon we can

364

change our flights and get back to you—'

'No! Please don't do that or I'll think I've spoiled things for you,' Grace broke in.

'I still think, and your mother will too, that we should come back.'

Her father's voice was firm, decisive. Grace's heart sank. She had to be left alone to get through this. She *was* managing to get through it. All she had to do was convince her dad of that.

'My new shop is going well, Dad. I had a marvellous order for a big wedding in St Bride's today. While I was in there decorating the church I met Donald Muir. He asked me to tell you that his wife was coming up for this wedding and is going to stay on here.'

'So they're talking things over and trying to work things out. That's good! Perhaps that's what you and Paul ought to be doing, Grace?'

Her spirits sank even lower. She hated to disappoint him but it had to be said. 'It's too late for that, Dad, because Paul's met someone else.'

'It might not last,' he broke in.

Grace closed her eyes and prayed that she would be able to make him understand. Then she spoke, gently. 'It needs to last, because they are adding another child to her family. So they want the divorce to go through quickly. It's Alison, who used to help me in my shop,' she finished with a rush.

'Oh, my poor wee girl!'

He had said that so often when she was a child, and sometimes during her teen years. To hear it now almost robbed Grace of her composure. She must not break down. She must be strong and convince him that she could survive her marriage breakdown on her own. She clenched her hands and fought against the tears that burned behind her eyes.

'I really am fine, Dad, and really busy with my shop and all my friends here. I'm going to share a meal with one of them tonight. So please don't come back early. If you do, I'll know I've spoilt this trip for you and I'll feel bad about that. I'll ring you again in a couple of days.'

'No, we'll ring you, now we know you're at Faith's Cottage. We wondered why there was no reply when we rang your Cotswold number a couple of times.' He sighed. 'Now we know. Take care, my dearest girl, and God bless you.'

Two tears rolled slowly down Grace's face as she replaced the receiver. She brushed them away with the back of her hand and made her way up the stairs to take a shower and dress for her meal with Victor. Ought she to tell Victor about the visit Isla had made to her shop, and the way Isla had forced her into saying she had been at Birch Cottage with Victor when she hadn't? Or would it be better not to mention Isla's visit?

Laurel fought against the tiredness that engulfed her as she struggled out of bed and went down to the kitchen to make tea. If her mother was not already up she would take some to her. The days of acute anxiety were taking their toll now of both of them, but Craig was coming home today so things would be easier. They had not told Craig about his dad's illness until last night when he had phoned to say what time he would be home. He had been horrified that they had waited so long to tell him and had demanded to know why.

'Mum didn't want you worried just before your exams,' Laurel explained.

'But Dad might have...' Her young brother could not get the dread word past his lips.

'He didn't, and he's on the mend now. So don't upset Mum by making a fuss because she didn't let you know before. After all, it was only three days ago.' Laurel spoke more sharply than she had intended because by now those three days of living with acute fear and without food were affecting her.

'All right, big sister, keep your hair on!' Craig retorted. 'Have the nosh ready for twelve. I'll be with you by then. Or I can come tonight if you'd rather.'

'Leave it till tomorrow morning. Dad's out of the Acute Care Unit. The rain's belting down here and some of the roads are flooded. Just keep your speed down when you do come because Mum's had enough worry without you adding to it. She's in the bath right now, so I won't bring her to the phone.'

Laurel had gone to bed then, to lie awake wondering if they would be able to manage without her if she went back to Scotland on Sunday. She had already stayed twice as long as she had planned to do and there would be a full house at Glen View next week for the clan gathering. Calum would need her there. He had said she was not to worry, only to think of her parents' need of her, but she could not stop worrying and she could not stop aching for the feel of Calum's arms about her again. It could not really be less than a week since she had last seen him. It seemed so much longer than that.

It was still raining heavily as she poured boiling water into the big brown teapot and left the tea to brew while she went to pick up the *Yorkshire Post* which had just come through the letterbox.

The headlines were ominous. They spoke of more cases of foot and mouth disease only a dozen miles away. What if, in spite of all the precautions they had taken, it reached this farm and her parents' animals? What would that do to her dad's already precarious health? This terrible epidemic could ruin all their lives in the days to come.

Her hand trembled as she poured the tea into two mugs and carried them up the stairs to the front bedroom where her mother was sleeping alone in the double bed beneath the patchwork quilt. 'Wakey, wakey, Mum!' she said softly as she put down the mug and forced herself to smile.

Twenty-Three

Victor found himself becoming edgy as the time for Grace to arrive drew nearer. While Robbie was still keeping him busy it had been easier to push into the back of his mind what he must say to her. Now, with the table set and the food prepared, he paced from the living room to the kitchen. With the clock moving on towards seven thirty he was beginning to panic. The polo-neck sweatshirt he had put on because the rain had brought chill to the air seemed to be choking him. He opened the living-room window wide to let in more fresh air and the curtains billowed madly in the strengthening wind.

It would have been easier if he had not liked Grace so much. He could have made a joke out of what he had told Calum to some of his women colleagues in the army; could have laughed it off and known they would do the same. Grace was different, because Grace was only just beginning to recover from the immense hurt inflicted on her by the collapse of her marriage. Grace was vulnerable. So he would have to lead very carefully into how he had come to tell Calum that she was his partner, and hope that she would understand. If she did not understand, he knew he would lose her friendship.

Dear God, what an idiot he had been to take that risk. Only a bloody fool would have taken such a risk just to save his job at the Glen View. There must be other places where he could use his skills, to pay the mortgage and educate Robbie, even if he had to move away from Rowanmore to find them. Only Grace would not be there in those other places. Grace would still be here in Rowanmore, trying to put together the broken pieces of her life.

All of a sudden it hit him that he was in a no-win situation. If he rang Calum right now and told him that he and Grace were not partners at all, he would lose his job and probably have to move away to find work. If instead he confessed to Grace just how he had managed to save his job here, he would lose her friendship. That thought was intolerable to him.

The urgent ringing of his front doorbell startled him. He frowned. It could not be Grace yet because he had not heard her van pulling on to his drive. Surely not Isla, come to embarrass him yet again? Reluctantly he moved across the hall and pulled open the door. His eyes widened when he saw that it was, after all, Grace. Though not the Grace he was so accustomed to seeing, with her short black hair crisply arranged about her neat head and her plain but immaculate shirts, sweaters, slacks or long skirts crease-free. This was a Grace who had a distinctly dishevelled air about her. The thin sweater she wore clung wetly to her shapely body as the water fell in heavy droplets from damp curls to soaking shoulders.

'Grace! I didn't hear you drive up...' He stared into her scowling face with astonishment, and opened the door wider.

'That's because I didn't drive up! I couldn't, because that damned van packed up on me halfway here and I couldn't get it started again. I tried the garage on my mobile, and they were closed. I couldn't contact the breakdown service because I'm not covered by them yet, having only just bought the rotten van,' she finished explosively.

'Why didn't you ring me?'

'I knew you'd have got Robbie to bed and wouldn't be able to leave him.'

'So you walked, and got wet?'

'Yes! Wet and angry. Very, very angry with the guy who sold me the van.'

Victor could not take his eyes off her. This was a new Grace, a Grace full of life and fire and fury. A Grace who brought sensations

to his body that he had forgotten he possessed. A Grace he wanted to...

'What are you staring at? Haven't you ever
seen a wet woman before? How long are you
going to wait before you—'

'Oh Grace, I'm sorry! Come in. I'll take
your wet things...' His voice tailed off. Now
he'd put his foot in it for sure. She was
glaring at him.

'What am I going to wear? Something of
yours, or something of Robbie's?' she asked
crossly.

Quite suddenly her mood changed. She
caught sight of her reflection in the hall
mirror and began to laugh. 'I look like a
drowned haggis, don't I?' she gasped.

Victor caught her changed mood and
began to laugh with her. They rocked together, within touching distance of each
other, locked closely in their shared mirth.
Then he reached out to put his arms about
her shoulders, and the nearness of her, the
damp sweet fragrance of her, engulfed him
in a swift tide of desire which he found
difficult to control.

'Grace, you are really wonderful when
you're angry. So, so wonderful!' The words
poured out of him spontaneously; words
that only a few minutes ago he had not
known he would say.

The laughter died in her throat as she
turned round and stared into his eyes. 'Do

373

you mean that, Victor?' she whispered.

'Yes. I've never seen you like this before. It's as if you've suddenly come alive for me.'

She frowned at him now. 'What are you trying to say? Tell me!' The spark was there again, the fire in her eyes, the hot colour in her cheeks. 'Are you making fun of me, Victor?'

'No, I'm quite serious. I've only ever seen you in calm or even melancholy mood.' He stopped, then went on, 'Though I was prepared for you to be very angry with me when I told you tonight what I had done.'

'Angry with *you*? Why?'

'It's quite a long story, and you are a very wet girl, so you need to change into dry clothes before we talk about it. Whose will you have, mine or Robbie's?' he finished with a grin.

Grace laughed again. 'Neither will be a good fit, but I'd better go for yours.'

'I'll get you a bath towel. You know where the bathroom is.' He let go of her reluctantly and stepped back from her.

'I've made you all wet too,' she said as she saw the spreading dark stain on his red sweat-shirt.

'It was worth it,' he murmured as he made a move towards the kitchen. A moment later he was back with a large warm towel. He placed it round her shoulders gently, then began to dry her hair with movements which were slow and sensual. 'It was worth it, Grace,' he said again as he kissed her mouth, just once, long and hard. 'Go and have a hot shower, but don't be long because I do need to talk to you.'

He went to his bedroom and opened his wardrobe. What could he give Grace to wear when she was so small and slender? There was a spare bathrobe, a deep blue towelling garment that came only as far as his knees. It would have to be that. He lifted it from the hanger, then carried it down the stairs until he reached the bathroom door. There he came to a halt. The sound of the shower died away. Grace would be drying that slender but shapely body now. Ought he to wait until she emerged wrapped in a bath towel, or should he tap on the door and drop the blue bathrobe at her feet? More than a year of solitary, monastic existence had not prepared him for this experience.

Yet the decision was made without him being aware of it. He put out a hand to tap on the door as Grace opened it. Moisture still glistened on the ivory flesh of her shoulders. There was a tantalising glimpse for him of her breasts, just visible above the large towel. She was so lovely that the sight of her made the breath catch in his throat. All the feelings he had known for her before, the caring, the liking, the sharing, were engulfed by this new emotion. A much more powerful emotion. His need of her was immense, and unexpected. It was so earth-shattering that he stood there with the bathrobe crushed between hands that ached to caress her, to love her, to possess her.

'Grace, Grace, you're so beautiful that I can't take my eyes off you,' he murmured.

She held out her hands for the robe. He saw then, as he reached out for her, that her eyes were full of tears. As she shook her head, some of the tears splashed on to the hand he was reaching out to remove the towel and gaze with wonder at the loveliness of her smooth, ivory skin.

'I'm not!' she cried. 'I'm not beautiful any more! Why do you think Paul couldn't go on living with me? Why do you think he could no longer bear the sight of me unclothed?'

He drew back, appalled by her reaction. 'I don't understand, Grace. You are very beautiful! You're beautiful in every way to me.'

Slowly, silently she allowed the towel to move downwards until he was able to see the healed wound which marred the smoothness of her skin. Victor's glance did not falter. He raised his eyes to rest on hers, and waited for her to speak.

'Do you still think I'm beautiful, Victor?' she asked quietly.

He smiled, and would have pulled her into his arms if she had not drawn back. 'I *know* you are even more beautiful now that I've seen more of you,' he told her.

'Would you still have told Isla that *I* was your lover if you had known about this?' she said.

Shock waves washed over him as her words took root in his mind. She could only have said those words if Isla had told her that he was making use of their friendship to try and cool her own desire for him.

'Oh God, Grace! What have I done?' He was appalled that she should have found out what he had told Isla. How much worse it would be when he confessed that he had been forced to tell a similar lie to Calum in order to save his job at Glen View. Shame kept him silent for a long moment during which Grace remained absolutely still, only a short step away from him. 'What can I say to you? How can I ever make it up to you?' he managed to utter at last.

Amazingly, Grace was smiling now; a smile which had pushed away the tears and brought radiance to her face. 'You've already made it up to me by not flinching when you saw my scars,' she told him. 'You've convinced me that I can still be beautiful to someone who might love me enough.'

He dropped the bathrobe at her feet, stripped off his still damp red sweatshirt and flung it away from him. Then he turned so that his back and left side were facing her.

377

Her eyes widened as she saw the scars left on his body by the bomb which had killed his wife. A moment later he was facing her again, speaking to her again..

'Dear, beautiful, Grace, will I live long enough to love you as much as you deserve to be loved?' he was asking her. 'Will you ever feel able to give your love to me?'

Grace dropped the bath towel and moved closer to him. Close enough to blend the warmth of her own body with the power of his as she put her arms about his neck. Close enough to ignite a blaze of passion between them that would not be denied.

'Do you want to eat first, my darling?' he asked as they came up for air from their first long, long, shared kiss.

Grace laughed. 'Do you?' she murmured.

'Are you sure you'll be all right now, Mum?' Laurel was desperately anxious to get back to Scotland now that her father was out of hospital and back at the farm, though not yet allowed to do any work.

'Yes, quite sure. You must go back to your job now or you may lose it, and jobs won't be so easy to find around here if the tourists don't start coming soon. Besides, it isn't just your job you want to get back to, is it, love?'

Laurel found it hard to meet her mother's searching glance. Of course she wanted to be with Calum again. It seemed so long

378

since they had been together, even though in fact it was only nine days. He had phoned her every evening, telling her how much he was missing her, but it was not the same as being alone together in Kingfisher Cottage when their work in the hotel was over, to share a meal, to talk, to make love.

By late this evening they would be together again. Immediately after she had finished the big breakfast shared with her parents and her brother she would begin the long journey back to Glen View Hotel. She still felt a bit guilty about going when her dad was only just out of hospital, but during his phone call last night Calum had told her that the agency chef would be leaving today because she had a holiday job already booked on a cruise ship. The clan gathering guests would be arriving the day after tomorrow and Glen View would be full to overflowing then. So she must be back in time to do some advance cooking of special desserts, pâtés and soups.

'Who is this guy?' Craig wanted to know. 'Some braw Scot with a knife in his sock and a sporran on his kilt, I suppose.'

They had not had much time to talk since Craig had come home because there had been such a lot of work for them all to catch up on about the farm.

'Don't tease her, Craig,' his mother broke in. 'Calum has a lovely accent and I'm sure he's a nice fellow.'

'If he's not, he'll soon regret it if I get my hands on him.' That was Laurel's father. 'And what will we tell your ex-boyfriend if he turns up here again?'

'Tell him to get lost!' Craig put in. 'I don't know how he had the cheek to show up here like he did, after the way he carried on down in London. Then to ring you again and try to talk you into going for this interview in the place where he works was a colossal cheek.'

'He won't be welcome here,' her father broke in. 'He'll be sent packing.'

'He won't come back here, after what Calum said to him,' Laurel told them.

Instantly they were all attention. 'Do you mean he got in touch with Calum?' Craig said incredulously. 'Why would he do that?'

'To make trouble for me. He told Calum he had lined up an interview for me with the head chef at this hotel in Manchester where he's working now. I suppose he thought if I lost my job at the Glen View I might be more likely to go back to him. He was wasting his time, and mine,' Laurel added crisply as she got to her feet ready to leave the table.

She wanted the goodbyes over with quickly now, because there was the beginning of a lump in her throat at the prospect of not seeing her family for some time. She knew that her mum would not leave her dad to take the few days' break in Rowankirk that they had been planning.

'Will you come and see us when you get your time off in October, love?' her dad asked as he got up and began to walk to the back door with her.

Laurel sighed. She ought to explain that she was going away with Calum to somewhere special in October while the hotel season was quiet. Only she couldn't do that now. Not since those frightening hours she and her mum had spent in the special care unit while the staff fought to save her dad's life. She turned her head away from her father's face and looked into her mother's eyes.

'You're going away with Calum then, aren't you?' Mary Appleby said quietly. 'You'll be looking forward to that.'

Laurel found herself shaking her head as she gathered words together that would sound like the truth. 'No. I'm not going away with Calum then. We've changed our plans. He's having some more work done at Glen View – an extension – so he wants to be around to supervise the work himself. So I'll be coming home.'

When she saw the way their expressions lightened, the way the forced smile became a real one in her mum's eyes, and the way her dad seemed to relax, she knew she had

381

done the right thing in uttering those untruths. Even Craig looked relieved.

'He must have decided on these alterations while you've been down here,' her mother commented thoughtfully.

'Yes, he did. He only mentioned it to me when he phoned last night,' Laurel lied cheerfully. She walked away then to where her car was waiting with her luggage already inside, along with some personal items from her room to make Kingfisher Cottage a bit more homely. They followed her and waited for her to open the driver's door. Then, one by one, they hugged her and told her to drive carefully, to look after herself, and to let them know she had got back safely.

Craig whispered, 'I'll see they use the cash you've left, as soon as they need it, and I'll see Fern's pups go to good homes,' when he crushed her to his chest and ruffled her hair.

Laurel switched on the engine of her small car and steered it through the farm gates as Fern gave her a noisy send-off. She turned her head and gave them a swift wave, then gathered speed as she turned into the moorland road that would lead her to the motorway and, many hours later, to Rowankirk.

She was looking forward to going back to the work she enjoyed at the Glen View, the up-market cooking which gave scope for her creative talents. She was also looking forward to seeing the friends she had made there: Fergus, Victor, Grace, Maggie Reid and young Ben. Most of all she was looking forward to being with Calum. The one thing she was not looking forward to was telling Calum that she would not be able to go away with him in October for that special holiday he had planned.

Twenty-Four

Grace yawned, then smiled across the kitchen table at Victor. Her hair was tousled, her eyes dreamy. They had just finished eating. He reached out for her hand, lifted it to his lips and kissed it. 'I love you, Grace,' he said. 'Shall we...?'

'I'll have to be going home,' she murmured.

'You are home, now, my lovely Grace.' This time he reached for her lips. 'Stay with me, please.'

She shook her head. 'I can't. I have to get some sleep. I need to make an early start in the morning because I've got funeral flowers to do.'

'You can make an early start from here. Robbie'll make certain you do that, he's usually awake by six.'

'I can't be here then! Someone could see me leaving!'

'Surely that doesn't matter...'

'But it does matter. It matters a lot to me! I'm not free yet of my marriage, and it's only recently that my father was the minister

384

here.' Grace was on her feet ready for flight.

'He's not here now, so I don't see...' Victor stood up to give her a puzzled stare.

'He'll know, the minute he gets back, because this is a small place and someone will tell him, even if they don't mean to.' She was gathering her clothes, which had been drying round the Aga, into her arms ready to dress. The dark blue towelling robe was all she wore.

'Some people know already,' Victor pointed out.

'Do you mean Isla? She only knows I sometimes have a meal with you. That's not the same as staying the night with you.'

'There's Calum too.' Victor frowned as he told her that. He ought to have told her last night, as he had planned to do. Only the moment he had seen her standing there in his hall with the wet garments clinging to her, and with her whole personality alive with fury because her van had broken down, he had known that he felt far more for her than friendship.

'Calum? What do you mean?' She halted as she reached the kitchen door on her way to the bathroom to dress.

Victor felt his heart plummet. 'I ought to have told you earlier, I meant to tell you, only I got so carried away with what I felt for you that—'

'Told me what?' she broke in.

385

'That I had given Calum to understand that we were already partners, Grace.'

She took a deep breath, and he watched hot colour stain her cheeks. 'What made you do that? Were you so certain I would...?'

'No, of course not. I didn't know then how I would feel about you now.'

'Why then? Why?'

Nothing but the truth would do, and she would hate him for that truth.

'Calum told me that he was very concerned about the way Fergus was behaving towards me, because he thought I was responsible for the breaking of his engagement to Isla. He said it was creating a very unpleasant atmosphere in the staff-room, and the hotel guests would soon become aware of it. It was also upsetting Laurel. So he would have to get someone else to do the garden. I told him it was unlikely to continue now that Isla knew you were my partner.'

Grace gasped, then words poured out of her. 'So that's what it was all about, all the sweet words, and the rest! No wonder you wanted me to stay here with you tonight! Damn you, Victor Thorpe! I wish I'd never set eyes on you; never begun to trust you; never let myself love you. The sooner I'm out of here and away from you the better.'

She was out of the room, afraid he would see the tears that so swiftly took over from the anger, and locking herself into his bathroom so she could fling off the blue bathrobe and hurl it into his bath. Then she dragged on the sweater and skirt she had discarded earlier. They were dry now but badly creased. It did not matter, she was past caring whether anyone would see her as she ran home through the darkness of midnight.

'Grace! Listen to me, please listen to me,' Victor said from the other side of the bathroom door. 'You can't go like this. We have to talk.'

Grace flung open the door. 'There's nothing left to say. In fact you've said too much already.'

'I haven't said enough yet. I haven't said I'm sorry.'

He looked into her face as he spoke and saw the hurt reflected there. Then the hurt was gone and bitterness took over.

'Sorry for having to behave as if you really loved me? Is that what you mean, Victor?'

'No! Oh God, how can I make you see that I do love you, and that I do need you,' he said in a low voice as he reached out to put his arms about her.

She was hesitating, weakening, wondering, when the anguished cry came from the back of the house as Robbie woke from a bad dream.

'Your wee boy needs you,' she said as she

pulled away from him and made her escape.

The long, long drive was almost over now and in less than half an hour Laurel hoped to be pulling into the space outside Kingfisher Cottage. She had been delayed by bad weather and roadworks, so instead of arriving in time to see Calum before dinner it was going to be much later than that. The rain which had followed her relentlessly from England was still beating against the windscreen as she followed the winding road round the shore of the loch and turned into the narrow lane that led upwards towards the mist-shrouded heights which hid the Glen View Hotel from her sight. She was so weary now that she had to force herself to concentrate on negotiating the sharp bends, where it was so easy to come to grief even in good visibility.

It was with a tremendous sense of relief that she saw the open gates of Glen View ahead of her with lights shining out into the gloom from all the front windows. Thankfully, she dragged herself out of her car and flexed her shoulders to ease the stiffness brought on by too many hours of driving. By the time she had unlocked the door of Kingfisher Cottage and stepped into the tiny hall she was feeling unsteady on her feet. Of course she ought to have made time for coffee and a sandwich at the last stop she made to fill up with petrol and visit the toilet. Only she had been too impatient to reach the place where she would be reunited with Calum.

By now she was long past feeling the need for food or drink. All she wanted was to lie down, because the walls of her cottage were moving crazily as though they were about to fall on her. The sensation was alarming. So alarming that she staggered into the bedroom, kicked off her shoes and collapsed on to her bed, to fall at once into the deep slumber of utter exhaustion.

When midnight was close, the hotel guests in their rooms and the locals long since returned to their homes in the village, Calum wandered out into the grounds. The rain had stopped but the mist remained, drifting eerily in white ribbons about the upper reaches of the mountain. Where was Laurel? She ought to have been back hours ago. Had her car broken down somewhere on the long journey from Yorkshire? If so, why had she not used her mobile phone to let him know? She must have guessed how anxious he would be when she failed to turn up in time to share a late meal with him in his top-floor apartment as they had planned.

'I'll come across and join you there as soon as I've had a quick shower and changed,' she had told him last night when he phoned her. 'I can hardly wait to see you, darling.'

They had not been in the habit of meeting up there in his private apartment because both felt it wiser to avoid causing gossip among the other staff, but with his mind firmly fixed on making his love for Laurel public as soon as possible, Calum had decided they would eat there rather than in Kingfisher Cottage. He had told Laurel that in his late night call to her home the previous evening, so why had she not turned up yet?

Fear had a tight grip on him as he scanned the area far below the hotel, hoping to see her car headlights moving upwards. It was difficult to banish from his mind an image of the vehicle reduced to a tangle of crushed metal. Or perhaps her father had been taken ill again and her mother had contacted Laurel and urged her to go back home? Ought he to ring her home and try to find out what had happened? Or would doing so cause needless anxiety to her family, if Laurel had simply been delayed by the bad weather which the radio had said was widespread?

He must get a hold on himself and not give way to panic. There would be a perfectly logical explanation for her failure to appear. There had to be. A brisk walk down the road that led to the village, and the steep uphill walk back would help to restore calm to his mind. The rain had stopped and a thin moon was pushing a weak beam of light through the clouds as he strode out. It was not long before the exercise and fresh air were having a steadying effect on his nerves. By the time he was walking upwards again, at a slower pace, he was castigating himself silently for behaving like a love-sick youth. This thought made him halt in his tracks. He was neither a youth nor a newcomer to love. Before he met Laurel, long before he met Laurel and fell in love with her at the Skellkirk Abbey Hotel, there had been Katharine.

They had met at university and discovered that they were both Highland Scots with a lot in common. All his plans for the conversion of his family home into a luxury hotel had been shared with Katharine. They had worked together to make it the success it became within a few years. He had wanted them to marry just before the hotel opened for business, but Katharine insisted they should wait until the place was firmly established, when they would be able to leave Fergus in charge while they took a leisurely honeymoon visiting members of the Clan McLeod in different parts of America.

So their marriage had been postponed,

and the hotel had prospered so much that every time the subject of them marrying was brought up by Calum it was brushed aside by Katharine arguing that developments at Glen View had to take priority. In the end this had led to a series of disagreements between them. Their final argument, which ended with a colossal row on the night Fergus and Isla were celebrating their engagement with a party at Glen View, had brought the truth from Katharine at last. The truth being that she had known for a long time that she would never marry Calum.

He had been furious with her. 'Why didn't you tell me before, when you first decided that?' he had demanded. 'Why did you keep me hanging on for so long with all those excuses about the time not being right?'

'Because I didn't want to have to leave my job here,' had been the reason she gave him.

'Why not? There are other hotels where you could find reception or management work with your experience,' he had argued.

'Not in places where I'd be able to see Fergus every day.'

Calum had felt stunned when he heard her say that. Yet later, when he came to think about it in calmer mood, he was able to recall times when he had seen Katharine staring at Fergus with an almost rapt expression on her face.

'Fergus is engaged to Isla,' he had reminded her.

'He is now. He wasn't when he first came here to work with you,' had been her answer.

'What will you do now? Obviously, you can't stay here.'

'I don't intend to stay here. I've already been offered another job. A much better paid one than I'll ever get over here,' she had replied coolly. 'So I'll be leaving as soon as possible.'

'That will suit me. The sooner the better.'

Calum had kept his anger under tight control but had been furious to discover that Katharine had been using their engagement and her job at the Glen View as a means of trying to make Fergus fall for her. Yet a few hours later he knew he was relieved to be free of a relationship which had been deteriorating for some time. Very soon after that the fire had broken out at the Glen View and wiped everything else out of his mind. It had been a nightmare which Calum would have liked to be able to banish from his mind for good, but the memory of crackling timber and choking black smoke kept coming back at intervals. He had thought at the time that all those in the hotel had been accounted for as they gathered in the front garden of Glen View and watched the spectacular blaze grow ever fiercer. .

Then someone recalled not being able to find Fergus, who had gone back into the building to find his labrador. Calum had gone back into the burning building to search for him. He had run straight into the path of the collapsing roof timbers, which knocked him out and resulted in him suffering smoke inhalation before the fire and rescue team got to him and sent him to hospital.

The vivid memories of the events which had taken place on just such a damp and misty night as this brought a faint sweat to Calum's brow. He wiped it away, and saw close at hand a young deer, graceful in her movements, then another, and another moving towards the back gardens of the three cottages belonging to Glen View. Going in search of food perhaps. He stayed quite still watching them and enjoying the sight of these lovely creatures as they moved closer to the rear of the cottages. The sound of an owl hooting made him turn his head sharply to the right. It was then that he caught sight of Laurel's car parked up close to the door of the centre cottage.

His heart gave a great lurch. The owl was forgotten, the deer were forgotten. All he wanted now was to see Laurel, to hold her, to kiss her, to make love to her, to tell her how much he had missed her. He could not wait to do that. The deer took swift, startled escape as he ran to Kingfisher Cottage. Once there he stared at the windows, perplexed because there were no lights to be seen in the front room or the hall. With eager steps he went round to the back of the buildings, moving quietly so as not to disturb the occupants of the other two cottages, which had been let to tourists. All three dwellings were in complete darkness. Since there were no walls or fences at the rear of the properties it was easy for Calum to make his way across the grass which the deer had just vacated and peer through the kitchen window of Kingfisher Cottage.

The security light above the back door came to brilliant life as he was doing this and showed the place to be as Laurel would have left it when she departed for her trip to Yorkshire, immaculately tidy. That left only the bedroom window to be scanned. Calum hesitated. He did not want to be accused of invading her privacy. Yet surely if she were in that room there would be lights on? Unless she was ill...

As the thought came to him he acted on it, his eyes staring hard to where he knew the bed was. What he saw increased his sense of urgency. Laurel was lying sprawled across the bed, minus her shoes but still wearing her jacket and slacks. There was an air of total abandonment about her, as though she had simply walked into the room and crashed out. Crashed out without even letting him know that she was back. Why should she do that? It could only be because she was feeling too unwell to even lift her phone to get in touch with him.

Alarm was forced down as he thought quickly about what he ought to do. If he went back to his apartment and telephoned her at well past midnight it would probably, considering the state of her father's health, alarm her. If he went back to his apartment and did not phone her to see if all was well, he would be awake all night worrying about her. The answer then was to get hold of the skeleton keys to her cottage from the reception desk and let himself in. That way he would be certain all was well with her. Though she certainly might not be pleased with him for doing that.

Deciding, almost at once, to take the risk, he hurried round to the front of the cottage again to where her car was parked. Profound uneasiness led him to look through the window of the vehicle. Her luggage was still inside, a weekend case and a holdall. Why hadn't she taken them indoors with her? His heart began to thump when he saw that the keys were still in the ignition. The driver's door, when he tried it, proved to be unlocked. That was all he needed to send him sprinting to the other side of the trees which screened the three cottages from the hotel building and across the car park, through the porch and into the hotel. His fingers were trembling as he found the skeleton keys for Kingfisher Cottage and sped back there to insert them into the lock.

As he bent over Laurel's prone body to check her breathing an enormous feeling of relief swept over him. She was alive! His beloved woman was warm and breathing. All that ailed her was probably extreme tiredness. Since the night air felt distinctly chilly he found the spare blanket, thick and soft, which he knew was part of the furnishings in every room at Glen View and laid it gently over her. Then he left her and walked back through the hotel garden. She would tell him in the morning why she had been too exhausted even to let him know she was back. He would tell her then about the plans he had made for October.

Victor hurried into Robbie's room and lifted the little boy into his arms. 'It's all right, Robbie, Daddy's here. Hush my wee boy!' He dropped a kiss on the silky tendrils of hair that were damp from the tears Robbie had tried to rub away, then carried him into the living room where he hoped he might see Grace coming back to him. His watch was in vain. Grace was already out of sight. He dropped on to the sofa and waited for

Robbie to fall asleep again. It was only minutes before this happened, but it was long enough for Victor to tell himself what a fool he had been to get things so wrong that he had ruined the relationship which had brought new hope and promise to Grace's life as well as his own. Now he had lost Grace's friendship as well as her love. His eyes ached as he fought the tears he could have shed for the loss of something so precious.

Twenty-Five

Laurel woke to feel the sun warming her body as it poured through the window of Kingfisher Cottage. At first she was puzzled about why she should be still wearing her clothes. Then she remembered how strange she had felt at the end of her long journey; the way the walls of the cottage had seemed to be moving so crazily about her that she had stumbled into this room and collapsed on to her bed. Had she remembered before that happened to ring Calum and tell him she was back, but not feeling well enough to go and share the meal with him that they had planned? There was only one way to find out. She rang his number and waited to hear his voice. As she waited she could hear birds singing in her back garden and the murmur of the sheep which grazed the lower slopes of the mountain. Then there was Calum's voice, warm and caressing, asking if she felt better this morning.

'So I did ring you last night to tell you I wasn't feeling very well?' she asked.

'No! You had me worried when you didn't

turn up and there was no message from you. In fact I was almost out of my mind, wondering about whether you'd had an accident. I was still looking out for you at midnight when I took a walk down the hill, and saw your car parked outside the cottage on my way back. I looked inside it and saw that the luggage was still there, and the door wasn't locked. So I locked it and brought the keys back with me.'

'Oh Calum, I'm sorry you were worried. The weather was so awful that I had to almost crawl along at times, then I got stuck at roadworks for ages. I couldn't ring you because I forgot to take my mobile to Yorkshire. I was feeling so dizzy that I crashed out and didn't wake until just now. I hope I haven't overslept.' Panic was setting in now. She had so much to do before the guests arrived for the clan-gathering events.

'It's only six o'clock, my darling. Are you coming up to have breakfast with me?'

'Oh yes, that sounds good! I'll be over as soon as I've had a shower.'

'Don't be long, I've got so much to tell you, and I love you.'

'I love you too, Calum, and I've got lots to tell you.'

As she stripped off the crumpled clothes which she had been wearing for almost twenty-four hours and stepped under the shower, Laurel reflected that Calum would not be pleased with everything she had to tell him. He was certain to be disappointed that she would not be able to go on holiday with him because she had promised to go and visit her mum and dad again. She was not looking forward to telling him that. Yet when Laurel did break the news to him, after a very early breakfast shared equally between food and love, he did not seem to be as disappointed as she had feared.

'Don't worry about it, dearest, I understand. In fact I've been half expecting something like this to happen, so I've made alternative plans,' he told her with a teasing glance from the silver-grey eyes which were such a striking feature of his long, lean face.

'What sort of plans?' she wanted to know.

'Much more exciting ones than my original plans, but there isn't time to say any more than that now because we've both got work to do. The first Americans are arriving a day earlier than we expected, and they want to talk to us about a wedding reception while they are here. So we have to get moving.'

Get moving they did, for the whole of that day, with Calum arranging an extra ceilidh at short notice while Laurel plunged into making pâtés of venison, pheasant and smoked salmon. She also made more luxury desserts to add to those already stored in the big freezers. The traditional haggis they would serve at some meals in the Scottish way, with mashed tatties and neeps, would be supplied by a local butcher whose small shop window was awash with certificates which proclaimed him to be a champion haggis-maker.

Early in the afternoon, when she would usually be taking a few hours off duty before cooking dinners, Laurel made scones and Scotch pancakes to serve with the butter shortbread and rich Dundee cake which were always part of afternoon teas at Glen View. She was taking a short tea break, and carrying a tray of scones and tea to Calum's office, when she heard a gasp from behind the reception desk where Isla was catching up on some paperwork.

'Look at that! It's definitely in the millionaire class.'

Since Isla was not easy to impress, Laurel looked, and looked again at the stretch-limousine which seemed to dwarf the other vehicles in the car park. 'Who are we expecting in that class?' she asked.

Isla did not need to check the bookings diary. 'Americans! Here a day early for the clan gathering. I'd better let Calum know.'

'I'll tell him. I'm just taking him some tea,' Laurel told her.

Calum looked up from the papers he was scanning as she tapped on the door of his office and entered. 'You don't need to do that,' he said with a grin.

'I do in working hours,' she insisted.

'You're supposed to be off duty at this time.'

'Not today, with so much catching up to do. The first Americans are here already.'

'Are they? I must welcome them.' He was on his feet instantly. 'This clan gathering is good business for Glen View.'

'When you see their car you'll get an idea of just how good,' she chuckled. 'It's a beauty. A real film star touch.'

The Americans were coming up the steps which led into the spacious front hall of Glen View, a big powerfully built man with a thick thatch of hair which might be blond or silver-grey, and a tall slender woman some years younger whose rich auburn hair fell in shining waves over the shoulders of her green silk shirt. Her eyes, as they took stock of everything about her and then came to rest on Calum, were an amazing emerald green.

'Calum! It's wonderful to see you again after so long!' There was no trace of an American accent in the woman's voice, but more than a hint of Highland Scot. She was holding out a hand to Calum, who seemed unable to move. Then she was reaching up to offer her mouth for his kiss. 'Aren't you going to say you're glad to see me?' she teased.

Calum came to his senses slowly. 'Yes, of course I'm glad to see you, Katharine.'

Laurel felt the breath catch in her throat as she waited within the door of Calum's office, watching and listening. What she heard next confirmed her guess.

'Glen View looks really marvellous, even better than it did before the fire. Don't you think so, Gray?' She was speaking to the big American, who came to stand with an arm about her slim shoulders.

The American shrugged. 'Can't say I can recall exactly how it looked before, honey. I guess you've forgotten I was only here for a couple of days.'

'Long enough to offer me a job with your own hotel chain,' she reminded him.

'So that's where you went,' Calum said calmly, already recovering from the shock he had experienced at the unexpected sight of the woman.

'Didn't I write and let you know? I'm certain I did.'

'If you did, I never received the letter.' Calum smiled then. 'Though with all I had to do once I came out of hospital, chasing up the insurance, planning the renovation and refurbishing of Glen View, and then moving down to manage a hotel in Yorkshire, I suppose it could easily have been mislaid.'

Katharine laughed. 'I don't think it

matters to either of us now. It's yesterday's news, and we've both moved on. You're in business here again, and I'm about to marry Gray.'

Calum smiled again. 'My congratulations!'

'We thought it would be great to have our wedding reception here, after our marriage at Inverness Cathedral. That's why we came a day early for the clan gathering. So we could arrange everything with you. Gray's folks were Highland Scots way back. I forgot to introduce you. My partner, Graham McDonald, my old friend, Calum McLeod.'

Laurel did not wait to hear any more. She took an escape route through the conservatory back to her kitchen, where she banged down the tea tray and stood with clenched hands while she silently uttered some very uncomplimentary words about this woman called Katharine who had been insensitive enough to come back without warning to a place where she had obviously once caused problems for Calum. She recalled the stunned look on Calum's face when he had got his first sight of her, in the moment before his expressive face had closed up. But Katharine had just said that was all yesterday's news, and so it was. Today's news was that Calum loved her. Calum had told her so when he had spoken of his plans for October. Laurel went back to her cake decorating with a smile on her face and a sparkle in her eyes.

Grace had spent most of the night lying awake, miserably asking herself whether she had acted too hastily when she blew her top and walked out on Victor. After all, she had gone along with his efforts to discourage Isla's fancy for him by allowing Isla to believe that she and Victor were having meals together almost every evening rather than only once or twice a week. She had done that to protect Victor. So what was so different about Victor saving his job, the work he loved at Glen View, by telling Calum that he and she were partners?

Would she have exploded into that burst of foul temper if she had not learned of this so soon after Victor had made love to her? Probably not. Maybe she just could not bear to believe that Victor did not love her as she loved him? Did it matter whether he loved her or not; whether he thought she was beautiful or not? All that really mattered was that she loved him, and that if she had not completely lost her rag with him she could have still been part of his life, and part of Robbie's too.

Since she could no longer bear to dwell on her own stupidity, she abandoned all attempts at sleeping and got up before five o'clock to shower, drink tea and make a start on the funeral flowers. It was only when she was about to start on the sheaves and wreaths of flowers that she remembered that many of the flowers were still in their boxes in the back of her broken-down van. She would have to walk to where she had abandoned the van and collect them before she could begin her work for the day. The funeral service was at noon, so there was no time to spare.

The fresh breeze that swept along the main street of Rowanmore felt good as she jogged along the empty pavement in the trainers she wore with her slacks and soft blue sweater. She would put the trauma, and the sweetness, of last night out of her mind and give all her thoughts and her energy to her work. If she was unable to make a successful and lasting relationship with Victor, at least she knew that she had the ability to build up a successful business. She had done that in the Cotswolds, and she would do it again here in Rowanmore.

As she rounded a corner which brought her into the square where her van had broken down, she was able to see the vehicle. Freshly painted, it bore in graceful white script the words *Fresh Flowers from Grace's Flower Basket*. It was bad luck that the engine had let her down last night. How differently things might have worked out if she had not got so soaking wet on her way to Birch Cottage that she had to shower and change into Victor's blue bathrobe. She and Victor would still have been friends this morning, and she was going to miss Victor's friendship so much.

This thought made her eyes sting and brought a rainbow mist of tears to obscure her view of the pavement ahead of her. It was not until she was only feet away from it that she saw the pushcart that was parked up close to the fence which enclosed the churchyard. Grace stopped running so suddenly that she almost pitched forward on to her face and only managed to right herself by grabbing the painted iron railings.

'Grace! Grace!' cried Robbie, waving Eddie Bear vigorously at her.

Grace stared at him through the moisture which was starting to escape down her cheeks. Her heart gave a huge lurch, then steadied as she caught sight of Victor bending over the open bonnet of her van. He looked up as he heard Robbie greeting her.

'What are you doing?' she managed to say after she had gulped down the lump in her aching throat.

It was Robbie who answered. 'Mend Grace's van. Daddy mend Grace's van,' he crowed.

'I should have thought of this last night,' Victor said quietly as he looked away from the sadness in her eyes. 'Then we would still have been friends this morning. I wouldn't have got carried away as I did by the sight of you looking so beautiful, Grace. I'm going to miss your friendship so much.'

Grace rubbed away a tear, swallowed again, then began. 'You don't have to miss it. I'll still be here when you need someone to talk to.'

He turned his head to look at her again. His dark eyes were desolate. The smudge of oil on one cheek made Grace long to take a hanky from her pocket and wipe it away. She wanted to wipe away so much more than the oil; she wanted to wipe away all the bitter words she had flung at him last night.

'I won't be here though.'

The words were said in such a low voice, perhaps because he did not want Robbie to hear them, that Grace was not sure she had heard him aright.

'What did you say?' Her heart was thumping again and there was a sick feeling in the pit of her stomach.

'I won't be here to talk to you, Grace. I must put things right by telling Calum the truth when I go to Glen View this morning. It's the least I can do. I should never have involved you as I did, no matter how strong the temptation was to do so. Maybe you'll find it easier to forgive me when I'm not around.'

Grace took a deep breath. 'If you leave

now I'll know it's because you haven't been able to forget some of the things I said to you last night. Things I wouldn't be saying this morning. Don't tell Calum the truth, please! Leave things as they were yesterday.'

'What are you saying, Grace?' he murmured, while Robbie talked to the blackbirds which had come down from the trees to peck at the biscuit crumbs he had dropped round the pushcart.

'I'm saying we should start again. That we should be friends, and let those who want to think we are more than friends do so.' Her words were the wishes that she wanted to share with him. She held her breath as she waited for his reply.

'Do you really mean that?'

'Yes. We can't waste a friendship that was so good for both of us.'

Victor smiled then and moved towards her, rubbing oily hands on the side of his jeans. 'Oh Grace, lovely Grace, you know I want so much more than friendship from you.'

Grace thrust a hand into her pocket and brought out a hanky. She reached up to wipe the grease from his cheek. 'You'll have to make do with friendship at this hour in the morning when I've got funeral flowers to do before ten o'clock,' she told him with a shaky laugh. 'I can manage without the van, but not without the flowers.'

410

He stood aside while she opened the back doors of the van and began to lift out the boxes of blooms. They filled the air with their fragrance. She was lifting out the final box when Victor spoke again, whispering the words as their hands met and clasped firmly beneath a heap of gold and white chrysanthemums.

'I can't manage without either your friendship or your love, Grace.'

'Mend van! Daddy mend van!' Robbie reminded him.

They exchanged laughing glances. 'We'll talk about it later,' she promised.

Victor watched her walk away with her arms full of flowers. Yes, they'd have a lot of talking to do later, but he had something else to do first.

'Daddy mend Grace's van now,' he told Robbie.

Laurel kept her head bent over the huge cake she was icing with the clan crest even though she was aware that Calum had come into the room where she was giving all her concentration to the task in hand. The room was small and cool, and had, in the days when Glen View was still a family home, been the butler's pantry. She did not turn round to speak to Calum but waited to hear what he had to say to her. They had not spoken since Katharine's arrival.

411

'Will you have dinner with me tonight, Laurel, up in the flat?' he asked quietly. 'We have a lot to talk about now you are back.'

'Yes, Calum. I'll need to tell you then what I was going to tell you last night if I hadn't flaked out so suddenly.'

He frowned. 'You're not thinking of taking that job in Manchester, are you?'

'No! Of course not! Whatever made you think I might?'

He hesitated. 'It was what you said just now – something you would have told me last night...'

Laurel laughed. 'It was nothing as drastic as that. I love being here with you at Glen View. I wouldn't ever want to leave. Unless you didn't want me here any more. You will tell me if...' Her face sobered suddenly.

'I'll tell you later what I have in mind for you and Glen View. I'll tell you in a better place, and at a better time, than this. Until ten o'clock, my love...'

Calum left her then to go on with icing the cake, and to go on worrying about what he would say when she told him their October holiday was off.

It was the final night of the clan gathering. Tomorrow, the guests who had crossed the Atlantic to take part in a week of reunions, of Highland Banquets, Highland Games, Celebration Ceilidhs and visits to places connected with their family histories would be departing. Before they went there was to be the wedding reception for Katharine and Gray McDonald, who were to marry that morning in Inverness Cathedral in the presence of many members of Katharine's family who lived in the Highlands, and some of Graham's who had come from America for the ceremony. Calum had been invited to the wedding service.

'I'm glad you're going after all,' Laurel told him as they met at Kingfisher Cottage very early that morning. 'Katharine might have been hurt if you had decided not to.'

'There's something else I have to do in Inverness, while I'm there. That's why I'm going as early as this.'

'It must be something important.' Laurel was puzzled.

'I'll tell you about it when I come back. Give me a kiss before I go, or maybe more than one,' he ordered with a laugh.

Laurel obeyed. Then it was time to stop kissing and start going their separate ways, he in the splendour of his full Highland dress of kilt, sporran and dark jacket, and she in her chef's whites with her hair piled on top of her head in a knot. She watched him drive away down the mountain on the beginning of his journey to the Highland capital. In a few weeks from now they would leave Glen View together to travel down to

Yorkshire, where Calum would meet her parents and her brother and they would make arrangements for their wedding at the village church next March.

In the meantime there were the finishing touches to put to Katharine and Gray's wedding reception this evening. Grace was coming up to Glen View at seven o'clock to do the flowers for that. They would be able to have a quick coffee together before Laurel cooked breakfasts for the guests who wished to make an early start. She was longing to know whether Grace's friendship with Victor was still just that, but of course she could not ask. All she had to go on was the glow there seemed to be about Grace these days, and the brightness that leapt into Victor's face whenever Grace appeared. It would be so wonderful if these two who had suffered so much could find happiness together, as she and Calum had done.

By mid-afternoon Laurel was back at Kingfisher Cottage, enjoying a couple of hours off duty before it was time to set out the wedding buffet which was to be served early in the evening when the wedding guests were all back from Inverness. Ten hours on her feet, with only a couple of short breaks for meals, were taking their toll and she was asleep in a garden chair when Calum spoke from behind her.

'Wake up! I've got something for you,

414

Laurel,' he said softly.

She yawned and stretched. Calum pulled her to her feet and led her into the cottage. He lifted her left hand to his lips. Then he took the ring from inside his jacket pocket and placed it on her finger. 'It was my grandmother's,' he told her. 'I got it from the bank in Inverness this morning. I hope you like it.'

'I love it, and I love you,' she told him as she stared at the sapphires sparkling beside diamonds.

The wedding party went on for hours. The guests enjoyed delicious food and superb wine; they danced for hours to music from fiddles and accordians; they met old friends and made new ones. It ended, as all the best Highland parties do, with a piper arriving at midnight to salute the newly married couple before they left for a secret destination. The music the piper played on that starlit night drifted through the clear air to where Laurel stood with Calum on the terrace of Glen View telling their good news to Fergus and Isla.

'Will you hold the fort here for us in October when we go down to Yorkshire to arrange our wedding?' Calum asked them.

'Sure! It's great news!' Fergus said without hesitation.

'I don't know if I'll be here then.' Isla

looked uncomfortable as she told him that. 'Ian and Isobel McDonald have invited me over to stay with them in North Carolina.'

'You will come back. You must come back.' Calum and Fergus spoke together.

'I'll come back when I've got used to the idea of seeing Victor and Robbie with Grace,' Isla told them with tears in her eyes. 'I have to get used to that, don't I?'

'You *will* get used to it, and I'll be here to help you,' Fergus said. 'Just give yourself time.'

The lively music was changing now as the stretch limousine came to the front entrance of Glen View. A different but well-loved melody was bringing the party to an end. Fergus led the singing with his fine baritone voice. 'Should auld acquaintance be forgot, and never brought to mind? We'll tak a cup o' kindness yet, for auld lang syne.' As he sang his eyes never left Isla's face. Then other voices joined in as Calum took Laurel's hand, Laurel took Fergus's hand and Isla found her own hand taken by Fergus.

They sang on, still holding hands, as the bride and groom drove away.